LOOK
CLOSER

STEPHANIE ROGERS

ALSO BY THE AUTHOR

1

HE WATCHES AS SHE sits on the bed, a bath towel wrapped loosely around her. She's combing her long, damp hair and, as a tangle gets caught in the comb, she winces then gathers it up, twists it and secures it on top of her head. Her bedroom is dimly lit and cosy, but he barely registers anything but her. Pleasure ripples through his groin when she stands and removes the towel, dropping it onto the floor. Her skin is flushed pink from her bath or shower. He settles back in his chair, gets more comfortable. The ringing phone makes him jump until he realises it's hers in her bedroom. She bends over to pick it up from the bed, which elicits a small grunt of satisfaction from him.

'Hi. Yes. Ten minutes,' he hears her say. Ten minutes to what? Where's she going? What's she doing? He hopes she's not going out.

'I'll ring you later,' she says and tosses the phone back onto the bed.

Disappointed, he watches as she pulls on her underwear; little scraps of lace now cover her best bits.

He moves back instinctively as she walks over to the laptop and sits down, her face looming large in front of him. She breaks out in a smile and starts tip-tapping on the keys. A response, probably to a Facebook message. She's never off it. Every night, Twitter, Facebook, Instagram, Snapchat, Pinterest. She's a social media junkie. He leans in again, taking in the snub nose that turns slightly up at the tip, and the eyes, multiple shades of green, framed by thick lashes. She's so close he can see a smattering of freckles that dot the bridge of her nose and spill onto her cheeks. His fingers trace them on the screen, like joining the dots, while she laughs at something she reads. When she leans back and stretches her arms above her head, her lace-encased breasts push up and forward towards the screen, and a rush of heat pins him to the chair.

She gets up from the desk, pulls on a long, floral robe and ties it tightly, then leaves the room, leaving the lights on. He breathes out slowly. He can wait. She'll be back before long. He reaches out and pops the tab on another can of beer, makes himself more comfortable in his oversized office chair and settles in to wait and watch some more. He's lost track of how many he's done this to, but this one is different. Better. Special. He smiles at the thought. He remembers reading a book about the climber, George Mallory, who died attempting to climb Everest. When Mallory had been asked why he wanted to climb the mountain, his reply had been 'Because it's there.' He sits up straighter as she returns to the room and begins to dress, scrutinising her. If anyone were to ask him why he did this, his reply would be 'Because I can'

2

I WAS IN THE kitchen at work, playing Candy Crush Saga and waiting for the kettle to boil to make yet more coffee to keep myself awake. The people I worked with were perfectly nice and everything, but it wasn't the most exciting place in the world. Was any solicitor's office party central? My new shoes were pinching me horribly, and I had just slipped one off when someone walked in. I jumped and jammed the phone behind my back before I realised it was *him*. *He* was Chris, an IT contractor who worked on the floor above.

'Gotcha,' he said, laughing.

I rammed my foot back in my shoe, knocking the blister that had formed. So much for looking cool. He must have been aware of the stir he'd caused since he started working at our place a few months ago: he was totally gorgeous, with a magnificent, muscular body. Not that I'd done much looking! Word was, he worked out all the time, and he certainly looked like he did—he was all angles and hard edges. I smiled at him as he squeezed past me. His aftershave was lovely, kind of musky and lemony, and he stooped as he towered above me with his six feet one to my five feet exactly. He leaned in and peeked at my phone, still hidden behind my back.

'What score you on?' he asked, reaching past me for a mug.

'Fifty thou.'

'What level?'

'Six hundred.'

'Managed a colour bomb on a stripe?'

'Not yet.'

'Ah! That's where the big points are.'

He smiled. He had a mesmerising mouth, sort of peachy, with a full bottom lip. When he smiled, one side sort of turned up first and the other side played catch up. It illuminated his whole face. It was a slow, spreading, lazy smile that did things to people, or women, at least. I was sure he knew it.

'The kettle's broken on our floor,' he said, reaching past me again for the tea bags.

Embarrassingly, my hand shook as I poured milk into my coffee, and some jumped out onto the side.

'Oops, butterfingers!' he said, mopping it up with a cloth from near the sink.

I felt like a clumsy oik and tried not to spill anything else as I lifted the cup. How had such a simple task turned into a major feat? He dropped the cloth into the sink and eyed the carrot cake on the plate behind that I'd already cut into small pieces.

'Ooh,' he said. 'That looks nice. Can I have some?'

'Help yourself.' I moved to one side so he could grab a slice.

He shoved the entire piece into his mouth and rolled his eyes. 'That's gorgeous. Who made it?'

'Erm... me. It's for Janice's birthday.' Now he would probably think I was some kind of boring, domesticated person, bringing homemade cake in.

His eyebrows arched above deep chocolate-brown eyes. 'You made that?'

'Mmm.' I nodded and he snatched another piece.

'That's better than shop-bought. You're good.'

I felt a flush of embarrassment mix with pleasure on my face.

'Thank you.'

'So, is that a thing of yours, then? Making cakes?'

Was he making fun of me? He didn't seem to be.

'Yeah. It is, really. It's my thing.'

He looked me up and down. 'You don't look like someone who makes cakes.'

I laughed. 'No.'

It had been said before. Everyone thought of Mary Berry when they pictured bakers.

'I'd better get back,' I said.

I shoved my phone in my pocket, put my coffee on a tray, along with the plate of cake, and he held the door open for me.

'Thanks.' I flashed him a smile.

'See you later, sexy cake maker,' he said as I left.

'Bye.' I looked back at him over my shoulder. He just called me sexy! His eyes were fixed on me and I had to work hard not to hobble in the stupid shoes. Then the door swung shut, and he disappeared from view.

If I concentrated hard, I could still smell his aftershave.

***

''S'cuse me, can you spare some change?'

In my rush to get home, I almost missed him as I left the Underground. He was sitting, hunched over, against the wall, with a grey blanket wrapped around his shoulders. A red, ragged woollen hat was pulled low over his forehead. Underneath the dirty beard and matted hair, I reckoned he could only be in his thirties. I'd never noticed him here before.

I opened my purse to get a couple of pound coins. Dammit! There was only a tenner. I'd forgotten about the magazine and bottle of water I'd bought earlier. He looked up at me, expectant and grateful.

I smiled, fished out the tenner, and pushed it into his hand. His fingers were freezing.

'Thank you. Have a nice day.' His voice was quiet, with a soft Scottish lilt.

'You shouldn't give them money. They only spend it on alcohol or drugs. It's best to give them food,' a woman next to me said.

'Yeah, well. Funnily enough, I don't have a sandwich on me,' I snapped, trying to hurry away, even though my shoes were crippling me. God save us from these sanctimonious gits who always knew better. What he spent the money on was no concern of mine. I glanced back before I turned the corner. He was sitting with his head bowed while people almost stepped over him. What the hell had happened to him that he was living this life?

3

IT WAS A HALF-MILE walk home from the Tube, but it felt more like five miles. Finally reaching my flat, I limped up the stairs, unlocked the door and pushed it shut behind me. I eased off the hateful shoes and threw them into the corner.

'I'm in the kitchen,' Leanne called out.

I found her making coffee.

'Want one?'

'Yeah, please.' I sat down at the table, hoisted one foot onto my thigh and massaged it. The ache got worse as I pressed harder. A groan sneaked out of me.

Leanne glanced at my feet and smirked. 'Not as good as they looked on the website then?'

'I know, I know... anyway, how was your day?'

'Boring as ever. But Kath was out, so at least she wasn't breathing down my neck all day.'

'Well, that's something, at least. Hey, listen Lee, I've been thinking. Would a vlog be a good idea? You know, along with the blogging?'

She put my coffee on the table and sat down. 'To promote the business?'

'Yeah.' Even if there was no proper business at the moment. You had to start somewhere, right?

Leanne pressed her lips together, which meant she was concentrating, something I learned on our first day at high school. We were both terrified, and she'd spotted me huddled in a corner, made a beeline for me and said, 'I'm Leanne Watson.' All I could focus on was her towering height, her wild, red hair and her intense green eyes. I tried not to smile now as she stroked the long, fiery ringlets, which meant she was preoccupied. And she was still loads taller than me, though that wasn't hard.

'Mmm, I think it would be good,' she said. 'A lot better than just blogging. Your personality could really come through.' She looked around the small kitchen. 'We'd have to clean this place up, though, if you did it here. Have you looked at any other people's?'

'A few. Just film yourself baking and talk about what you're doing.'

'You know, I think it could work. And you could capitalise on your looks! The gorgeous, husky, Latino baker,' she added. 'Ooh, I know—Sultry Sarah's Sizzling Scones,' she said, making quote marks with her fingers. 'You could wear short skirts and low-cut tops while hand-whisking cake mix vigorously.'

I snorted. 'Don't be daft.' I switched feet and rubbed the other one. 'I have no Latin blood, anyway.'

'So what? You've still got that Eva Longoria look about you,' she said.

'Yeah, so you keep telling me. I've heard she's a short-arse too, so that is one thing we have in common.'

'It's petite, not short-arse.'

My fingers found the massive blister on my heel; it was bigger than ever. No wonder it had been killing me all day. Maybe I could get a refund on those shoes. But I'd worn them from Shepherd's Bush all the way into central London and back now. The soles would be all scuffed and god knows what I might have stood in. What a bloody waste of eighty quid.

'So, what are we doing for dinner?' Lee asked.

'Don't know. Takeout?' I knew I shouldn't have said it as soon as the words left my mouth. Lee shook her head.

'No. Waste of money. What was it you were saying the other day? No unnecessary expense if you're to get a business off the ground? We'll have omelettes or something. We've got loads of eggs. And cheese. I'll cook.'

'Fine by me. I'll do the washing up then. I might just go and have a look at some YouTube videos and decide what to put in mine if I do one.'

I picked up my coffee and wandered towards my bedroom; the carpet was heaven under my feet. I passed the hateful shoes on the way and resisted the urge to kick them hard. Lee was right, though. I did need to start saving money. It was the internet that was the problem; it was just so easy to buy things. If I didn't watch it, my credit card would be maxed out soon. I'd hidden the last two statements from Leanne to avoid the lecture that I'd get if she saw them. But there were so many gorgeous things online. Still, there was one good thing; if I spent this evening looking at baking videos and planning my own, I wouldn't have spent any time shopping, would I? And I was absolutely determined to leave my job and start my own business; I wanted my passion to become my job. Plus, it was one of the few things I was any good at. Leanne and Emma said all the time how good my food was as they stuffed it in.

I loaded up my laptop, which took an age as always, and checked out some baking videos on YouTube. Most of them were on the boring side, to be honest, especially the ones in expensive, middle-class, gorgeous kitchens, with huge marble-topped islands and bi-fold doors in the background. Too Nigella.

For me, they lacked a certain realism that made them hard to relate to. I was sure I could do a better one. I could link it to the blog and do a Facebook page. I still hadn't thought of a good business name, though. As ideas began to take shape, I scribbled them down. I could video myself making some stuff this weekend and take some pictures for the blog as well.

While Facebook was loading, I checked my emails on my phone, which were full of rubbish as usual: marketing crap and annoying links from people I'd never heard of that didn't go anywhere when you clicked on them. My phone vibrated as a text came in. It was from Adam.

Still on for Thursday? Xxx

I typed *yes x* then deleted the kiss, then added two and deleted them. What was the right amount for a second date? Before I could agonise any more about it I sent it. Ten seconds later he sent *:) xxx*.

Two hours later and I'd written another blog, announcing I was going to start vlogging. Might as well jump right in. I added some pictures of the carrot cake I'd taken into work today, plus one I'd made last night (milk chocolate with tiny violets piped on top). I also included one of the empty plate at work with just a few crumbs left. I read the blog back and couldn't believe how crap it sounded. I'd gone for a punchy, breezy tone but ended up sounding like a total airhead. Sod it; it was only a bit of fun anyway, and I didn't think many people would read it. I'd only been doing it for two months.

Leanne, sitting cross-legged on her bed, looked up from her laptop when I went into her bedroom. Her sewing machine took up most of the space on her dressing table. There was a good layer of dust on its cover.

'What are you looking at?' I asked.

'Nothing much. Just Facebook and emails.' She closed the lid and eyed me. 'What? You look sort of giddy.'

'I've just announced it on my blog. That I'm going to post some videos.'

'Sounds like you've made your mind up.'

'I have.'

She looked at me, her smile fading.

'What?'

'Mum just rang me a few minutes ago,' she said quietly. 'He's out.'

My heart stuttered. 'Already? Are you sure?'

'Time off for good behaviour.' Her eyes were glistening.

'That's so shit. He bloody raped somebody!'

She put her hand to her forehead and rubbed away at the skin. 'I still can't move on, Sarah. It could have been me. I was going to marry a rapist. Would have, if she hadn't come forward. It still haunts me, you know, the gentle cajoling when I wasn't in the mood, not taking no for an answer until I gave in, the way he liked to control everything I did and said. You know, I thought it was because he cared, at first, and was taking an interest. How could I have not seen it?'

'But you didn't know then, did you? Hindsight is a wonderful thing. He's barely been in prison for two years, if he's out already. Heaven knows what that poor girl is thinking. If she knows. Oh god, do you think she does?'

'I don't know. It's a kick in the teeth for her.'

'It is.'

'I just think, if that's the sort of men I pick, I'll stay on my own, thanks.'

I touched her hand. 'It was one bad decision.'

She shook her head, not convinced. Her face was white.

'You're not worried he'll find out where we live, are you?'

She shrugged. 'I don't know. You saw the letter he wrote from prison, saying he still loved me and that we had unfinished business. He sent it to Mum's. I know we've moved since then, but people can find out these things easy enough, can't they?'

'He wouldn't dare, surely. Is that restraining order thing still current?'

'Yes. But it might not stop him. He still maintains he was innocent, that she was lying and she wanted it as much as he did.'

'But, even if that were true, he still cheated on you. The scumbag!'

She nodded, put her laptop on the floor and got into bed. 'Anyway, I'm tired. I'm going to have an early night. I don't want to think about him. He's not worth it.'

'No, he's not. Night,' I said, going out of her room and back to mine. I couldn't believe Craig was out. He *did* rape that girl while he was engaged to Leanne, and serving two years of a five-year sentence was just a joke. If that was justice, then what was the point? He'd more or less got away with it.

4

AT LUNCHTIME, I WAIT *in the café where she's meeting her friend. I read it on her Facebook page. The one she thinks is private. I know her login. She uses the same password for everything.*

Hacking her computer was easy. I heard her giving out her email address and with one email, I was in. She clicked on it and bingo. The keylogger I installed means I can follow everything she does on it. Every website she visits, every email she writes, checking her bank.

I'm facing away from the door. In my bulky winter coat and cap pulled down low, she won't notice me. She's really not that observant. Her friend gets there first and sits down two tables away. I recognise her from a Facebook photo: Emma. She's the chunky one with the horrible dyed-red hair that's cut in that unflattering earlobe-length swingy style. She's doing something on her phone. She's a minger, barely a two out of ten. She's wearing a green coat that only just buttons up and has a handbag the size of America, probably to keep her make-up in, judging by the amount plastered over her face. A woman with a noisy kid sits at the table between us, eating a sandwich and ignoring the whingeing sprog that's trying to get out of the buggy.

She arrives not long after, oblivious to everything but her friend. If I angle the phone towards them, I can see their reflections in the mirrored screen. They do that air-kissing thing and sit down. I can't hear much of what they're saying thanks to the whining brat.

The minger talks a lot and waves her hands about all over the place. Finally, she stands up. It's a wonder she can swing her arse round in such a tight space, but she manages it somehow and goes off to the counter. I risk a glance over my shoulder, back at their table. She's taken out her phone and is messing about with it.

The minger returns with food, and they eat. I'm getting bored and considering leaving when the minger looks at her watch and drains her cup then stands up. Thank God, she's going. The minger leaves, holding the door open for a woman coming in with a child. I finish the last of my cold coffee and watch her in my phone screen for a while longer as she sits there, still doing something on her phone. She smiles and types something in, then gets up to go. She doesn't glance my way. Who's made her smile? It could be anyone.

I can hardly wait for tonight. She'd better be home because I've got the whole evening planned. Watching her. My favourite pastime.

5

ADAM PICKED UP TWO menus and handed one to me. His right leg was jiggling like crazy under the table.

'What do you fancy?' I asked, opening the menu and trying not to yawn. The heat from the log fire in the corner was making me drowsy.

'I don't know. I've had a few meals in here. They've all been nice.'

I closed my menu. 'I'm not that hungry. I might just have the tomato soup.'

He looked up. 'Are you sure that's all you want? I'm starving. I think I'll have fish and chips.' He got his wallet out and stood up. 'I'll go and order.'

I watched him as he walked up to the bar and leaned on it. He turned to look back at me and smiled, his fingers drumming out a rhythm on the wooden surface. He was really nice-looking with a mouth that flicked up at the corners, whether or not he was smiling. His skin was tanned, and his floppy golden-caramel hair glinted as the lights above the bar reflected off it. He was more surfer boy than bad boy, with that lean frame, narrow hips and long legs. We met in the local supermarket, of all places. He was on his own with a hand basket (four-pack of Carlsberg, chilli con carne and tinned chocolate pudding!) and I was with Leanne, who was pushing a small trolley. Unfortunately, we were choosing toilet roll at the time and arguing about the value cheap stuff your fingers go straight through (Leanne's choice) or aloe vera enriched quilted (mine). I lost.

I looked around the pub. The Worthy Arms was one of those olde-worlde affairs, all black oak beams and faded, patterned carpets, just around the corner from my flat. Adam only lived a couple of streets from here, too. He turned to the girl behind the bar when she went to serve him. She smiled and preened, tossing her hair back as she took his order, obviously flirting with him. Hmmm! Bloody cheek! When he wound his way through the jostling crowds with two more cokes, her eyes were fixed on him all the way. He was oblivious.

'How's your day been? Does it get quieter around Christmas?' I asked when he'd sat back down next to me.

His eyes fixed on mine. He leaned forward and steepled his fingers. I could feel the rush of energy and enthusiasm as he talked.

'God, no. It's madder than ever; businesses putting new security systems in while they're closed over the holidays. We're rushed off our feet. This is the first night I've finished before ten. I told Nathan there was no way I was doing a late one tonight. I had something much more important on.' His cheeks flushed and he picked up his drink, taking a swig of his coke.

I thought back to the business card he gave me in the supermarket, that was on the hall table at home. 'A & N Security. Let me guess: Adam and Nathan?'

'That's right.'

'Is it just you two?'

He nodded and swirled his coke around, causing a white froth to fizz. 'Yep. And neither of us is good at the paperwork, so our office is a right mess.'

'So, what have you been doing today?' I asked.

When Adam put his glass down, his hand crept nearer to mine. 'I've been putting new security cameras in a theatre in the West End. Their old system was ancient. I'm surprised it still worked. I think Noah had one on his Ark.'

That made me laugh. 'They probably got destroyed in the flood.'

'Yeah. You should have seen the size of them. They weighed a ton. Nathan almost dropped one on his foot. It would have broken it if he had.'

'That would have been all you needed, a trip to A & E.'

I picked up my drink. His hand went back to his own side of the table and he picked up a beer mat, turning it over and over between his long fingers. His leg began to jiggle again. I knew it was only our second date, but the silence was kind of awkward. All I knew about him so far, apart from his security system business, was that he had an older sister and lived with his twin brother, Luke, a trainee doctor. He seemed more intent on asking about me, wanting to know everything.

'Oh, I forgot,' he said, 'My sister, Debbie, asked me to ask you about doing her wedding cake. I told her about you.'

My first wedding cake? Wow! 'Really? That'd be great. When's the wedding?'

'Ages away yet. September next year.'

'I'd love to do it.' I sipped some diet coke and fished the slice of lemon out of it with my fingers, dropping it on the table. I hate lemon in coke. What's the point of it? It doesn't even go. The condensation on the glass dripped onto my dress and I wiped my fingers on my tights.

Adam shifted in his seat, took a knife out of the cutlery pot in the middle of the table and started to fiddle with it. 'Do you have any brothers or sisters?'

'No. I'm the only one.'

'Aw! Were you lonely?' He nudged me with his shoulder.

'No. But I think I was a spoilt brat.'

Adam burst out laughing and just then our food arrived.

'That was quick,' I said, when the waiter put my soup and bread roll in front of me.

Adam's fish and chips were massive. I hoped he wouldn't mind if I pinched a few chips. Some men hated sharing their food. This soup wouldn't fill me up for long, but it was the cheapest thing on the menu, and I didn't want to assume he was paying for mine. I liked to pay my own way, and I'd made up my mind to definitely stop wasting money.

'Want some chips?' he asked, pointing with his fork. 'I can't eat all this.'

'Go on then.'

He piled some chips on his side plate and pushed it over to me. With my bread roll I made a chip butty, which made him laugh, especially when I slathered brown sauce on it. We ate, and when he'd finished, he put his knife and fork together across his plate. He had managed to finish it. I opened my purse and got enough money out for my soup and drinks.

'Don't be daft. I'll get them,' he said.

'No, I'll get mine.'

'Put your money away. My treat.' He started to rip the beer mat into tiny fragments.

'Okay. Well, thanks.' I checked the time on my phone. 'I suppose I should be getting back.'

'Aw, come on. One more drink? A proper one.'

I looked at his eager face, at the fire crackling in the fireplace, and thought of the December chill outside. 'Go on then, you've twisted my arm. I could murder a glass of dry white.'

'Great. I'll have a pint then,' he said with a grin and went off to get them.

I leaned back in my seat and watched him again as he laughed with the girl behind the bar. She definitely fancied him. Even though she knew he was with another woman, she was using every trick in her arsenal: chest out, hair flipping and twirling, touching his arm, leaning closer. Breaking the sisterhood code. It just wasn't on. But again, Adam seemed oblivious.

When he got back, he handed me a massive glass.

'Is that okay?'

'Perfect,' I said, determining not to get drunk. Tomorrow was a workday.

Two hours later and I'd lost count of how many I'd had. The room felt like it was starting to tilt. We'd talked about our jobs, childhood pets and families, and what we liked on telly; I'd learned Luke was training to be a surgeon in something or other. And I'd gone on about baking and wanting to set up my own business far too much. But he hadn't complained. In fact, he'd been a great listener. We'd spent the last ten minutes talking utter crap, from what I could remember. And now I really, really couldn't drink any more. I picked up my phone from the fragments of several beer mats littered all over the table and peered at the screen.

'Look at the time. It's late. We've both got work tomorrow. And I'm drunk. You're a bad influence,' I said, reaching for my coat.

'Sorry,' he said, looking anything but. He picked up his leather biker's jacket and put it on while I zipped up my thick, winter coat.

It was freezing out and we made our way down the road, me tottering slightly in my high boots. Adam took my arm and steadied me when I stumbled. The biting chill sobered me up some, but not enough. Outside my flat, I rummaged in my bag for my keys.

'I've had a great time. When can I see you again?' Adam inclined his head and kissed me gently on the lips. Beer and chips mingled in with his own smell, of leather and something musky. It was nice.

'I'll call you,' I said.

He nodded and thrust his hands in his pockets, smiling. 'Great. Night Sarah.'

'Night.'

The stairs up to the top floor seemed longer than ever. How come they never got any easier? In the living room, Leanne was watching TV. Her eyes slid past me as I walked in.

'On your own?' she asked.

'Yes. Adam's gone home.'

She got up and walked to the window, pulled the curtain back a fraction and peered down onto the street. I felt like she was expecting to see Craig standing outside under a lamppost, staring up at our flat. Instead, she dropped the curtain back into place, said nothing, and resumed watching TV.

6

'SHIT!' I SAID AS my trainers slipped on a patch of black ice and my legs went from under me. I banged my knee on the metal bin and grabbed it to break my fall. It hurt so bad I couldn't speak.

'He looks like fuckin' Bambi, don't he, Shanksy?' Paul said, with a snort of laughter.

I was too busy trying not to smash my head in on the litter bin to punch him one, as I skidded again. As soon as I could stand upright, I'd smack him if he was still laughing.

Shanksy looked wary, like he wanted to laugh but thought it was probably a bad idea. Sensible guy.

'You're heading for a smack in the gob,' I told him. 'I'd fuckin' shut it if I were you.'

His smile disappeared. 'Just joking, Col. No offense. Jeez!'

'Well, watch it, next time.' I nodded at his pocket. 'Any stuff left?'

He pulled out a tiny packet of foil from his jacket and handed me it. 'Not much. Here, though, you can have it.'

I put it in my pocket for later. 'Right, you twats. I'm off. I'm not staying out all night freezing my balls off with you couple of pussies.'

'You off to school tomorrow?' asked Shanksy, shielding the cig in his cupped hand as a gust of wind whipped around our faces.

'Dunno. See what I feel like when I wake up. Probably will, just to get away from my Ma. See ya.'

I walked away from them. I should go home but couldn't face it just yet. Dad's house was near here. He'd probably be in bed with some *slag, or pissed up and flat out on the sofa. I didn't want to go in there either. My fingers clutched the foil packet. I needed somewhere sheltered to take it. I jogged down a couple of streets and round the corner, cutting down the back alley behind Dad's garden. The fence, or what was left of it, was only four foot high, and I leaped over it without breaking my stride. Dad's shed door was already busted, but it wasn't like there was anything in there worth nicking. It hung at an angle on one rusted hinge and I crouched down to get through the small gap. It was still cold in here, but at least it was out of the wind.*

A tattered piece of cloth covered half the window, but the glass was so dirty no one would see in anyway. I sat on a black bin bag, overflowing with rubbish, and took out the foil packet, unwrapping it carefully so I didn't spill any of the powder inside. An old table had just enough clear space for me to chop it up and snort it through a rolled up bus ticket. My nostrils burned as I sniffed hard, and the coke shot through my body with a burst of energy. There was enough for three small lines and I had it all.

I wouldn't sleep if I went home to bed now. There might be some booze under Dad's sink if I was lucky. The one thing you didn't nick off him was his booze; if he caught you, he'd kill you. But I wanted some, and I wouldn't get caught. No way. I left the shed and picked my way through the cat shit and piles of litter in the back garden to the back door. It wasn't locked but the chain was on, and I couldn't get my hand through the gap. No matter. I jogged round the front and turned the door handle. Locked. I lifted the stone next to the door and got the spare key. Everyone round here knew it was there, but no one would break in. Not only was there nothing to pinch, my old man would beat the living shit out of anyone who tried. There was no chain on the front door, so I slipped the key in and turned it.

The handle was stiff, and the door always creaked if you opened it too fast, so I eased it slowly inwards, listening to where he might be. Upstairs light off. No shagging sounds. Snoring coming from down the hallway where the living room was. The kitchen was on the left, but the light was off. I couldn't risk putting it on, so I crept over to the sink and opened the door to the cupboard underneath. The roller blind was up and there was a streetlight right outside. I waited a few minutes for my eyes to get used to the dark, hardly daring to breathe. For all he was

22

pissed and snoring, the old man could go from fast asleep to wide awake and roaring in an instant. Many times, I'd been belted for assuming he was snoozing when he really had one eye cranked open, just waiting. Finally, dark shapes in the kitchen took on form and substance but it was all for nothing; there was fuck all to drink under there. The bastard had supped the lot. Best not to hang around much longer.

On the way back to the front door, I spotted his car keys next to the rusty fridge. I lifted them. His car, parked outside, might be a pile of shit, but it still ran. I closed the door behind me and crept down the path, keeping close to the hedge. It was about half ten at night, but there was always someone skulking about this place. Sure enough, there was a couple up the street walking a dog the size of a guinea pig, but they were going the other way.

I unlocked the car door, jamming the key into it quickly; no central locking shit here. The car looked older than my Ma and that was saying something. I felt lit up like a Christmas tree under the streetlight, so I started the engine, leaving the seatbelt off. It was the first time I'd been in a driver's seat. At fifteen, I was two years off even having lessons, not that there was any chance of me being able to afford them, and my folks weren't the type to pay for them. There were other things they'd rather spend their dough on than us.

The engine caught first time, then stopped after lurching forward. Shit! Forgot about the clutch. Shanksy's brother was a mechanic and he'd told us the basics though, course, we couldn't have a go in the customers' cars. This time, I left the clutch down, put it in first and let the handbrake off. Nothing happened when I revved it. Clutch. Left foot. Release slowly. Shit, it was moving! The blood pumped faster round my body and I let out a whoop. I kangarooed up the street at first and a cloud of thick black smoke followed me up the road. Despite it being dark, I could still see it billowing out behind the car. Shitty exhaust. When I got a car, it wouldn't be a crock of crap like this. This wouldn't pass an MOT, but I'd never known the old man take it for one.

At the corner, I turned left without stopping. Safer than turning right—I might stall it again. The streets were quiet as the pubs round here didn't always chuck out when the law said. Lock-ins were common. Our estate wasn't a place the cops liked to come if they didn't have to, so they tended to save it for the big stuff. I was heading towards the shops and there were more streetlights and cars around. I was getting the hang of the steering wheel and pedals. I was a natural, probably. Wouldn't need lessons at this rate. The speed limit was thirty round here, and it felt really slow. When I accelerated, so did my heart rate, and soon I was up to sixty going past the park and the school. Whoo-hoo! I turned the radio on, and Linkin Park came booming out. I turned it up full, so the bass thumped me in the chest. Past the park, I did a wide u-turn, bumping up the kerb on the other side and stalling it again. It was darker here, the shops being half a mile away. I set off again, pedal to the floor. Nickelback came on and I started bellowing out How You Remind Me, swaying my head to the music. The streetlight here was bust, and it was dark. A cat startled me by running straight across the road in front of me and I hit the kerb, just missing a rubbish bin. A woman with two little kids was just coming out of the off-licence. The kids were way too young to be up at this time. Funny the things that go through your mind, even in the blindest panic. The car sort of ricocheted back into the road as I pulled the wheel way too hard the other way, and I was heading straight for the kids, up onto the pavement.

'No! No!' I yelled, trying to brake. In my panic, I hit the accelerator instead. The kids came closer at an alarming rate. The woman looked up and I saw her eyes go wide. We both screamed as the car ploughed into the kids. I didn't stop, and pressed down harder, pulling the car back into the road, my mind screaming Shit! Shit! Shit!

I took the first right turn off the main road and drove back to the old man's as quick as I could. Every bit of me was shaking, out of control. I hadn't looked back in the mirror, but I was pretty sure I went over at least one of the kids. I'd felt a bump and a bang. I was back at Dad's in minutes and I stopped, ran up the path, returned his keys and got the fuck away. He was still snoring and by the smell of the booze coming out of the living room, he was more out of it than I'd first thought.

When I got home, my sister was in her bedroom, but Ma wasn't there. I'd expected her to be on the settee, with an empty bottle of vodka on its side next to her, like most nights. I hammered on my sister's door.

She turned her music down and opened up. She was in her pyjamas, a cig burning between her fingers.

'What?' she said, scowling.

'Where's Ma?'

'Fucked if I know.' She closed the door in my face.

In bed, the shakes just wouldn't stop and I was icy cold with dread and fear. What if the kid was dead? What if the woman saw my face? It was dark, and I had my hood up as it was cold, so maybe she didn't. I knew one thing. I was never having coke again.

7

HE LOOKED LIKE A tramp. He was half-concealed, slumped between two wheelie bins in a front garden on Gaulk Road and had a good view of the blue front door of Westmoreland House, where she lived. It was six thirty in the morning and the street was beginning to wake up, though dawn had not yet arrived. The odd commuter had begun to leave, but no one had seen him yet. He wasn't that bothered if they did. He'd just move on. That was what tramps did, wasn't it?

It was damn cold. He was glad of the layers he'd put on under the thick coat. The ragged blanket around him was just for effect. Once he was on the move, he wouldn't want to look like a hobo. He'd want to blend in, just another commuter going about his business. The woolly hat he was wearing would be discarded in one of the wheelie bins, along with the blanket.

He jerked when the front door of the house whose garden he was in cranked open a fraction.

'Go on, boy,' a woman said, and he turned his face slightly to see a small black and white dog, a Jack Russell, trot out. The door closed. The dog couldn't fail to see him. The garden was about four metres square, if that. Whoever shooed it out must not have looked outside.

It stopped when it saw him and raised one front foot.

Please don't bark, please don't bark. The dog looked around uncertainly. It ventured forward slowly, its tail ramrod straight and quivering, neck stretched forward. He could hear it snuffling the air. He moved his hand, and it leaped back with a low growl. He hid his face and hoped it would just go away. It sniffed him but soon lost interest, trotting off to the other side, where it cocked its leg up on a weed. The yellow, stringy plant looked like it got this treatment every day and had given up trying to grow.

Snuffling again. It came closer, stopping a few inches away. He could hear its paws scrabbling about on the gravel. What the hell was it doing? He moved his head a fraction so he could see. Aw, jeez. It was only having a dump.

The door opened again.

'Come on, Frank. Hurry up.'

The dog was called bloody Frank! The dog stood, shook itself, and cocked its leg up for a final pee. The door closed again.

For Christ's sake! It'd pissed on him, the little bastard.

By seven thirty, stiff with cold and with a stinking, wet leg, his patience paid off when the door to Westmoreland House opened and she came out in a thick coat with a scarf wound tightly around her neck. He couldn't take his eyes off her. The dog hadn't come out again and nor had its owner. No one had seen him. She turned left and hurried down the road. He got up, wincing at the pain in his back from huddling in the cold for so long, and stuffed the hat and blanket in the bin. The dog in the house started barking and scrabbling at the door. He hopped over the low garden wall, ignoring the clammy trouser leg that was sticking to him, and followed her up the street. She turned left at the end. Bus or Tube? Both were up this way.

She didn't look back. She was huddled up in her coat, her shoulders hunched. He was wearing a baseball cap now, with the peak pulled low. If he couldn't see her face, she wouldn't be able to see his. She was going for the bus. *Shit!* Tube would have been better. He was going to have to get the same bus. Was it too much of a risk? He followed her to the bus stop. There was a queue. Maybe if he got on at the last minute, she wouldn't spot him. He hung back, leaving his decision until the last moment. He was going to risk it.

The bus arrived and the queue moved swiftly. He lost sight of her. He ran and jumped on at the last minute, flashing his Oyster card and keeping his head down. She'd managed to get a seat halfway down. All the other empty seats were at the back. He was going to have to walk past her. If she looked up, she'd be bound to see him, but the beard he now had concealed half his face. She was taking out her phone, plugging earphones into it, head down. He averted his face as he went past, holding his breath so hard he thought his eardrums might burst. There was a vacant seat right at the back. He made for it, the breath exploding out of his lungs. From here, he'd be able to see when she got off.

The bus moved slowly at this time of the day. Rush hour. He tried to imagine what job she was going to. He had no idea where she worked now, so he gave up trying to guess. He'd find out before much longer, anyway.

8

ON MY WAY TO work, the homeless guy was sitting outside the Tube station again, his ragged, red woolly hat standing out against the dull grey brick. It was the first time I'd seen him in two weeks. I stopped a moment, watching him. He was speaking to everyone who passed, but he might as well be invisible. After a five-minute detour to the café over the road, I stood in front of him with a cup of coffee and a bacon sandwich. He squinted up at me through weary eyes. I did a quick check—no empty beer cans or bottles of cider scattered anywhere near him, just a large Starbuck's cup with a few coins in it.

'I thought you might be hungry. It's freezing out here,' I said.

'Thank you.' He took the paper bag from me. The smell of the bacon sandwich seeped out when he opened it, and he took a massive bite. I handed him the coffee.

'Three sugars.'

'Thank you. I'm very grateful.' I was no good with Scottish accents. It could be anywhere from Aberdeen to Glasgow for all I knew.

While he had another bite, I took a foil package containing two cherry muffins out of my handbag. One for me, one for Pauline, who sat next to me at work. I placed it on the blanket he was sitting on.

'Pudding,' I said. 'Homemade.'

He stopped chewing. 'What's your name?' he asked, his attention moving from the sandwich onto me.

'Sarah. What's yours?'

'Ben.'

I nodded. 'Well, Ben, I'd better get going. I'll be late for work.'

He held the bag up towards me. 'Thanks again.'

***

After work, I sat at my little desk in the bedroom. The phone call I'd been hoping for had come this lunchtime, and I'd hardly been able to keep still all afternoon. Last weekend, I had a mad baking session and took loads of stuff to a newish deli that had opened up five minutes away from our flat. My stuff sold out and they wanted more. I flexed my fingers and started to type a blog post.

Partybakes

Tuesday 16th Dec

Just want to share my fantastic news. A deli near me is selling my Christmas goodies, so look out for my Christmas bombes and spiced Christmas brownies in Delish in Brook Street in Shepherd's Bush. If you try some, let me know what you think (if you like them, that is— if you hate them, perhaps better keep it to yourself!).

This is an extremely short blog as I am an extremely busy cook! Hope to blog again before Christmas. If I don't, have a good one and I'll be back in the New Year with some videos of what I've been making during the holiday. Check them out on my YouTube channel here.

Ps, please keep emailing me your lovely comments and recipes. It's lovely to hear from you all.

Happy Christmas

Sarah xxx

I posted the blog. I was beginning to hate the Sarah who wrote it. She sounded nothing like me; she was so wet and bland and polite. Plus, I lied—hardly anyone was getting in touch about it: two nice comments and a troll on Twitter. But at least the bit about Delish placing an order was true. My first order! I could hardly believe it. I wanted to tell Leanne, but she wasn't home yet. I didn't know where she was.

After it was posted, I checked my bank balance and got a shock. God, it was bad. Had I really spent all that? I leaned forward and put my elbows on the desk, as if being closer to the screen would make it say something different. Most of it had gone on ingredients for the cakes and bakes, way more than I'd realised. The direct debit for the lottery tickets I bought every week stared me in the face, taunting me. If only I could have a big win. My parents had never been well off, even though Dad had had a decent job. They still lived in the council house I grew up in in north London. I'd love to win the lottery just to give it to them. Mum would sit at a big pine table in the massive kitchen of a country pile, and Dad could have a veg patch and keep chickens.

The front door banged and Lee poked her head around the door a second later, still in a coat and scarf. At the sight of her anxious face, something twisted in my gut. I got up too quickly, knocking the stool over.

'What's up?' I swallowed hard. 'Is it Craig?'

She stood there, knitting her fingers together. 'No one knows where he's gone. Mum's been trying to find out.'

I picked the stool up. 'He won't try and find you, surely. That'd land him straight back inside. Wouldn't it?'

'I suppose. What should I do?'

'Look, you knew this would happen eventually, didn't you? Carry on as normal. He won't come looking for you. Surely he wouldn't be that stupid.'

'I hope so. It's the not knowing where he is and the 'unfinished business' stuff. It's freaking me out. I can't stand the thought of him. He makes my skin crawl.' She chewed her bottom lip, and I went to hug her. Her body was tense and unyielding against me.

'You should tell the police if you're scared, Lee.'

'He hasn't officially done anything, has he? Anyway, you're probably right about him not coming here. I'm probably just panicking and being stupid.' She squared her shoulders and tossed her ringlets back. 'He's not worth wasting time talking about.' She lingered in the doorway and folded her arms. 'So anyway, when's your work's Christmas do again?'

'Tomorrow night. Don't remind me.' I pulled a face at the thought of it.

'Cheer up. You said they're never as bad as you think. Think of all the free booze.'

'I'll have to. It's the only thing going for it. At least Donna and Katie will be there.'

'I'm going out tomorrow night too. With Emma. She's dragging me out.' Leanne didn't look too enamoured with the idea.

I knew Emma was. I'd asked her to. Well, begged, and promised her a red velvet chocolate cake. If Emma couldn't cheer you up, no one could. 'That's great. It'll do you good. Where are you off to?'

'Pictures, I think. Emma said it's a surprise, then gave it away by talking about the new Chris Hemsworth film that's just come out.'

Typical Emma.

I noted the dark circles under her eyes, how tired she looked. 'You're late, aren't you? Where've you been?'

'At the shop. Late night opening. Kath decided I could do the first one. I forgot to tell you. It was a waste of time. No one came in. Honestly, if she expects me to sell loads of clothes, she needs to stock better stuff. Or let me do the buying.' Her eyes went sparkly when she mentioned it. It would be her dream. 'Well, I'm off to have a long bath,' she said. 'Do you need the loo first?'

'No.'

My heart felt heavy in my chest, like a lump of lead, as she left, her shoulders slumping slightly. I knew she was thinking about Craig. I'd met him a few times, and he seemed nice. Charming and considerate. A bloody good actor. Wherever he was, I hoped it was a long way from here.

The day of the Christmas party dawned freezing cold and sleeting. I dragged myself out of bed, looked in the mirror and there it was: a massive zit, right there on my chin. It looked like Mount Vesuvius about to erupt. A quick squeeze only hurt and made it angrier. I'd need a boatload of concealer to cover it. The shower graced me with its customary trickle of lukewarm water and I got ready for work, dressing in layers, four-deep. The party was straight after work so I was taking my outfit with me. I'd got the most fabulous dress from a new vintage shop that had just opened up on the Uxbridge Road. I'd hired it as it was three hundred to buy. I wished it were mine. I ran my hand over the silver brocade fabric and folded it carefully into tissue paper, then packed it into a carrier with a black bag and shoes. I could sort my hair out later in the toilets. It'd be shoved under a woolly hat on the way to work so it'd be in a state when I got there, anyway.

Nobody seemed to be working too hard. Pauline, at the desk next to mine, hadn't been with the company for long. She was nice but very quiet most days, not one for office gossip. I'd put her somewhere in her fifties. She'd told me she had two grown-up sons. Husband worked as an accountant.

'Are you looking forward to the party tonight?' she asked as I sat down.

'It'll be alright. It's your first one, isn't it?'

'Yes. What are they usually like?'

'It depends on what you class as exciting.'

'Oh, that good!' She laughed and went back to her work. I started my computer and checked through what I had to do. The usual, basic, bog-standard admin.

Adam texted me twice in the afternoon. *Are we still meeting tomorrow xx*

Depends on how much I drink tonight ;)

He sent back *Have a good time xx.*

After work, I went to the toilets to change. The dress was gorgeous and fit me as if it was made for me. I turned my head upside down and ran my fingers through my hair. When I threw my head back, it fell in glossy, wild waves, my favourite look. I scrutinised myself in the mirror. I may have dark colouring, but I couldn't see the Eva Longoria connection. My nose was too large. A quick refresh of my make-up and I was done.

I got another text: *We're ready.*

It was from Donna. She and Katie were waiting for me downstairs. Katie worked on reception and Donna did admin-type things like me, but for a different bunch of solicitors, who we hardly ever saw. They were both good fun, my best friends from work. They were dressed to kill, as I knew they would be, and I envied their height as they towered above me in skyscraper stilettos. They were quite similar, with blonde waves cascading down their backs, large smoky eyes and full-on red lips. Donna was in scarlet, in a tight-fitting body-con dress and red jewelled high sandals. Katie was wearing purple, something beautiful that managed to be both clingy and floaty.

'You look gorgeous, Sarah. That dress is stunning,' Katie said, her hand stroking the fabric. 'Amazing colour.'

'Thanks. I love what you're both wearing. You look amazing. And really tall!'

We left the lobby and headed out into the night. It was raining and snowing at the same time. The party was at a hotel just a few doors down and we ran as best as we could in our high heels.

'My God, it's freezing. And I'm never going to last all night in these shoes,' Katie moaned. 'They're killing me already.'

'When you've had a few drinks, you won't notice the pain. Come on,' Donna said, putting a spurt on.

A welcome blast of hot air hit us when Donna pulled open the door to the room where our party was. The dimly lit room was large and airy, with circular tables draped in red and silver everywhere. Balloons and party poppers adorned the tables, and wine glasses gave off sparkling glints as the light bounced off a large silver disco ball that rotated high up in the ceiling. A DJ was playing eighties hits, at the moment more background music than the ear-splitting cacophony it usually turned into by the end. I looked around the room with interest. There was a lot more female flesh on show than on your average office day. The women strutting around reminded me of peacocks on display.

Not that the three of us were any different. Almost as one, we pulled our shoulders back and headed straight for the bar at the far end of the room. My goose bumps had faded and I was starting to feel a nice warm glow. I'd rather have been at home creating something in the kitchen, but I was going to enjoy it now I was here. The loud chatter was almost drowning out the disco music and the DJ inched up the sliders in competition. I glanced around the room and my eyes landed on Chris, over on the far side. I'd barely seen him since that day in the kitchen, other than a couple of 'hellos' in passing. He looked as if he'd come straight from the office and just taken off his jacket. His tie was off, and his shirt sleeves were rolled up past his elbows. He ran a free hand through his dark hair, which somehow always looked on the verge of needing a trim. I suspected it took a lot of work to look so unbarbered. He was lifting a pint to his lips when he caught me looking. He stopped with his glass poised and looked at me long and hard. Then he smiled and nodded. I smiled back, trying to ignore the flip my stomach performed, and tuned back into my friends' conversation.

It was an open bar tonight, so I'd only brought enough money for a taxi home. At the bar, trays of glasses filled with wine were lined up, and Donna shoved a glass of something white and bubbly into my hand.

'Thanks.' We clinked glasses then drained them. Not very ladylike, but, hey!

Donna picked up another three and passed them round. 'Start as you mean to go on,' she muttered, raising the glass to her lips.

We sat together and by the time the meal was served, we were tipsy. The food was the usual Christmas dinner fare, overcooked and lukewarm. After the meal, the big boss (who I'd never met or spoken to) made the obligatory speech and people laughed in all the right places. He was actually quite witty. The laughter got louder when someone's mobile phone went off with a naff ringtone, just as the boss got to a serious bit. He carried on regardless after saying 'the show must go on'.

At last, the meal and speeches were done. I picked at the mince pies left on a plate in the centre of the table. The pastry was too thick and the filling was dry, but at least you could taste the brandy. Mine were much better. Donna and Katie were up dancing, having discarded their shoes. I couldn't be bothered. I picked up my coffee and moved to a lounge in the back corner. My head was spinning, and I'd lost track of how many drinks I'd had, and what they were. There was an oversized, comfy-looking sofa with its back to the rest of the room, and I leaned into it, closing my eyes and tipping my head back.

The cushion next to me gave way when someone sank into it. Assuming it must be Katie or Donna, I kept my eyes closed until a strong smell of aftershave wafted over me. *Aftershave?* I opened one eye, then the other, and sat up too fast when Chris came into focus. He was right up against me and our thighs were touching. The wine sloshing about in my stomach made me feel nauseous.

'Hello,' he said. He was holding two enormous glasses of wine, which he placed on a coffee table.

The effort of sitting up proved too much for my spinning head, and I closed my eyes fast. What did he want?

9

CHRIS DIDN'T MOVE AND I squeezed my eyes together tighter, waiting for the nausea to pass. He cleared his throat and I felt a light touch on my thigh. Or did I just imagine it? My eyes sprang open. The wine sloshed again and for a brief, horrid moment I thought the mince pies might make a reappearance. Chris's hand was on his own knee. He smiled again and I had to lean in slightly to catch what he was saying over Clean Bandit's *No Place I'd Rather Be*.

'You look beautiful. Stunning. Easily the most gorgeous woman in the room. A ten out of ten from me.'

A rush of heat infused my cheeks. Was he serious? He looked gloriously rumpled, as if he'd just rolled out of bed. It was incredibly sexy and made me think he could be dangerous to be alone with. I looked around, trying to spot my friends, but the sofa had its back to the rest of the room. There were empty armchairs to both sides and a fireplace with a massive oil painting of a landscape above it. If we couldn't see anyone, no one could see us. His presence was unsettling and exciting, and I shifted about on the sofa, unsure what to say. He didn't seem to notice the awkward silence and carried on.

'I like your dress. It suits you.'

'Er, thank you.'

'I've never seen one like it. Where's it from?'

'Oh, erm, it's from a vintage shop on Uxbridge Road.'

'Looks expensive. I like a lady with expensive tastes.'

'It is expensive. Which is why I've only hired it.'

'Ah! I like a thrifty one even more.'

He nodded approvingly as his eyes roved over the dress. I grasped the hem and tried to tug it down my thighs, conscious that the lace tops of my ultra-sheer hold-ups were peeking out. It must have ridden up when I sat down half-pissed. He batted my hand away.

'Well, it looks great. Stop pulling at it and relax. I won't bite.'

His mock scolding made me smile. He shifted further into the sofa and spread his arms along the back, his left arm disappearing behind my shoulders. I tried not to look at the dark chest hair that was visible from the open neck of his shirt. He leaned forward, picked up a glass of wine and handed it to me. I took it on autopilot, and he reached for his own. He clinked his glass against mine. 'Cheers.'

'I've had way too much already,' I said, gazing blearily into the glass. I really didn't want any more.

'Well, it's a party. Let your hair down.' His eyes followed where my hair tumbled over my shoulders and his mouth lifted slightly at one corner.

I sipped it, before putting it down on the table. The damn dress rode up even more when I leaned forward.

'So, tell me about yourself, sexy baking girl,' he said. His eyes seemed to capture mine and I couldn't look away. I was captivated by how startlingly blue they were, and I'd kill for the thick black lashes he'd got.

'Well, there's not much to tell,' I said, feeling my face go hot again.

'What do you like to do in your spare time?'

Before I knew it, I was telling him all about my plans for the business, the blogging and the planned vlogging over Christmas. I prattled on for about ten minutes before I tailed off.

'Sorry, I don't know when to stop. I must have bored you rigid.'

'You haven't. I'm interested.'

'So what about you? What do you like doing?'

He shrugged. 'This and that. Playing Candy Crush Saga. Top score four hundred and eighty thousand.'

'No way! Really?'

We both laughed. He tapped the side of his nose. 'That's for me to know and you to find out.'

'God, I don't think I'll ever get that many.' I thought I felt his finger on the back of my neck and my hairs stood on end. Then again, I could have just imagined it.

'My contract's up at the end of January, so I'll be moving on,' he said.

'You're leaving? I didn't know that.'

'Yeah. The job's almost done. I've got a contract somewhere else.'

'What exactly is it you do?' I asked, not that I'd understand. All I knew was he'd been hired to write some software program or other.

'Set up new security systems. More difficult to infiltrate, you know, so clients' details are safe and such like. You'll be using it soon.'

'So what's the new contract?'

'Similar sort of thing somewhere else. Anyway, no talking shop tonight,' he chided. 'It's not allowed.'

'Okay... so what do you like to do in your spare time? Apart from playing Candy Crush Saga.'

'Me? I like to hit the gym and hang out with my mates. Usual stuff really.'

'Yeah, you look like someone who lifts weights.' *Lame!*

'Do I?' He looked pleased and glanced down at his body. 'I try.'

I wanted to say, 'and it's appreciated by most of the women in this building', but I didn't. Instead, I had some more wine. My head lolled back and I swivelled it to look at him. My eyes seemed to follow a split second later. He too was sitting with his head tipped back, scrutinising the ceiling. Sia's *Chandelier* came on. One of my favourite songs. I played it constantly on my phone.

'I like this song,' said Chris.

I was already humming to it. 'Me too.'

'Are you seeing anyone?' he asked.

Was he really interested? In me? Thoughts of Adam sprang to mind. 'I've been out with someone a couple of times, but it's early days. You?'

'Nah. No one special,' he said. 'Although there is someone I like. A lot.' He gazed at me and I couldn't look away. He had the most perfectly defined Cupid's bow and a deep five o'clock shadow. When he leaned towards me, the smell of him was intoxicating and I breathed it in. When his lips brushed lightly over mine, I didn't stop him. I couldn't. His hand lightly stroked the back of my neck and my nerve endings were on sensory overload. I watched his mouth coming closer again, the tip of my tongue touched the tip of his and desire shot through me as the kiss went deeper. Thousands of tiny fireworks ignited inside me.

He pulled back to look at me and kissed me again. My brain was singing *please don't stop*. I was deflated when he pulled away, leaving me wanting more. Seconds later, Donna and Katie appeared and threw themselves down into the armchairs at either side. *Did they see us?*

'Here you are,' said Katie. 'We've been looking for you everywhere.'

She was clutching a full glass and weaved slightly as she spoke. Donna, too, had a similar vacant expression and for the first time they noticed Chris sitting next to me. He removed his arm from the back of the sofa.

'Oops, not interrupting anything, are we?' asked Donna, way too obviously for my liking. To my horror, she sent me a big wink that can't have gone unnoticed by him.

'No, course not. We were just chatting.' My face was burning and I daren't look at Chris. When I glanced at Donna, she was doing something on her phone. I think Katie had fallen asleep.

Chris got up abruptly. 'Well, I'm going to get off home. I'll see you at work.'

'Yes, okay...' But he'd already gone.

10

HE WAS WALKING IN the park, with the raw wind whipping his hair around his chapped face, just following the path to wherever. It was bitter, made him shiver, but he loved it. He'd forgotten what it was like to just wander.

A brown spaniel came racing towards him with a stick in its mouth. It circled him three times, and he couldn't help but laugh at the sight of the long, floppy ears flying up every time it bounced. A man over the other side of the park whistled and it hared off like a mad thing.

He flopped down onto a nearby bench, just another stranger sitting in a park in broad daylight with nothing better to do. All he did was think and never got any nearer an answer to what he was going to do next. Maybe he should send her some flowers. He pulled his scarf tighter around his neck to block out some of the cold. He couldn't stay here much longer or he'd freeze. His fingers wrapped around the small packet in his pocket. If he'd learned anything since it happened, it was that you could do what you want. You just had to be better at it and not get caught. He glanced over to the next bench. Two women with pushchairs were chatting and unstrapping their kids. One of the kids was wriggling like mad, desperate to get out of its restraints quicker. He knew how that felt, to be desperate to throw off the shackles and snatch back freedom, and the irony was not lost on him.

On another bench was a man, sitting on his own. He couldn't see his face from this distance, but he was older, with greying hair bushing out from under a cap. He was staring straight ahead, stock still. Didn't react when the kids ran, screaming, past him. What was his story then? Wife got cancer? Or himself? Missus ran off and left him? Pension gone tits up? Who knew?

He banged his hands together to get some feeling back into them. Yes, he'd send flowers. Women liked flowers, didn't they? And he wanted her back. He loved her. She was the only one he'd ever loved. The way he'd felt when he'd seen her and followed her to work only confirmed that. He was sure he could win her back if he could just get to talk to her. She'd been crazy about him. They were so good together. He stood up and left the park, suddenly desperate to get out of the cold. It was only a short bus ride away to his mum's.

On the journey, passing boarded-up shops covered in bright graffiti, his mood dropped. He hated this unfamiliar part of London, where his mother, his only family, had had to move when he got sent down. He got off the bus, walked around the corner and stopped dead when he turned into his mum's road. The low front garden wall of the council house had been decorated with spray paint, thick and blotchy in red, black and blue, obscuring most of the brick.

It said SCUM.

It hadn't been there this morning. An icy feeling gripped his guts, colder even than the biting wind. Without realising, he squashed the packet of Rohypnol in his pocket, crushing it until his fingernails dug into the skin. He broke into a trot and crossed the road. No one seemed to be around, but he imagined he could feel eyes on him from behind the dark windows of the other houses and flats. Who was responsible?

'Mum?' he shouted, pushing the front door open and slamming it behind him.

He followed the sounds of weeping to find his mother huddled on the sofa. He sat beside her, not sure what to say. Both of them leaped up when a brick came hurtling through the window, cascading showers of glass exploding around them. A note was tied to it.

WE DON'T WANT YOUR SORT HERE

11

THE MORNING AFTER THE Christmas party, I woke up with a massive hangover. My mouth felt woolly and disgusting, and the next thought that popped into my head was about what happened with Chris. We were kissing, and all I could remember was how intense it felt. Just thinking about it made me all tingly, despite my headache. I hauled myself into the shower, got dressed and left for work without breakfast, the thought of which made me feel sick.

The morning was arduous, and the headache just wouldn't go. Pauline looked better than me but then, I don't suppose she got drunk and started snogging the face off a colleague. Just before lunch, I went to the toilet and came out of the cubicle to find Donna in front of the basins, applying lip gloss. She didn't look half as bad as me.

'Hi,' she said as her eyes met mine in the mirror. 'Someone's puked in the toilets on our floor, so I've had to come down here.' She pulled a face.

'Urgh!' My stomach heaved at the thought. 'How are you this morning?'

'My head's killing me,' she groaned 'How much did we have?'

'I don't know. You kept doling it out.' I splashed cold water onto my temples. Did she see me and Chris kissing? I shot her a look in the mirror. I'm sure if she had, she would have said something.

She caught me looking. 'What?'

'Nothing. Just this bloody headache.'

'You and Chris looked cosy last night. What were you talking about?'

'Just rubbish, really. This and that.'

'Do you like him then?'

'I like the look of him. Who doesn't? But I don't really know him, haven't spoken to him more than a handful of times. But he seemed nice last night. Friendly.'

'Yeah, he is. He sits near me. He's a laugh when he wants to be.'

'Is he as rough as us this morning?'

'Dunno. I haven't seen him. I don't think he's in today.'

She rummaged about in her bag and pulled out some paracetamol. She gave me two and took two herself.

'Is Katie in?' I asked.

'Yes. She looks a million dollars. As if she stayed in last night and had an early night. I don't know how she does it.' She picked up her bag. 'Better go. See you later.'

She dashed out of the door and I swallowed my paracetamol, trying not to gag at the bitter taste on my tongue. When I got back to my desk, I finished up the bit of work I had to do, then googled Christmas recipes. Tomorrow should be a good day. I was baking for the deli and their sister deli on the South Bank. I'd have to stay up half the night to get it done, but I wanted everything to be just perfect. If those two placed regular orders, it would be huge for me.

When I got home, I realised I'd forgotten to cancel seeing Adam. I knew he wouldn't be pleased, but I didn't feel a hundred percent. I got out my phone and typed out a long text but before I could send it, he rang the bell downstairs. I opened the door and pasted a smile on my face. He looked like he'd gone to an awful lot of effort.

'I was just sending you a text,' I said.

He gawped at the state of me, taking in my scruffy jogging pants and baggy old T-shirt. 'Oh dear! Good night, was it?' He frowned. 'I thought we were going out.'

I pushed some stray bits of hair back into my ponytail. 'Do I look that bad? I knew I did.

'You just look a bit tired, that's all.' Adam smiled at me and my face burned at the memory of kissing Chris.

'I am tired. And I'm really sorry, Adam, but I've got a load of stuff to do for the delis. I'm going to have to get up about four. I meant to tell you earlier I can't go out. It just sort of went out of my head.'

He put his hands on his hips, and his mouth tightened.

'I'm really sorry,' I said again.

Then he sighed, shrugged and looked disappointed. 'Ah, well. Okay then. How come you don't make the deli stuff before bed instead of having to get up that early?'

'It won't be as fresh.'

'Only by a few hours.'

'I know, it's daft but...'

'I could help you get started. If you like.' He raised his eyebrows but didn't look keen.

I didn't want him mucking things up. I'd probably spend more time redoing it.

'No, you don't have to do that. But thank you, it's good of you to offer.'

He looked relieved when I turned him down and he trudged back down the stairs. Guilt tugged at me. I hated messing people about, but my brain just wasn't firing right after last night. I'd make it up to him somehow. I spent the rest of the evening sleeping and feeling bad about Adam.

***

Saturday morning was manic as I had got to make the stuff for the delis and deliver it by nine. Both shops were having half each: four large bombes and eighty brownies. I had the added stress that I didn't trust the stupid, piddly little cooker in our flat. If it crapped out on me, I'd be stuffed. Thankfully, it heated up and valiantly maintained its temperature throughout. At quarter to eight, I dashed down the road carrying two boxes and practically threw them at Jenny, the owner.

'Thank you. Sandra's waiting for you at the other shop,' she called after me as I went back out the door.

Dad turned up promptly at eight o'clock to help me get the stuff there in his car. If he hadn't offered, I don't know how I would have got it all there. I hadn't thought of it, to tell the truth.

As we loaded the car, I snuck a look at him. Once tall and strong, he now seemed smaller somehow, stooped and grey, looking all of his sixty-two years. After taking early retirement, he now spent most of his time looking after my mum, who had severe arthritis and needed help more and more.

'Thanks for this, Dad,' I said, as he closed the boot. 'I really appreciate it.'

'No problem, love. Glad to do my bit.'

We set off in his old Fiat, which also decided not to be too temperamental. Dad, as ever, commented on everybody else's bad driving and grumbled about the risks the cyclists took, driving up the side of buses and lorries that were trying to turn left.

'They're going to get themselves killed one of these days,' he said as yet another one had a near miss. He wasn't wrong. I spent much of the journey with my eyes closed. Even though I'd passed my driving test, I'd never had a car. Never needed one and didn't want one. Driving in London would scare the living daylights out of me.

We arrived at the South Bank, going past the London Eye, museums, cinemas and art galleries. I loved it here. The Thames, as always, was full of boats, from pleasure cruisers to speedboats. Dad slotted the car into a loading bay at the rear of the deli and stayed inside while I took the boxes out of the boot. The tall woman behind the counter, who looked up as I entered the shop, glanced at her watch and rushed over to help.

'Hi, I'm Sandra. You must be Sarah. Well, you're certainly punctual.' She grabbed the boxes from me. 'I can't wait to try these.'

'I hope you like them,' I said. A churning started up in my stomach. What if they hated them?

As she opened one of the boxes, a tendril of light brown wispy hair escaped from the clip holding it off her face.

'Ooh, these look great.' She began to take the white chocolate brownies out, piling them onto trays behind the counter. She paused with a pen in her hand.

'What's this one again?' She pointed to one of the bombes.

'Raspberry and white chocolate truffle.'

She wrote it on a small square of pink card in fancy lettering, along with the price of a piece. Then she gave me £100 out of the till.

'These look fantastic. I'm sure our customers will love them. Thank you.' She slid the empty boxes back over the counter to me, surely a good sign.

'Thanks. I'll keep my fingers crossed.' I shoved the folded notes into my jeans.

'I'll be in touch in a few days. I'm sure we'll be ordering more from you.'

'Okay. Thank you.' I gathered up the boxes and went back to the car. When we'd set off, Dad looked across at me. The big smile on my face must have been catching, as he broke into a grin.

'You're on your way, kiddo,' he said.

'I know. It feels awesome just to know that somebody wants to buy something I've made.'

'Well, you deserve it. You work hard.'

'Thanks. How's Mum today?'

He pulled a face. 'She's having a bad day with it. Finds it harder to get going in the mornings but, you know...'

'She's not one for complaining, I know. I'll be over tomorrow. I'll do dinner then she doesn't have to bother.'

'She'll love that. I'll tell her.'

'I'll make some of that ginger cake she likes tonight.'

I could try filming it for the first time. Emma said she'd help with the videoing.

The journey back was much the same, like driving in Beirut or something; a constant cacophony of car horns accompanied by bumper to bumper traffic. When we pulled up outside my flat, I got my purse out. 'Let me give you some petrol money, Dad. And thanks again for helping me out.'

'Don't be daft, lass. Put your money away.'

I should have known he wouldn't take the money. I kissed him and waved him off, then struggled upstairs with the boxes. I dropped them just inside the door to take to the kitchen later. It was Leanne's Saturday to work, and the flat was quiet. I wandered into the bedroom and switched my computer on. When I logged onto my bank, my heart sank. How had that happened? I was in the bloody red! I leaned forward and scrutinised the transactions. I'd bought a watch for Mum for Christmas and... *shit!* I'd paid for it with my debit card instead of my credit card. That, and the direct debit on my mobile phone contract going out (which I forgot about every bloody month), had put me over my limit. The money I'd just made was all I'd got to last over Christmas. I couldn't afford to go out, buy anything or go anywhere. If I hadn't already made my mind up to cut spending, I was really going to have to now.

But looking was still free, right? Every site I went on was full of gorgeous things I couldn't afford. I clicked off Harvey Nichols' bag department and lowered my sights to ASOS. Ooh, they were having a pre-Christmas sale. A beautiful, silver beaded clutch bag caught my eye. It was only £40, reduced from £80. It would have been perfect with that vintage dress I wore for the Christmas party. Just for the feel of it, I clicked on it to put it in my basket. I hit checkout then removed it before it could go any further. No payment details had been entered so it couldn't go through, and I didn't have an account with them. My resolution to save loomed large in my mind again. I could and would do it. With a deep sigh, I closed the internet down.

12

SHE'S NAKED, AND IT'S a glorious sight. She's in her bedroom, rubbing some sort of bronzy lotion all over. And I've got the best seat in the house. I lean forward, closer to the screen, determined not to miss a thing. There's nothing better than watching a woman who's at her most relaxed. And there's nothing more relaxed than a woman who thinks she's alone. She puts one leg on the bed and pays particular attention to her thighs and knees, then bends over to do her lower leg. Then the same on the other side.

She doesn't get dressed but walks around the bedroom, doing something on her phone. It looks like she's texting. Who? And why is she wandering up and down? I look at the bottle of stuff she was applying: fake tan. That explains it—she needs to leave it a while before she can get dressed. Thank you, St Tropez! And thank you for the vanity of women, who long for bronzed bodies in the depths of winter. I'd expected her to be on her laptop tonight, on the obligatory Facebook or something. This is a huge and unexpected bonus, which just goes to show—you never can tell. Patience is a virtue, everything comes to those who wait, and all that other shit.

After five minutes, she spreads out a towel and sits on the bed. She hoists her left foot onto her right thigh, picks up a tub of cream and rubs it into the sole of her foot. Then repeats on the other side.

Once she's dressed (in nightwear, so she's not going out, then), she leaves the room and turns off the light. Damn. The problem with using her webcam is that I can only see into the room it's in. Luckily, she never, ever thinks to close the lid. So, what now? Might as well read her emails and have a general nosey round. Her bank account might be *a good place to start. Just looking, of course. I wouldn't steal from her. I'm not a thief.*

13

WHEN I SAW MY mum on Sunday, I was shocked by how ill she looked. Her face was drawn, and she was obviously in a lot of pain. But she smiled when she saw me and hugged me tight.

'You look healthy, love. You have a glow.'

'Out of a bottle. St Tropez rip-off. Me and Lee decided we needed a winter boost. But it's gone really orange on her. She's not happy,' I said. 'It's all my fault, of course!' I rolled my eyes and Mum smiled.

'Of course. Poor Lee. How is she?'

'Other than that, fine.' I wasn't about to tell her about Craig. It would only spoil the afternoon.

Dad and I made dinner while Mum sat on a kitchen chair and told us better ways to do things. While we ate, I told them about Ben, the homeless guy.

'I've been looking out for him, but he's not there every day. I've probably seen him ten times now. What happens in someone's life that's so bad they end up on the streets?'

Dad pursed his lips. 'All kinds of things. There but for the grace of God and all that...'

Mum nodded. 'It's a wonder they don't freeze to death. I think the Government should do more.'

'You know, it's awful how many people ignore him. They'd step over him if they had to. And I don't think he's a druggie or an alkie. There's no sign of anything like that.'

'So, what are you going to do about him?' asked Mum.

'Me? What can I do?'

Mum just looked at me then shrugged. 'I'm sure you'll think of something. These things have a way of working themselves out. What are you doing tonight, anyway?'

'Going out for a quick drink with Adam and having an early night.'

'So, when can we meet him?'

'Mum! We've only been out twice!'

'That's a shame. Does he set your heart racing then?'

'Mum!'

'Leave the poor girl alone, Stella!' said Dad.

Mum laughed and said nothing.

But when I met Adam later, I realised that although he was good looking and kind and funny and sweet, he didn't set my heart racing.

Ben wasn't outside the station the next morning and I put the sandwich I'd made for him back in my bag. Where did homeless people go at Christmas, anyway? I hoped he was in a shelter, keeping warm and dry somewhere.

It was dead in the office, just skeleton staff in, and everyone was in casuals. I hoped Donna or Katie were around as there wouldn't be much work to do today, other than answering the odd phone call. Maybe I could write another blog. Pauline had booked the day off and her desk looked bare with all her work tidied away.

I spent the day mainly answering the phone and responding to emails. Chris's name was on the work email list and my hand pushed the mouse over his name, where it hovered, the cursor blinking expectantly. I clicked it and the screen changed to a blank email with his name at the top. I hadn't heard from him or seen him since the party a whole four days ago. Maybe I could go up to Donna's floor with some lame excuse and see if he was at his desk? Maybe I wouldn't need an excuse. I'd just be going up to see my friend. What was wrong with that?

Just then, Terry, one of the solicitors I work for and who I hadn't seen since the Christmas party, walked past my desk.

He was wearing a daft green Christmas jumper with a reindeer's face on it. His stomach jutted out, stretching Rudolph's face to the limit. A lone flashing light in the middle of the red nose made me laugh.

'Oh, hi Sarah. How are you? Good party, wasn't it? You were worse for wear, if I remember rightly.'

'So were you.' I closed the email down.

'Yeah. I've only just got over the hangover.' He held up the glass of water he was carrying. 'Detoxing,' he mumbled, looking embarrassed. 'The wife's idea. I've told her it's bloody stupid, but she won't have it. Always nagging me about this.' He patted his ample belly.

I laughed. 'Bad time to detox, isn't it, over Christmas? It's more a New Year thing.'

'I know. That's what I think. That's why I've got some Quality Street in my desk for later. Come and find me if you want any.' He tapped the side of his nose and left, and I went back to wondering if I should go upstairs.

Just then, an email from Chris appeared on my screen. What were the chances? Was he psychic or something?

Hello sexy baker.

I pulled my chair closer and stared at the words on the screen. I'd been trying hard to ignore the fact that I'd thought about him way too much the last few days.

I wrote back *Hello* and sent it, grinning.

Are you busy?

Extremely

Doing what?

Now that was the question. Thinking about you? Remembering our snog? *Work type things* I sent back.

I waited. Nothing. What if he'd taken me seriously and now thought I was too busy to talk? Damn!

I sent another. *Not really. Googling Christmas recipes :)*

He didn't reply. What should I do now? I sat there, thinking back to the kiss and how it felt. What did it mean? Was it something he did, randomly kiss women? All women or just ones who fancied the pants off him? But there again, he had asked me if I was seeing anyone. I was trying to decide whether to send him another message when he walked in, pulled up Pauline's chair and sat down at my desk, right beside me. My heart briefly skittered crazily before getting back into its stride. My inbox was still on my monitor, our messages on display.

'Morning,' he said, his eyes sliding to my screen and back. His mouth twitched.

I couldn't help smiling. 'Hi, yourself. And I believe it's now the afternoon.'

He was in black jeans and a tight red T-shirt. Bulging biceps protruded from the sleeves and I couldn't tear my eyes away from them. He hadn't shaved, so he'd got more stubble than usual, thick and gloriously dark. I gave myself a stern talking to—*get a bloody grip*. I glanced around the room. There were only two other people in the big, open-plan office and they had got their backs to us.

'So,' he said.

I swallowed. My mouth felt dry. I tried not to lick my lips. 'So.'

'About the other night...' He raised one eyebrow. I couldn't read the expression in his eyes. He was sorry it happened. In case he was about to give me the brush-off, I decided defence was the best tactic.

'Look, I'm sorry about that. It should never have happened. I was drunk, and it was stupid and...'

'Was it?' he said. 'Why was it stupid?'

'Wasn't it?' My eyes fixed on his mouth. I wanted to kiss him again. He leaned back in his chair, stretching his arms up, and a gap opened up between the bottom of his T-shirt and the top of his jeans. Tanned, solid, a thick line of dark hair.

'Did you enjoy it?' he asked.

I looked up. 'Er...' Why did he always get me so flustered?

'Because I did.'

'I did, yeah. It was... very nice,' I said.

'Nice? I thought it was better than nice.'

'Well yeah, so did I. That's what I meant. Better than nice.'

My eyes shot between his mouth and that small strip of flesh above his waistband. I licked my lips without realising until it was too late.

'I wouldn't mind doing it again, myself. What about you?' he said.

I paused, chewing my lip. What about Adam? I did still like him. 'Erm…' I said, shuffling in my seat. Whump whump whump went my heart, loudly in my ears. It was a wonder he couldn't hear it.

'I really liked talking to you,' he said, leaning forward with his elbows on his thighs and looking down at his hands. The fingers of one hand were rubbing the palm of the other, tracing the love and life lines on it.

'I liked talking to you, too.' *Way too much.*

'What are you doing over Christmas?' he asked, picking up a pencil and flipping it idly back and forth over his knuckles and between his fingers.

'Family dinner with my parents. What about you?'

'Don't know. Haven't decided yet.'

So, did he not have any family then? He didn't elaborate.

'Have you done your Christmas shopping yet?' I asked, wanting to keep him there for longer.

'No. I don't have anyone to buy for, really. But it's not like you have to go out to get stuff these days, is it?'

No one to buy for at all? Really? 'Um, no, you don't; that's true. The wonder that is internet shopping! I *love* it.'

'Are you a shopaholic, then, Sexy Sarah?' He leaned back with his hands on his thighs and looked me right in the eye. It was impossible to look away.

'Possibly. I mean, I was.' I smiled. 'But my New Year's resolution is to stop all reckless spending and start to save.' Now I'd said it out loud to him, I was going to have to really do it.

'It's all about control,' he said.

'Are you a control freak then?' I teased.

He was quiet for a second, then gave a tiny nod. 'Quite possibly.' He smiled his lazy smile. 'How old are you? Or is it wrong to ask a lady her age these days?'

'Ask away. I'm twenty-five. How old are you?'

'Thirty. Last Wednesday.'

'Oh, sorry. I didn't realise it was your birthday...'

'Or you'd have made a cake,' he finished, laughing.

'Exactly. I would. Whatever your favourite is. What is your favourite, anyway? Just so's I know for future reference.'

Just then his phone rang, and he grimaced as he looked at it. 'Sorry. Work. I'd best get back.' He hurried out of the room, leaving me deflated. I didn't see him again all afternoon, but just before I left, I got an email from him. It said *What's your mobile number)* followed immediately by *I don't have a favourite cake. I like it all!!! Especially if you've made it x*

I emailed back my number.

Later that evening, still buzzing, I opened the door to our flats to see a massive bouquet someone had taken in and left where our mail was usually left. They were beautiful, blood-red roses and some white flowers I didn't know the name of. It was very festive, with green foliage and pine cones sticking out randomly. The card had Leanne's name on. I ran upstairs, my face half obscured by it, and shouted for her. She rushed out of her bedroom and stopped dead.

'They've got your name on,' I said, holding them out to her. 'Have you got a secret admirer you haven't told me about?'

She took them slowly and carefully, frowning, and pulled out the little envelope. Clutching the flowers to her, she opened it and pulled out the card. Her face went bone white and the flowers fell to the floor. She handed me the card, and I read the small type.

My dearest Lee, I love you. Please let me explain. C xx

14

2002

THE DAY AFTER I *ran the kid down in the old man's car, the local news was mad for the story. I got up to the news on the TV. The living room was fogged with its obligatory cloud of fag smoke. Ma was sitting watching the news reporter, with her head in her hands, looking shocked. She must have been having a rare moment of feeling something for someone else. Either that or she had another hangover; it was difficult to tell.*

'What's this?' I said, sitting at the other end of the sofa from her, swallowing hard. A nervous tremor started my leg jiggling and I leaned my elbows on my thighs to stop it.

'Accident,' she said, inhaling on her cig. 'Little girl's been killed.'

Killed? 'Where?'

'Outside Compton's shop. Hit and run.'

Icy fingers reached into my bowel, even though, deep down, I'd already known. It hadn't just been a bad dream. I picked up a flyer for a pizza place from the coffee table, and started to tear it into little strips.

'And her brother injured,' she added, shaking her head. 'Terrible, just terrible. Did you see 'owt when you were out last night?' Her eyes flitted to me and lingered.

'No. We never went near the shops.'

She turned back to the TV. There was police tape around the scene. 'Police are appealing for witnesses...' the reporter was saying. 'Treating it as a major incident. No one in custody as yet...'

Her words leached into my brain, even as I was trying to block them out. I couldn't watch it anymore. If anyone saw the car, it wouldn't take long to trace it back to my old man. I mean, how many shit-coloured Cavaliers of that age were there around here? I tried to calm down and think more clearly. Maybe it was too dark, things happened so fast, no one saw. I'd go to school, try and forget about it. I wasn't done for yet. Until they came for me. And they might not. No one saw me except the mother, and she wouldn't have been in a fit state. It was too dark with that streetlight out.

At school, everyone was talking about it. The teachers were subdued and serious, and there was a special assembly about it. My stomach was in knots and I couldn't eat a thing. What was I thinking? A killer at fifteen. And what if the other kid died, the boy? If I got locked away for this, my life would be over. As I sat alone, as far from everyone else as I could at lunchtime outside, ignoring a game of football that was going on nearby, it occurred to me that if I didn't get caught and stayed on this path, my life would be over, anyway. I didn't drink much, but yesterday, I'd gone to my old man's looking for booze. Yet I hated both my parents; what they were, who they were, the way booze ruled their life. I didn't want to be like them.

I got home at four. My sister and Ma were in the living room. They stood up to face me when I came in. I almost crapped myself when I saw a copper standing at the other side of the room. The blood drained from my face and my heart seemed to be beating right at the back of my throat. Were they arresting me? The school bag slid from my shoulder, hitting the floor with a thunk.

'Sit down, love,' said Ma. 'We've got some bad news.'

Love? She never called me love. And I couldn't sit down; my legs wouldn't bend.

'What?' I said. My voice caught, but that was okay, wasn't it? It was normal to be scared when there was a pig in your house.

'Your dad's been arrested. It was his car that killed that little girl last night. He was drunk.'

They'd arrested Dad? I couldn't speak. The relief was overwhelming. They weren't arresting me. Now I sat down as my legs buckled, collapsing onto the sofa. I could make it look like shock. With a bit of luck, he'd have been so drunk that he wouldn't remember *whether he'd driven or not. And no one would believe him. Everyone round here hated him. He'd been on his own when I went round there last night. At least I thought he was. If he was, then he had no alibi. It was his car, and I put the keys back where he'd left them.*

I looked at my mum, my sister, the police.

'My God,' I said. 'Dad? That's awful. How could he?'

15

IT WAS GREAT HAVING the full week off between Christmas and New Year. I got loads of baking sold as both delis had been open and they wanted more of my stuff, so I made some much-needed extra cash. Leanne helped me film some baking videos, and Emma posted them online for me. We had a real laugh and they both said I was a natural in front of the camera. I wasn't so sure. I felt stiff, stilted and silly, and I hated hearing myself speak. Did my voice really sound like that?

But behind her smile, Lee was still shaken by the flowers and the fact that Craig knew where we lived. How had he found out? The police told her the injunction against him was still in place, but as we hadn't actually seen him here, there wasn't a lot they could do.

Adam had been away on a last-minute holiday with Luke somewhere hot all Christmas, so I hadn't seen him at all. But I had had a few flirty texts from Chris.

On New Year's Eve, I managed to drag Lee out to the local pub for a drink. Emma would have come with us but she was at home, packing, off to America for six months tomorrow for work. Lucky cow! Her job as an account manager for an advertising firm sounded so glamorous to me. She was always running off here, there and everywhere doing exciting things. Jealous? Me?

The pub was noisy and hot, and we were alternating the wine with soda water. It could just be the alcohol, but she seemed more relaxed to me. Half an hour before midnight, I got a text. *Happy New Year Gorgeous xx.* From Chris. I felt the usual buzz and texted him back, wishing him the same.

The next morning when I got up, thanks to after-pub hot chocolates last night, we were out of milk. Lee was still asleep, so I put my coat on and grabbed my bag and umbrella to walk to the Tesco Express five minutes away. It was drizzling when I set out, but soon turned heavier. The Tube entrance was on the way to the supermarket and I spotted Ben's red hat long before I got there. I hadn't seen him in a while. I hurried towards him. He appeared to be asleep when I reached him, but opened his eyes when I stopped. His face was a horrible grey colour.

'Hi,' I said.

'Hello.' He tried to sit up but a barking cough made him hunch over. It wracked his whole body.

'Are you okay?' I asked, crouching down in front of him.

He tried to wave me away. 'It's nothing; just a cough.'

'You don't look so great.' I looked at the greasy spoon over the road that never seemed to be closed. 'Maybe a hot meal would do you good.'

His eyes followed where I was looking and then slid back to me. He looked confused, unsure what to say.

'Come on,' I said. 'I'd been wondering where you'd got to.'

He struggled to get up and put the blanket from around his shoulders, plus the one he was sitting on into a carrier bag that he took out of his coat pocket. He winced as we started to walk. He was limping quite badly, not putting his full weight on his right knee. I tried to cover both of us with the umbrella but almost poked his eye out. I dropped it down instead.

'What's wrong with your leg?'

'Old injury,' he said. 'Cold makes it worse, is all.'

'Battle scar, eh?'

His face went sort of pinched and tight. I must have said the wrong thing.

In the café, he went off the toilets to clean himself up. His hands and cheeks looked pinker when he returned, having scrubbed some of the grime off. He sat with the menu in front of him but didn't read it. He seemed to be somewhere else, far away.

'What do you want to eat?' I asked. 'Ben?' I leaned forward. He blinked. Came to. Looked at me.

'Anything,' he said. 'Anything. Thank you.'

I ordered shepherd's pie with extra veg for him and coffee for us both. While I was at the counter, I took my phone out and snapped a picture of him while he wasn't looking. He was miles away, staring out of the window.

'Why are you doing this for me?' he asked when I sat back down.

'It's only one dinner.'

He didn't answer. When someone behind the counter dropped a plate on the floor with a crash, Ben jumped to his feet. His eyes were wide and he was shaking and looking frenziedly around him. The other occupants of the café looked across in concern.

I stood up. 'Ben? What is it? Someone just dropped a plate. It's fine.'

He sank slowly back into his seat. 'Sorry,' he whispered.

I sat back down.

He pulled the hat off and gripped it tightly between both hands. His hair was a stringy, ratty mess. His eyes were still wide, giving him the look of a rabbit frozen in the glare of headlights. He was still broad-shouldered and well-built., and he looked younger with some of the dirt cleaned off his face.

'Ben, how long have you been living like this?'

He hung his head and stared into his coffee. 'Over a year.'

'What happened to you?'

His voice was quiet, and I had to strain to hear what he was saying. 'I was a soldier. In Afghanistan. Came back five years ago and... here I am.'

It was the shortest and saddest story I'd ever heard. I'd read about men like him. 'And they've abandoned you,' I finished. Something flickered behind his eyes.

'Don't you have any family? In Scotland?'

'No,' he said, his voice flat and dull.

How sad that there was no one to look out for him. His meal arrived then and he devoured it. When he'd finished, he looked at me with keen, bluey-grey eyes while he finished his coffee.

'Better?'

He nodded. 'Thanks.'

'Stop thanking me all the time. It's only a meal.'

He dropped his gaze to the table. 'It isn't. It's much more than that. It's the most kindness anyone's shown in a long time.'

I leaned back, away from the smell of him, and hoped it wasn't too obvious. 'Well, you're very welcome. Anytime.'

He coughed again, another spasm.

'That doesn't sound good. You should see a doctor about that,' I said.

'It's nothing. Hazard of the lifestyle. It'll go.'

I smiled sadly. 'Where've you been over Christmas? I haven't seen you.'

'Here and there. Managed to get a few days in a hostel.'

'How do you cope with the cold on the streets?'

'You don't, not really.'

My mum's words came back to me. *What are you going to do about him? I'm sure you'll think of something.* I knew what she would do.

'Would you like to come to my flat? Have a shower, get clean and warm for a while. I can wash your clothes.' The words were out before I could take them back. Lee wouldn't be happy, me turning up with a strange man I knew hardly anything about, but it was the right thing to do.

He looked up slowly. 'Really? Are you sure?'

'Yeah.'

'Thanks. I'd love a shower.'

We left the café. It was raining again, and it stung my face like needles, but I didn't bother with the umbrella but put my hood up instead. It was also blisteringly cold. There was no way he could sit out in this. He wasn't well enough.

'I'm not an axe murderer or anything,' he said.

I burst out laughing.

'What?' he asked.

'I know you're not. And anyway, I could easily outrun you with that limp of yours.'

He laughed and nodded. 'Aye. I suppose.'

'Wait here,' I said. 'I need milk from Tesco.'

I rushed in to get it, glad he was still there when I got back. I wanted to ask him more but didn't want to pry and scare him off. It took a while to reach our flat as he couldn't walk very fast.

'Lee,' I called as I came through the door. There was no answer. She was probably still in bed. She'd been taking sleeping tablets lately and they made her dead to the world.

I beckoned Ben inside and closed the door behind him, trying not to breathe in. The smell was much stronger in here. I hung my wet coat on the hooks near the door.

'The bathroom's through here. Throw your clothes out and I'll put them in the wash,' I said. 'The towels are clean, and there's shampoo, shower gel, razors, anything you need, in the cupboard above the basin. And a packet of new toothbrushes. Feel free to use any of it. I'll leave a dressing gown out here for when you're done.'

'Thanks,' he said and went into the bathroom.

He opened the door a crack and threw his clothes out. I put some rubber gloves on to pick them up and put them in the washer. After that, I dug around in my wardrobe for an old blue dressing gown I no longer wore and put it outside the bathroom door.

Back in the kitchen, the water in the washer was filthy.

It was another forty minutes before Ben emerged, looking and smelling much better. Months' worth of beard had gone and his face had a few cuts on it from the razor.

His hair was wet and combed through. I suspected it took ages to get through the tangles. He was quite attractive now you could see his face properly.

'Might have used all your conditioner, sorry,' he said, pulling the dressing gown tighter. It was long on me but came halfway up his thighs and barely closed. He'd kept a towel wrapped around his waist. He looked strained and tired. When had he last had a decent night's sleep? You probably didn't sleep great in a hostel, though it had to be better than the street.

'You can get your head down, if you like. On the sofa,' I said. 'We won't disturb you.'

He shook his head. 'No, no, I'll go as soon as my clothes are dry. I won't impose.'

'You can't. They'll be ages yet. Come on. Through here.'

He looked grateful, and he wasn't in a position to refuse. 'Okay. That would be great.'

He sat down on the sofa looking anything but relaxed. I passed him a throw and he covered his legs with it. I heard Lee's door open.

'Back in a sec,' I told him, and rushed out, closing the door behind me. She was standing in the hallway with a sweatshirt over her pyjamas, rubbing her eyes.

'What?' she said when she saw me. I whispered to her, explaining about Ben. She took the fact there was a strange man in the house surprisingly well.

'Poor bugger,' she said, shaking her head.

Just then, the bell went and Adam's voice came over the intercom.

'Hi Sarah, I'm back from sunny Tenerife.'

'Okay, come up.' I released the button. 'He texted me earlier to say he was back.'

'It's a good job we weren't banking on a relaxing New Year's Day,' Lee said. 'I'll go make coffee and see if Ben's clothes have finished.'

Adam burst through the door carrying a package which he gave to me.

'I just signed for this for you downstairs.'

'I didn't know they delivered on New Year's Day, now.'

Adam just shrugged. I wasn't expecting anything. I put the package down on the hall shelf, wondering what was in it.

He thrust a little box into my hand. 'I brought you this back. Did you have a good Christmas?'

'Yes, thanks. What is it?' I opened the box to find a silver necklace nestling on tissue paper. It had a tiny butterfly on it with jewelled wings. 'Oh, Adam, it's gorgeous. Thank you. I love it. But you shouldn't have.'

'Why are you whispering?'

I filled him in on Ben, and he looked surprised. 'You're such a softy,' he said.

He took a step nearer and Lee came out of the kitchen.

'Hi. You must be Adam. Nice to meet you.' She inclined her head towards the living room door. 'Sarah's been at it again. She was always bringing home waifs and strays. Has your mum still got Treacle and Toffee?' she asked me, referring to the two tiny kittens I landed them with years ago, that had been abandoned, half dead, in a cardboard box at the back of the bookies.

'Treacle's still with them, just, but Toffee died a couple of years ago.'

We crowded into the kitchen, and I put Ben's clothes into the dryer.

'We'd better go back,' I said. 'He must be feeling really awkward, undressed in a stranger's flat.'

Lee surprised me by barging into the living room first, making Ben jump.

'Hi, I'm Leanne. And this is Adam...' She looked at Adam as she tailed off.

'Warner,' said Adam

'Adam, this is Ben...?'

'Um, Harrison,' Ben said automatically, standing up.

Well done, Lee. She just played a blinder. Now we had his surname. Unless he was lying but it didn't sound like it.

'Hi, mate,' Adam said cheerfully when we went in.

Ben pulled the dressing gown around him, not that it made much difference. 'Um, hello,' he said, flushing.

'I've just put your clothes in the dryer,' I told him. 'They'll be about an hour.'

'Thank you,' Ben said, copying us as we all sat down, and covering himself with the throw again.

Adam made Ben feel at ease by doing all the talking, mainly about his holiday, and the hour passed quickly. Soon enough, Ben was dressed and could not be persuaded to stay. Adam even offered his own sofa for a few days but Ben shook his head.

'You've all been brilliant,' he said, hovering in the doorway, clearly itching to be off. 'But I'll get going now. Thank you so much.'

Adam winked at me, mouthed 'call me', and left at the same time as Ben. I had a feeling he was going to have another crack at getting Ben to stay at his. I doubted he'd succeed.

When they'd gone, I remembered the package that Adam had brought in with him. It was still on the hall shelf. I turned it over, mystified; there was something hard inside. I hadn't ordered anything. I closed my bedroom door and ripped the bag open. Something wrapped in black tissue paper fell out onto the bed. When I tore the paper off, I just gawped at it—it was the silver beaded bag from ASOS that I saw on the website. The one I didn't order. I dashed to my laptop to check my bank. No money had gone out. I definitely didn't buy it. But who the hell had? And why?

16

AS I GOT DRESSED for work the next morning, my eyes kept going to the bag, sitting on the desk next to my laptop. I took an extra second to shove it in a drawer. If I couldn't see it, I might stop wondering about it. It just didn't make sense.

I shivered as I waited for the Tube on my first day back at work. Friday 2nd January. What was the point of going back to work for just one day? Most people were starting on Monday, but I had no more holidays left. Pauline wasn't due back until Monday, so there wouldn't be anyone to talk to.

I got off the Tube at St Paul's and walked out into a strong, gusting wind that made it hard to move. By the time I got to work, I looked a total mess and had to spend ten minutes in the loos trying to calm my hair back down. I made a coffee and waited for my inbox to load, which turned out to be just work emails from clients, mainly Happy New Year messages. Nothing exciting or different. The morning was uneventful and by lunchtime I was desperate for some fresh air so made for Café Sirocco around the corner. It wasn't a great place but it was close. I used to meet Emma here sometimes. It was hard to believe she was in California now. How much warmer and more pleasant would it be there?

A few tables were free, and I'd just sat down with a cream cheese bagel when the chair opposite was pulled out. I looked up, startled, to see Chris flop down into it.

'Happy New Year,' he said. 'Mind if I join you?'

I sat up straighter and resisted the urge to fiddle with my hair. 'Er, no. Feel free.' I tried to pull the corners of my mouth back down from the smile that was splitting my face. *Act cool, for God's sake! He'll think you're a moron. And don't say anything stupid.*

Chris shrugged off his jacket and put it over the back of his chair. His white-and-blue-striped shirt pulled apart at the chest when he stretched round, and I was distracted by the smattering of dark hair on his arms as he proceeded to slowly and methodically roll up his sleeves. Why didn't he just buy short-sleeved shirts? Every time I saw him in a proper shirt, his sleeves were rolled up.

'I'll just go get a sandwich,' he said and disappeared off to the counter. I studied him from the back: broad shoulders, neat waist, narrow hips. Peachy buns, though. He must have big thigh muscles; his trousers were pulled tight over them. The shape of sculpted muscles showed through the fabric.

He got served and carried his lunch back on a tray: a sandwich, a bag of crisps and some coke. He picked up his sandwich and began to eat, while I tried to work out what this was about. He said nothing, just caught my eye, smiled and chewed. He looked damn sexy, and it was hard to ignore the attraction. He must have been aware of me watching him.

I bit into my bagel. It was hard and dry in my mouth, and the knot in my stomach made it harder still to swallow. Chris opened his coke and had a long swig, burping silently after. He leaned over the table and I noticed his pupils were large.

'So, what have you been up to over Christmas, then?' His eyes fixed onto mine.

I shrugged. 'Nothing very interesting.' Neither of us looked away.

'Not out partying?'

'No. Except New Year's Eve down the local. When you texted. What have you been doing?'

'This and that, you know.'

I didn't know. He was quiet while he ate his lunch. I nibbled on mine but didn't really want it. I didn't want cream cheese all over my face. After he finished his sandwich, he said, 'We never finished our talk, did we? About the Christmas party?'

'Um. No, I don't believe we did.'

'I've been thinking about you all Christmas,' he said, lowering his voice.

I couldn't help but smile. 'Have you?'

'Yep. Have you thought about me?'

'Maybe.'

He looked pleased. 'So, Sarah. What exactly *have* you thought about me?'

He looked me up and down, his eyes snagging on the front of my blouse then lingering on my face. I glanced down to check I was buttoned up and took a sharp breath in, not sure how to answer. I'd thought about his sexy body, what it would look like undressed, how it would feel to be in bed with him, with his perfect lips all over me. But I couldn't say that.

'Well, that's for me to know...'

'And me to find out?'

I shrugged.

'Just tell me. I want to know. No games.'

'No! You're such a flirt. Stop it!'

'Well, I can tell you what I've been thinking about you.'

'Go on then.' A tang of his aftershave wafted across the table and I inhaled. A bolt of pleasure shot through my pelvis. What was wrong with me? I'd fancied men before, but it had been nothing like this.

He leaned forward. 'I've been thinking what it felt like kissing you at the party. I want to do it again.'

I rested my chin on my hand. 'I bet you say that to all the girls.'

His expression was mock-hurt. 'I don't, actually. Only if I mean it.'

'Oh, come on. You must know the stir you've caused in the office. Half the women practically have their tongues hanging out.'

He laughed softly. He was aware, all right. 'Are you one of them?'

'No.' I tried to sound cool.

He reached over the table and twined his fingers through mine. It was like an unexpected explosion of power erupted inside me, and I didn't want him to let go. I looked down: his hands were perfect, smooth, with long, slim fingers. He rubbed his thumb over the back of my hand. The white half-moon on the cuticle of his thumb was crooked, dipping more on one side than the other. Not so perfect, then.

'So, do you fancy going out sometime? Properly? I've given up waiting for you to ask me,' he said.

My nerve endings were tingling like mad. 'Alright. Yeah. And, for the record, I never ask men out.' Once more my eyes were drawn to his lips, which were curving into a smile again.

'Good.' His thumb stopped stroking. 'So, this business you told me about—are you serious about it then?'

He withdrew his hand to open his crisps, which broke the spell. Is that what he had me under—a spell?

'Er, yeah. I'm trying to. It's hard, though. I'm learning as I go along.'

'Have you done any videos?' *He remembered!*

'Yeah, although I'm not very good at it. For God's sake, don't watch any, will you?'

'I bet you are. Who wouldn't want to watch you?'

'Do you really think so?'

'Yes.' He looked at his watch, pulled a face and stood up. 'Don't want to, but I've gotta get back. I'll be in touch.'

He smiled and left, putting his jacket back on as he got to the door. I watched him go and my excitement dissolved as I thought about Adam. I had to break things off with him. I just needed to find the right time.

17

2002

·

SO, MY DAD HAD been sent down for running that kid over. I wasn't in court that day, but Ma and my sister were. They said he said nothing when he was pronounced guilty. No response whatsoever. That seemed to get taken as further proof of his guilt. No remorse, said both the headlines in the local paper and on that night's news. I'd managed to convince myself that maybe, somehow, he really did do it and I only dreamed I did it. The kid's mum even said it was the old man who was driving. Positive identification. Funny how the brain twists what the eye sees until it's convinced itself. She wanted to believe it was him. Wanted justice.

If I can only keep my mouth shut for the rest of my life, I may just be okay. I'm now the son of a murderer. Not that the kids at school have said much to me. None of them would dare.

On a cold day in March, a month after the old man got put away, I walked past a group of three kids in my year that were huddled round something in a boy's hands. The boy was Frankie McCabe, a kid from the more affluent part of Leeds, not the shit end where I was from. His blazer was always clean, without the frayed lapels and cuffs that mine had, and the sleeves didn't end way short of his wrists. It still even had the school badge on the breast pocket. Mine was ripped off in a fight last year and had never been replaced, although the badge had been the only thing of mine to get damaged. Same couldn't be said of the other lad. Frankie McCabe had very straight, white teeth (on account of his dad being a dentist and we all know how much they got paid). I'd heard their house was massive.

They were laughing at whatever it was they were huddled round. I stopped. What were they looking at? They hadn't seen me yet. Frankie and his best mate, Tommy Foster, always gave me a wide berth, since the day I'd whacked both their skinny arses in the showers after P.E. with the regulation tea towels they gave us to get dried on. I'd thought Shanksy was going to piss himself laughing, so I gave him one as well. That wiped the smile off his face. But that was two years ago now.

The lads were pointing at something, but I couldn't see what. When Mick Parker moved his big fat head to one side, I saw that Frankie was holding a Game Boy, working it like lightning with his thumbs. I'd never been one for stuff like that. Never really had a go on one. It wasn't as if I could ever have a computer. It'd have to come out of my folks' drink money and that was never going to happen, was it? Whatever they were engrossed in, it looked good fun.

'What you playing?' I asked, taking a step towards them.

Three heads looked up at me in one motion. They were seated around one of the plastic tables outside the dining room. None of them spoke, and their smiles faltered as they glanced at each other. Frankie eyed me warily and his knuckles tightened on the Game Boy.

'What is it?' I asked again, in a deliberately non-confrontational tone.

Frankie dropped the hand holding the Game Boy down by his side. I sat down on the one remaining available chair.

'Sonic Advance,' he said, his eyes dropping down to the table.

Tommy cleared his throat and tossed his head to one side to clear his eyes of his too-long fringe. He end up with a crick in his neck one of these days doing that. The tension between them was practically crackling. I don't know why they were so scared of me. I might lark around a bit and I stuck up for myself, but I wasn't a bully. I hated bullies. I'd been known to go in to bat for the underdog many times. There again, to the rest of the world, my dad had just killed a kid. I was a murderer's son.

Frankie looked defeated and put the Game Boy on the table, his fingers still locked round it.

'Can I see?' I asked.

He let it go and pushed it towards me. His fingernails were extremely clean. All their eyes were fixed on it as I picked it up. I held it in both hands, like Frankie did when he was playing. I placed my thumbs where Frankie's had been, and a blue cartoon character started to move on the screen in a jerky, robotic fashion. I pressed a few more keys and it changed direction or jumped up and down. It was funny. I could spend ages working it out, but I wanted a shortcut. I handed it back to Frankie.

'Will you show me?'

***

By the end of the month, Frankie and me were best mates. He let me take the Game Boy home sometimes. I'd become his protector, in some ways. He walked around with me and was cockier and more confident, relying on me to get him out of trouble if his mouth got him into it. But I didn't mind. He had something I wanted. The first time I went to his house, it was like stepping into another world. And his parents were normal. They cared, for a start: whether he went to school or not, what his grades were, what he ate. If he ate. At first, they were uncertain when they saw me. Everyone round here knew who I was, what my family were. His parents' eyes flitted over me. My trousers, hovering too high above my trainers, had stains on them that I couldn't remember the origins of, that never came out in the wash. My white school shirt had an old, faded blood stain on the collar and the front (where I cut myself shaving—Frankie didn't need to shave yet. I did it twice a week). I pulled my shoulders back and down and looked his dad in the eye. I may not have had much, but I had some pride. I was NOT like the rest of my family.

'Thanks for letting me come over,' I said. It came out stilted and I stuck my hand out awkwardly. His dad paused for an infinitesimally small amount of time, then shook it and smiled.

'It's a pleasure,' he said, touching me lightly on the arm.

I took that as acceptance.

Frankie had a computer of his own at home, along with every game in existence, it seemed. He showed me Grand Theft Auto, Ratchet & Clank, Splinter Cell and Halo. I was hooked from the first second, but starved of the chance to play. The time at his house was limited and I craved the feeling I got from being totally absorbed in that magical, addictive world.

At school, instead of being bored and switching off in lessons, I started to listen. Really listen. Turned out I had a good brain. Who knew? And it was going to be my ticket out of the hellhole I lived in. Frankie was a good student, one of the ones I always called a swot, and I borrowed his books, studying them every night. I caught up to the rest of the class a lot quicker than I thought I would once I put the effort in. A lot of the things I didn't think I'd learned had somehow made it to my brain after all.

'You have an analytical, enquiring mind,' said my maths teacher. 'It's good to see you putting it to use at last.'

Life at home was the same, but I learned to separate it from the rest of my life. It was just something to be endured. The less time I spent there, the better I liked it. The turning point for me was the new computer shop that opened up a mile from where I lived. It was a one-man-band affair. 'On-site repairs and servicing, we fix all makes and models, competitive prices' it said in the window. I pushed the door open and a thin, youngish bloke behind the counter stopped fiddling with a machine and stood up. His smile faded when he saw my empty hands.

'Can I help you?' he asked, looking me over.

'Will you teach me? I'll work for nothing.'

He looked taken aback. 'Er, I'm not hiring. I've only just opened.'

'I don't need paying. I just want to learn. Please?'

He sat back down on his stool. 'What are you good at?'

'Playing games. Well, I'm alright.'

'What do you know?'

'What about?'

'Computers.'

'Not enough. That's why I'm here.'

He nodded. 'Okay,' he said. 'I'll teach you. But you turn up when I say and do as I say. If you can't agree to that, don't bother.'

'I agree.'

'Alright. I'm Simon,' he said. 'What's your name?'

'Colin.'

After the shop had been open about two months, it got broken into. It suffered more in the way of damage than theft. Seemed whoever broke in was just a malicious bastard after money. Probably some crack-head. When all they found was computers in bits, they smashed things up, and left. When I got there after school that day, Simon had just about finished clearing up.

'What the fuck...?' I said as I came through the door.

Simon was still seething as he told me the tale. I listened, not speaking, right until the end. Simon lived a few miles away with his missus and baby, about a ten-minute drive from the shop.

'I have an idea,' I said, when he'd finished ranting.

He looked up from sweeping up the last bits of glass. It was gloomy, with the window boarded up. It matched his mood.

'What?' he said.

'I could move in upstairs. Clear out the boxes.'

There was a tiny flat above there which we mainly used for storage. There was a small kitchen area and a toilet. One small room, bed/living space. Nowhere to shower, but I'd had enough strip washes in my time, when the old boiler in our flat had been dodgy.

'But you're only fifteen,' he said. 'No, you're too young.'

'I was sixteen last week,' I lied.

'Oh. I didn't know that, sorry. Happy birthday.'

'It's okay. So how about it? If I lived on site, it might stop a repeat of today.'

He was actually considering it. I could get away from home and I'd only have to buy food. So what if it would be like living in a broom cupboard? I could do it. Plus, Simon did pay me; he paid me from day one. A pittance, but I also now had a paper round and a job collecting glasses in the local pub on a weekend. He was torn, I could see.

'Let's try it. Nothing to lose. And if it doesn't work out, then...' I held my hands up.

That did the trick.

'Alright, we'll give it a go,' he said.

No one at school ever found out. I don't think my family even noticed I'd gone.

18

IT WASN'T AS EASY as he'd thought it would be. He'd tried twice with the Rohypnol in the past few weeks but had had to abort it both times, as there always seemed to be someone watching him. How the hell were you supposed to get the stuff into someone's drink unnoticed? If there was a knack to it, he didn't have it. Of course, he'd had some sex recently, with willing women in clubs who'd taken him home, but it wasn't the same. He craved the sense of power it gave him, to know he was taking something from someone that wasn't being freely given. The release was so much stronger when he was the one in control. He couldn't help it; he'd tried, really tried. All he could do now was accept it and be more careful. Of course, it wouldn't be like that with Leanne. He could keep that side of himself separate, if she'd only try. But he daren't approach her yet, didn't know what she'd do. He'd had a visit from the police for sending her the flowers. Despite having told them he didn't go near her flat, that the florist delivered the flowers for him, they told him that he'd be back inside if he tried it again, and '*Did he really want that?*' the dumpy little PC had asked him sternly, looking at him over the top of her glasses. He'd suppressed the vision of her trapped under him, protesting, while he showed her how it should be. He would put his hand over her mouth to drown out the noise. That would shut her up. But all he'd said to her was, 'No, I don't want that.'

But he was going to have to act soon. The feeling was burning him from the inside out. Just once, that would be all for now, to release the anger, the rage boiling inside him. Soon. Maybe in a few days, perhaps at the weekend, when the pubs and clubs were busy, and the slags were walking around half-naked, like they always did, asking for it. Soon.

19

I WAS LYING ON the sofa thinking about Chris when Leanne walked in and dropped a newspaper straight onto my face. I sat up with a yelp and it slithered to the floor, sending pages everywhere.

'What was that for?'

'Page twenty-three.' She sat on the battered armchair opposite and curled her feet under her. 'Honestly, you'll thank me.' She turned on the TV, smoothing her hair as she settled down to watch The Great British Sewing Bee, which always bored me stupid.

I grabbed the piles of pages and found page twenty-three. A story about a missing cat, mugging of an old lady, something about a local MP trying to stop a library closure.

'What? There's nothing here.'

'Are you blind? Bottom left-hand corner.'

An advert in a box about an upcoming wedding fair.

'I'm not with you.'

'What's the point of wedding fairs? To sell things? *Your* cakes, perhaps? You could see how much it is to rent a stall. There's a contact number there, for traders.'

I stared at it. 'Leanne, you're bloody brilliant. It's only two weeks away, though. I thought the pitches for these things sold out straight away. They must have some left. It'd be a mad rush to get enough cakes done... but I could do some modern ones as well as traditional, you know, cupcake ones and those chocolate tower ones as well.'

She laughed. 'Yeah, you could.'

'But what if there are some other cake makers there, you know, really professional ones, and they're much better than me? Mine would look crap.'

'There probably will be others, and if they are better than you, then learn from them. If you work hard enough, you'll get enough cakes done. I'll help you.'

I dropped the newspaper onto the floor, on top of a pile of old magazines, underneath which I spotted a pair of shoes I'd been looking for for ages. 'Do you think I should? I could, couldn't I? I could do this!'

'Look, do you really believe you're good enough to make a living out of it?'

'Yes,' I said, in a small but firm voice. I really did. But there was always a little voice in my head that told me I might not be.

'And so does everyone else. Put it this way, you've got nothing to lose, have you?'

She was right. I went over and gave her a big hug. 'You're the best.'

I spent the next hour researching wedding fairs. Leanne could really be onto something here—there were so many of them, up and down the country. Why hadn't I thought of it before? I could hire a van for the ones further away, buy one when I'd done a few and sold loads of cakes. I was getting carried away, but I couldn't help it. This was a great start to a new year.

***

I slammed the door to the ladies' toilet viciously behind me, jumping out of the way just before it caught my heel.

'What's up with you? You look fed up.'

I started at the sound of Chris's voice.

'Nothing,' I said, shrugging. 'Well, nothing you can help with, anyway.'

'I'll decide that. Look, it's nearly lunchtime. Do you want to meet me outside at one o'clock and you can tell me all about it?'

'Alright,' I said.

He was waiting outside at one o'clock on the dot.

'Fancy a walk?' he asked.

'Okay.' I buttoned my coat right up and put my gloves on.

He pointed the way and we started walking past the other offices that lined the street, in the direction of Blackfriars.

'Go on then, shoot,' he said.

I took a deep breath before launching straight in. 'Well, basically, my flatmate, Leanne, suggested I try my luck at a wedding fair, to promote the business. To try and get some orders for wedding cakes and stuff. It's only two weeks away.' It was easier to tell him all this when we were walking side by side. That way, I couldn't get distracted by looking at him.

'Yeah, so?' He waved his hand about in a *carry on* gesture.

'I rang them up, to enquire about a stall and everything, and it would cost me about £500 by the time I've hired the stall and bought the stuff to make the cakes. And I haven't got £500, have I? So, I can't bloody do it.' I stared mutinously across the road at nothing.

'I can lend you the money,' he said.

I stopped walking. I didn't know what to say. I didn't want to borrow money from him or anyone else.

'Er, thanks, but I wasn't hinting. I am grateful though.'

'I know that. And you didn't ask. I offered. I can afford it, it's no big deal.'

'Thanks, Chris, it's really kind of you, but I can't let you do that.'

'I want to. This could be just what you need. This could be your big break. You can't not do it.'

Damn. He was right. If I refused his money, would I be cutting off my nose to spite my face? I hesitated, but Chris was insistent.

'Look, is there anyone else you can borrow it off? No, else you would have.'

I turned to look at him.

'I want to,' he said, his face inches from mine. 'Let me help you.' He took out his phone and started pressing the screen with his thumbs.

'Give me your bank card. I'll put the details in here and transfer it straight into your account.'

'Are you absolutely sure about this?'

'What are friends for? Now—bank card.'

He held out his hand and I reached for my bag to get my purse. I didn't want to borrow his money but I really wanted to do this wedding fair; it could be the start of something big. I gave him my card.

'Thanks, Chris. I do appreciate this. I'll pay you back as soon as I can,' I promised.

Chris input my bank details at lightning speed.

'Done.'

We walked over the road into a park and spent the next ten minutes strolling and chatting about daft things. I didn't want to go back to work. He kept calling me Sexy Sarah and at one point he reached for my hand and pulled me down a little path leading to a sheltered bench. When we sat down, he kissed me, lightly at first, teasing my mouth with his, then deeper, like at the Christmas party except this time I was stone cold sober. I didn't want to stop. All I could think about was going to bed with him. Maybe he was thinking the same about me.

'Get a room,' someone shouted and we drew apart. I flushed, embarrassed, but he just laughed. I was also more than a little breathless.

'They're just jealous,' he said.

All I could think about was how turned on I was. It was as if he'd obliterated all other thoughts from my mind.

'We'd better get back,' he said, pulling out his phone. 'Look at the time.'

When I got back to my desk, I realised I hadn't had any lunch. And I was starving. I could still taste him.

20

SHE WAS LOOKING AT a blouse on ASOS last night, and some new shoes. I think they'll suit her, though they're not as nice as the bag. She didn't buy them, of course. When I checked her bank balance, it was shocking. She has no idea how to manage her finances, although I do believe she's trying to mend her ways. I hope she keeps her New Year's resolution not to spend unnecessarily, like she's said on Facebook and in her emails to her friend in America. To break a resolution so quickly would indicate weakness, and I despise weakness. It denotes a lack of character, and that's no good at all.

The thing about Facebook is that the life people put on there rarely matches up to the reality. It's full of lies and I don't like liars.

Weakness and liars. I do hope she doesn't turn out to be a person like this. It would mean I was wrong about her and I don't like to be wrong.

21

SO, I RANG UP the number in the paper and booked a place. It was that simple. At the weekend, I made a start on the traditional fruit cakes. The sponges I wanted to do would be more last minute as I didn't want to have to freeze them. I was plagued with nerves every time I thought of the fair itself and what I was going to have to do—talking to all those people. Strangers.

The weekend was so busy, it was almost a relief to get back to work on Monday for a rest. When I turned my computer on, there was an email from Chris. *Lunch 12.30? x*

Okay, I sent back. He'd been on my mind all weekend. I owed him for giving me this opportunity to really get my business going. Adam had been texting all the time too and I'd agreed to see him tomorrow night. I was going to call it off and I was dreading it. I was no good at that sort of thing. Not that anything much had happened between us yet anyway, but he seemed so keen. Plus, he was nice, and I hated the thought of hurting him.

Chris met me outside the office again.

'Sorry, but I won't have long,' he said. 'I'm snowed under with last-minute things to do before I leave. But I wanted to see you.'

I deflated. He always seemed to be rushing everywhere. And soon I wouldn't see him at work at all. He was due to leave next week. We walked the few minutes to Café Sirocco, got sandwiches and took them to an empty table.

'How come there are always tables free in this café at lunchtime?' I asked as he unwrapped his food.

'Cos the food's shit,' he grunted. 'It's hard to get down.' He took a massive bite of his BLT.

'You're managing pretty well.'

He shrugged. 'I'm hungry and not fussy.' He ripped apart his bag of crisps. 'Crisps are okay here cos they don't make them. It's one of the few things they can't ruin.'

I opened my cheese salad sandwich, which managed to be both dry and soggy at the same time. I picked out a dry bit of bread to eat.

'I wanted to talk to you,' he said.

'Oh? What about?'

'Have dinner with me tomorrow night and I'll tell you then.'

'Dinner? I can't. Not tomorrow.'

'Why not?'

I'm seeing Adam. To call things off and I'm dreading it. 'Well, er, I've got all the cakes to do for the wedding fair.'

'Don't be daft. You can tear yourself away for one evening, surely. Anyway, I've already booked a table. All I'll say is it's a business meeting. You need to come.' He fixed me with a meaningful look.

'What kind of business meeting?'

'You'll find out soon enough. There's someone I want you to meet. Get dressed up. Look business-like. We're going straight from work.'

'I'm intrigued. Tell me what it's about.'

He grinned. 'No. Just be ready.'

He wasn't going to tell me. He opened a can of coke.

'What did you do this weekend,' I asked. 'When I was tied to the kitchen.'

'Worked some. Did some weights. Chilled.'

'Sounds much more relaxing than mine.'

'It was okay. Nothing special.' He finished his coke, then got up to go. 'I'll see you after work tomorrow. Can't wait.'

Then he was gone. I walked back to work alone, wondering who he wanted me to meet. At least I wouldn't have to wait long to find out.

***

The next morning, I rifled through my wardrobe, trying to decide what to wear. Business-like didn't mean it couldn't be sexy, right? I settled on a deep-red pencil skirt that finished above the knee, with a semi-sheer white blouse. With a nude, lacy camisole underneath and a Wonderbra jacking me up, it should look good, especially with two or three buttons undone, showing a hint of what was underneath. And if it made Chris's eyes pop out, I wouldn't be complaining. I packed them carefully into a bag, along with the bag from ASOS. I was no nearer to finding out who sent it, but I might as well use it. I put on a grey trouser suit and set off. The day dragged by and I got more impatient and excited as the afternoon went by. I'd been putting off telling Adam I had to cancel, knowing he wouldn't be happy. In the end, I decided the truth was best.

Hi Adam, sorry for short notice, but I can't do tonight. I have a business meeting. I'll explain later x

He didn't text back, which probably meant he was really pissed off with me.

At five twenty, I disappeared into the toilets to change. When I'd dressed and done my make-up, I studied my hair in the mirror. Up or down? Definitely down. After a quick shake, it was wild and wavy; perfect. I checked the buttons on the blouse, undoing two. What the hell—I undid a third. There was more than a hint of cleavage on show. Too unprofessional? Chris would tell me if it was too much. The same dark grey jacket and black heels I came to work in looked okay. I went back to my desk and put the clothes I'd changed out of into my desk drawer. I'd pick them up tomorrow.

Chris was waiting for me by the lifts, looking heart-stoppingly attractive. He was in black jeans and a casual striped shirt. I bet he'd got changed at work as well. He looked me up and down as I approached and gave a low wolf-whistle. His eyes lingered on the front of my blouse.

'Wow,' he said and pressed the call button. The doors opened straight away.

'I hope I'm not too dressed up,' I said.

'You look just perfect.' He ushered me into the lift with his hand resting lightly on the small of my back.

'Where are we going, anyway?'

'You'll find out soon.' He pressed the button for the ground floor and the doors closed.

To my disappointment, he didn't try anything in the lift, just checked his watch and his phone. We dashed out into the dark evening and into the underground car park around the corner, where Chris led me to a gleaming silver sports car. It must have cost a fortune.

'God! Is this yours?'

'Yeah. New toy,' he said. 'Do you like it?'

'I love it. It's absolutely beautiful.'

He unlocked the door and got in. I was still looking at the car and he pushed the passenger door open for me. 'Well, get in. Or are you just gonna stand there all night?'

He patted the seat beside him, and I tried to climb in elegantly in my tight skirt. The inside of the car was pristine, as if it had just left the factory. Chris smiled over at me.

'Ready?'

'You bet.'

The engine was throaty and deep, and the vibrations roared through my chest as we accelerated up the ramp and onto the street. I was soon lost as we drove through twisty and turny back streets. A smooth jazz track filled the car. My body melted into the seat and excitement bubbled in my stomach. Where were we going?

Eventually the car stopped. I had no idea which bit of London this was. Chris had already left the car and was opening my door, letting in the biting cold which went straight through to my bones. It was barely above freezing and he noticed me shiver.

'Cold?'

'Freezing.'

He held out his hand and led me to a restaurant. Its exterior was painted a very pale pink colour, almost white under the streetlight. Gold and black lettering emblazoned across the window in an arch spelled out the name *Porter's*. Very simple and very stylish. Through the window, the lights were dim, and it looked warm and inviting. I followed Chris, who was already inside and talking to an overweight black man with a shaved head, dressed in clean chef's whites.

'Sarah, this is James Porter, a mate of mine. He'll be be looking after us tonight.'

James shook my hand in a gentle grip. 'Hi, Sarah, pleased to meet you. I've heard a lot about you.'

Had he? Like what?

'This is your table here,' he said. He led us to a small alcove at the back. Very private.

After we were seated, James left us. The table was small and round, covered in a pristine white cloth with pink napkins. A waiter returned with two menus, took our drinks order and left.

'How do you know James?' I asked.

Chris opened his menu and started to read through it. 'He's just someone I've known for years,' he said, without looking up.

I opened mine, hoping I could read it in the dim light.

'Ready?' he asked, a few minutes later.

'I can't decide. It all sounds fantastic.'

Chris beckoned the waiter over. 'What do you recommend?'

'The sea bass, sir.

'I'll have that, then,' he said.

The waiter looked at me.

'Yes, I'll have that too. Thank you.'

He took our menus away with him, and a second later our drinks arrived. I tried my house white, which was delicious, while Chris downed half his beer.

'Chris, I need to talk to you about the money. I meant to ask you yesterday. How much should I pay back a month? Will £100 be okay?'

'Whatever you can afford. Don't leave yourself short, though.'

'Great,' I said. 'I still don't understand what all this is about, lovely though it is.'

'Eat first.'

Just then, my phone rang. It was at the top of my bag. *Adam*. Damn! When it stopped ringing, I turned it off.

'Who was that?' Chris asked.

'No one.'

While we waited for the food to arrive, we chatted. Every time Chris caught my eye, he smiled and my heart flipped over. He eyed my cleavage plenty. Dinner arrived.

'Bit small,' Chris grumbled, examining the plate.

I shook my hair off my face and slipped my jacket off, looking down to check myself. Another button had come undone. What the hell—Chris wasn't complaining.

The food was gorgeous, and I savoured every mouthful. I didn't know what the wine was, but it was the nicest I'd ever had. I was more of a cheap plonk kind of girl.

'Do you want dessert?' he asked.

'You bet. I want to see what the competition's like. I'm having tarte au citron.'

'I'll have that as well, then.'

'No, have something else, then I can taste it.'

'Alright. What do you want? You pick.'

'The profiteroles.'

When it arrived, we had half of each other's, Chris feeding me the first mouthful off his fork. It was so intimate, like long-standing lovers would do. And the desserts were just delicious. I was on my third glass of wine, feeling slightly light-headed. This was turning into the best evening I'd ever had.

Over coffee, I asked him about his past.

'Not much to tell,' he said. 'Nothing of note to talk about. Pretty average, in fact.'

It seemed that that was it. He beckoned James over. I guessed that conversation was done then.

James pulled a chair over and sat, taking up all the available space in the small alcove.

'Your food is amazing.' I gushed.

He inclined his head. 'Thank you. I have a proposition for you.'

'Oh?'

'Chris has told me about your new business venture. In fact, he brought me a brownie and some chocolate bombe the other week, from that deli you supply. I must say, I was impressed. You have a knack for mixing flavours, and I like your textures. How would you feel about supplying my restaurant with some samples and seeing how it goes? I'm sure my customers would like it.'

My jaw dropped in surprise. 'What? But surely with chefs of this calibre, you don't need me. Dessert was fantastic.'

James laughed. 'Don't talk yourself out of a job, Sarah. You're right, I don't need you, but I would like to help if I can. Chris is a good mate of mine.'

From the corner of my eye, I saw Chris lean back in his chair and fold his arms.

'Oh. Okay. In that case, I'd love to. Thank you so much.'

'Good. We'll sort something out.' James got up, held out his hand to me and we shook, before he disappeared again, into the darkness at the rear. Had I just sealed a deal? Wow!

I looked at Chris. 'I don't know what to say or how to thank you. I can't believe you went to all that trouble, going to the deli and bringing it here.'

'Glad to help,' he said. He reached over the table and took my hand. My nerve endings fired up at his touch and the rest of the room sort of melted away. 'Listen, I've been thinking, I could do you a website for your business, if you like.'

'I can't ask you to do that. You've done so much for me already.'

'It won't take me long. Stuff like that's a busman's holiday for me.'

'Maybe, but...'

He held his hand up. 'The offer's there.'

I did need a website. Why didn't I think of it before? 'Okay, if you're sure. But I insist on paying the going rate for your time.'

He sighed and smiled. 'If I asked you to help me, you would, wouldn't you?'

'Well, yeah, but...'

'If I asked you to make me a cake, would you charge me?'

'No, but—'

'Okay, pay me if it makes you feel better.' He leaned forward, still clutching my hand. His thumb was stroking the sensitive skin on the inside of my wrist. It was heaven, both relaxing and arousing at the same time. 'Anyway, I could link it to your blog and other pages, and it'd probably bring more work in. It could really showcase what you do. Have you got any pictures I could use?'

'Yes, loads.'

He smiled at me. 'Consider it done.'

'Thanks, Chris. Seriously, I don't deserve all this.'

He mimed a drinking motion to the waiter, but I jumped in.

'I've had way too much wine,' I protested.

'Shall we go then?'

'Okay.' I finished my wine. It was far too nice to leave it.

On the way back to the car, the biting cold found a way through my jacket, straight into me. There again, I hadn't exactly dressed warmly.

In the car, everything seemed to spin around me. 'I think I'm having a wine buzz. Are you alright to drive?'

'I've only had one. The rest have been alcohol-free.'

'Really?' I never realised. 'Look, I can get a taxi. Shepherd's Bush is miles out of your way.'

'Don't be daft,' he said, with a soft laugh. 'Anyway, what's your address?'

I told him, and he put it into the sat nav. Then I asked him the question that had been bugging me.

'I'm just being nosy and you can tell me to mind my own business if you like, but why would James do this for me? Or rather, for you?'

He looked over as he changed gear. 'I paid off a massive gambling debt of his years ago. Got him out of the shit. He owes me.'

'Ah. I see.'

We drove for a while with neither of us speaking. I kept wondering whether he'd kiss me when we got back. I kept sneaking glances at him as he drove, watching as the changing shadows played across his face. It was so hard to get a read on him. Was he playing games with me? But the silence wasn't uncomfortable and it was interspersed with chat. We managed to find a parking spot not too far away from my door.

'Do you want to come in for a coffee?' *Please say yes.*

He turned the engine off. 'Okay then.'

As we got out of the car, the Jack Russell over the road started its incessant barking in the front garden. Once inside, I could sense Chris's closeness to me as we went up the three flights of stairs to the top. As I went to unlock the door, he kissed the back of my neck very lightly, sending a shiver through me, making it impossible to get the key in. I giggled, and he spun me round and kissed me hard, pressing me up against the door. If this was a game, I wanted to play. He pulled away, grinning.

'Sexy Sarah,' he whispered in my ear. 'You're looking very flustered.' He tucked my hair behind my ear in an intimate gesture.

'I'm feeling very flustered, thanks to you.'

I unlocked the door and he followed me in. I needed to tell Lee we had a visitor.

'Wait there,' I told him.

He followed me into the living room. She was watching TV in her tatty old dressing gown. She stood up when she saw us, and clutched it around the neck, her face turning scarlet.

'Oh. I didn't know you were bringing anyone back.' She was clearly uncomfortable.

'Sorry. It was a spur-of-the-moment thing. This is Chris, from work.'

'Hello. Sorry, er, I'm not dressed for visitors.'

Chris shrugged lazily and said, 'Don't mind me.'

'Coffee?' I said.

'Please. Two sugars,' said Chris. 'Can I use your loo?'

'Back through there, first door on the left.'

'Okay. I won't be a sec.'

He closed the door behind him. Lee turned to me. 'Sarah! Look at the state of me. Where have you been? Who is he?'

'We've had a business meeting. I'll tell you all about it later. It's been brilliant. I thought I mentioned Chris.'

'I don't remember you saying anything about him. And do people usually get drunk at business meetings?'

I didn't like the way she inserted quote marks in the air with her fingers around *business meeting*. I took a deep, calming breath. 'I've got loads to tell you. He's helping me get the business off the ground.' I hadn't told her he'd lent me the money for the wedding fair.

'Why?'

'Because he's a nice person. He's got contacts and stuff. He's doing things I could never do.'

'And what's in it for him?' Her voice was getting louder.

What was that supposed to mean? 'Nothing, actually. You could try being happy for me.'

'And I might be if you didn't spring things like this on me. I'm off to bed. I'll leave you to it,' she said.

She left in a strop and I heard exchanged words as she bumped into him on the landing. God, could this get any worse? I busied myself making the coffee and he came looking for me.

'Have I upset her?' he whispered in my ear, encircling me from behind and pulling me close to him.

'No, it's not you. It's more to do with her. Just forget it. Anyway, thanks for tonight. It's been brilliant. Let's go sit down.'

He followed me into the living room, and I heard a clatter. He'd tripped over my hairdryer, which was lying on the floor next to the door, from this morning.

'Sorry,' I said, picking it up and putting it on the coffee table. He sprawled on the sofa, looking around the room. I saw the mess through his eyes—bras and knickers drying over radiators, clothes stacked up waiting to be ironed (even though our iron was broken), magazines thrown onto chairs and general clutter everywhere. The back of the TV was sprouting wires that trailed over the carpet. My straighteners were among them somewhere, as was my phone charger.

'Sorry about the mess. It's not normally like this.' Sometimes it was even worse.

'You're going to break your neck on that lot one day.' He nodded at the cables. 'It's not safe.'

'I know. There aren't enough plug sockets in this room, though. Or the whole flat, really.'

'Sit here. I don't want to talk about plugs.' He patted the cushion next to him. I sat close and we lingered over coffee interspersed with kisses. When he'd finished his drink, he sighed.

'I don't want to end this evening, but I think it's best if I go.'

He raised his eyebrows and inclined his head towards the door. He probably meant Leanne. He got up, took my hand and led me back to the front door. I put my finger over my lips as we crept past Lee's bedroom. At the door, he turned and kissed me gently, burying his fingers in my hair.

'See you at work,' he whispered as he opened the door and slipped through it. No sooner had he gone than Lee's door flew open.

'Were you kissing him just then?'

I bristled. 'Why? Were you listening?'

'Sarah! What's going on?'

'Will you calm down? What's the matter with you? He works at my place. He took me to a restaurant tonight, one that his friend owns and...' I stopped in frustration. She was taking the shine off this for me now I was having to justify everything.

'And what?'

'And James, the owner, asked me to supply him with some cakes and desserts to see how it goes.'

'Why?'

'To help me out with the business. And I was really happy about it until now.'

'Well, I'm sorry I don't like you bringing complete strangers into our house unannounced.'

'Why are you being so aggressive? He's not a stranger.'

'He is to me.' She folded her arms, still looking fierce.

This was stupid. We both needed to calm down. 'Look, I've said I'm sorry about that. I told you it was a spur-of-the-moment thing. And it's my home too, if you've forgotten.'

'Clearly that's all that matters. And what about Adam?'

'I'm going to finish it with him, if you must know. It's not working out.'

'Have you slept with Chris?'

'No! I haven't. Not that it's got anything to do with you.'

'But you want to. It's obvious.'

I don't answer.

'You do need to tell Adam. Anyway, I thought you were seeing him tonight.'

'I was. I had to cancel.'

She looked at me for a long time. 'I hope you know what you're doing.'

'I do. Anyway, what have you been doing tonight?' I asked, trying to defuse the situation.

'Research,' she said, cryptically.

'About what?'

'Ben.'

'Ben?'

'Oh, and another parcel came for you from ASOS. I thought you were supposed to be stopping spending.'

'I haven't ordered anything,' I said.

She went into her bedroom and closed the door quietly. I spotted the parcel on the hall shelf and ripped it open. All the hairs on the back of my neck stood up. Shoes and a blouse I didn't order. The exact same ones I was lusting over the other night. Once, okay, but twice? This was weird. I didn't like it. What the hell was going on?

22

THE HALL WAS BUZZING when Dad and I arrived at the wedding fair in Hammersmith. He'd given me a lift with all the boxes, which were packed tightly into his boot and all over the back seat. It was a wonder he could see out of the back window. Once inside, we were shown to my table and pretty much left on our own. Dad helped me unpack the car and carry the boxes to my stall. When he'd piled them onto my table, he looked round nervously at all the wedding paraphernalia. The ratio of men to women was about one to ten. Or maybe twenty.

'I'd better get back and help your mother with the washing. I'll see you at half five,' he said.

'Thanks, Dad.'

I kissed his cheek and he legged it, leaving me standing looking around the room, feeling very alone. Leanne was supposed to be here all day, but she'd ended up having to work as Kath, the clothes shop owner, wanted the day off at the last minute. I was disappointed, but relieved too. The atmosphere between us hadn't been great since we'd rowed about Chris.

I smoothed down the barely worn, midnight-blue wrap dress I'd dragged out from the back of my wardrobe. I'd been worried I might have been overdressed, but it was perfect. Everyone else looked as smart.

The venue was a function room in the Town Hall with windows round three sides and tables set up along all four edges. Two parallel lines of tables also ran down the centre of the room. I was on one of the outside runs of tables in between a flower stall and a local hotel, well known as a wedding venue. All the stallholders were busy setting up. I tried to ignore my thumping heart and wiped my clammy palms on my thighs. First thing was to find the box with the tablecloths I'd borrowed from Delish packed inside. For one horrible moment I couldn't see it and thought it must be still in Dad's boot, but no, there it was, underneath more boxes. I unfolded them and spread them out, smoothing away the sharp creases. There were at least another two cake stalls. Their stuff was bound to be much better than mine. A voice at my ear made me spin round.

'Sarah Haverland? A package for you.' A woman was standing there holding out a padded envelope.

'Oh, erm, thank you.'

I ripped it open and a pile of cards fell out onto the table. I picked one up. It was a beautifully embossed, thick business card with Sarah's Cakes in black and gold lettering on a cream background. My mobile number and a new email address Chris said he'd set up for me were underneath my name, along with my Twitter, Instagram, LinkedIn, and Facebook links. A simple ink sketch in black of a three-tier wedding cake was down the left-hand side. It was gorgeous. I turned it over. Who'd done it? A handwritten note dropped onto the table when I shook the envelope.

Thought you might be able to use these. Chris xx. Ps, good luck.

A huge smile spread across my face. How thoughtful. I didn't feel quite so alone now.

I worked quickly, setting up my stall, and tried not to pay too much attention to what others around me were doing. If you looked confident, people would think you were; Emma told me often enough. I put some of the boxes under the tablecloth to create a tiered effect, Jenny from the deli's suggestion, which elevated the cakes at the back and showed them off. My two favourite cakes, a dark chocolate tower oozing milk chocolate curls, white chocolate ribbons and a chocolate orange ganache, and a white, three-tier flat iced one with a hand-painted flower design in black, were in pride of place at the front. I had to admit it; my table looked fantastic. It had been well worth all the time it had taken me to get the cakes done. I propped up my beautiful cards at the front and fanned some out. They looked really professional and added the perfect finishing touch. I breathed out in relief at the finished stall. My worst fear had been that everything would have got broken in Dad's boot. I'd even had a bad dream about it the other night.

Most of the stallholders had finished now. The cake makers and florists had had the most work to do in setting up their stands. I stared at the wedding dress stalls, and an idea started to form. I shelved it for later. There was a drinks machine in one corner and I got myself a cup of tea. Coffee was the last thing I needed right now, despite the fact I was up until gone three doing last-minute tweaks. One of the organisers, the woman who gave me the cards, spoke into a microphone, announcing the doors would be opening in ten minutes.

I took my place behind my table, ignoring the quivering in my knees, and copied the others who looked like they'd done this a million times before. Some of them obviously knew each other and spent the last few minutes chatting. The organisers had spread the same sort of businesses far apart, so no two stalls of the same type were together. There was one cake stall in a corner at the far end from me and another at the opposite side of the room. The one opposite had a couple manning it, and the woman looked across at me and smiled. She nodded at my stall and gave me a double thumbs-up. Their stall was beautiful, and their cakes were all white, much more ornate (and also more traditional) than mine. I preferred mine.

It turned out to be a queer sort of day. You were either rushed off your feet talking to people or being ignored completely. It turned out, as I'd suspected, I wasn't very good at approaching people, and nobody spoke to me for the first hour, which was horrible. I watched how the woman opposite just kind of stepped forward and chatted naturally to people walking by, whether they were showing an interest in her stall or not. And she looked genuinely interested in what they were saying. It was a much better approach than mine (basically standing and trembling with fear) so I tried it. I got better as the morning wore on. Most of the brides-to-be were enthusiastic and happy to chat; it was their dragon mothers that could be awkward. And rude.

I smiled at one lady and she snapped, 'We've got the cake sorted,' as she marched past me, ushering her mousy daughter on towards the stall *she* wanted to look at.

'Mum!' I heard the girl say, obviously embarrassed.

'Well, you've got to let these people know,' her mother replied.

These people? Who did she think she was? But thankfully, most people weren't like her. Two people introduced themselves as familiar names who had contacted me on my blog, Dawn and Eileen, neither of whom were getting married but wanted to meet me, which was lovely. Dawn even looked after the stall while I nipped to the loo. They didn't stay long, but I was touched they'd come.

I got two orders and gave out a pile of cards and by mid-afternoon, my face hurt from smiling. I got a buzz from every compliment I received about my cakes and the chocolate one elicited the most interest. Kristen, a stunning blonde, was positively gushing about it.

'I've got to have that one. It's just so different,' she said to a woman who must be her slightly shorter, dumpier twin. In other words, she was only marginally less stunning.

'It is,' she agreed.

'This is Amber, my sister,' said Kristen. Kristen was a catwalk model, and she was lovely, not thick or bitchy at all. I got a crick in my neck looking up at her. I'd never heard of her, but she could be somebody really famous one day. If I could do her wedding cake, it might be good publicity.

'Can you do it as a rush job? The wedding's not far away. I know it's last minute, but I'd need it in two weeks.'

I said I could, and I was thrilled when she paid the deposit and ordered the chocolate one, but with an extra tier.

Thirty minutes later I'd taken another deposit and I realised I hadn't had any lunch when my stomach growled. I was also starting to flag. There was a vending machine so a Mars Bar and a packet of Quavers would have to do. A strong coffee perked me up and I went back to my stall bolstered by the sugar rush.

I checked my phone to find a text from Adam, asking if he could pop round tomorrow, which gave me a sinking feeling. I'd have to text him back later. I bent down to pick up an empty chocolate wrapper that had been kicked under my table, and a pair of men's black boots came into view. My eyes travelled up denim-clad legs, over a neat waist, white t-shirt and black biker jacket, ending at a handsome, stubbly face. I stood back up quickly.

'Chris! What are you doing here?'

'Thought I'd stop by. And see if you need any help.'

'Really? Thanks. I do.' I kissed his cheek to thank him.

'How's it gone so far?' He glanced around the room. 'Looks busy.'

It's gone really well. Several orders, lots of enquiries and compliments. Couldn't have gone better, really. And thanks for the cards. They're brilliant. I had forgotten to get some done.'

He picked one up. 'I thought 'Sarah's Cakes' was better than 'Partybakes'. More serious. Professional, you know. Is that alright? I can do some more if not.'

'No, you're right. It does sound loads better. I'm keeping the name. And the cards are gorgeous; I love them.'

He smiled, looking pleased. He glanced around. 'I thought your mate was gonna be here, anyway.'

'Oh, she had to work.'

'Have you been on your own all day, then? I'd have come earlier if I'd known.'

I wished he had. 'I've been fine. A bit scared at first. It's great to see you, though,' I said.

It really was. I was dreading him going. It was much more fun with someone else. And he looked gorgeous, like a film star or something. He stunned me by taking his jacket off and standing behind the table.

'I'll stay then. How are you getting back?' he asked.

'My Dad's coming back at half five.'

'Ring him. Tell him you don't need him. I'll drop you back.'

'Are you sure?'

'Absolutely. It's no problem.'

For the rest of the afternoon, Chris was a revelation. He cut pieces of cake and handed them out, along with the gift of the gab. He was the ultimate salesman and oozed charm. Plus, as the only sexy male in the room, women flocked round him, especially the dragon mothers. They were practically swooning over him and their eyes swivelled back to me in envy. Any queries, he directed to me, and more orders came in. I was also kind of proud he was with me. When there was no one at our stall, he stood close to me in a proprietorial kind of way. And the attraction between us was so strong, it must have been tangible. Every time he looked at me, my pulse sped up and my heart started twanging.

Eventually, the event drew to a close, and Chris helped me pack up the bits of left-over cake, after eating a good amount of it himself. A van was outside, and he walked over to it.

'Are we in that?' I asked.

'Yeah, well, we wouldn't get all these boxes in my car, would we?' he said, laughing.

I didn't tell him that they'd all gone in my dad's car okay.

23

CHRIS WOULDN'T LET ME help as he started to throw everything into the back of the van. I stood there shivering, watching him.

'You're freezing. You get in. I'll have this done in a second,' he said.

I slipped gratefully into the passenger seat, stifling a yawn. The adrenalin had finally run out.

'Tired?' Chris asked when he climbed in the driver's seat a few minutes later.

'Exhausted. But it was a great day. I'd do it all again in a second.'

'It was worth your while then?'

'Definitely. Thanks so much, Chris, for making it happen.'

'No worries.' He started the engine. The van was clean but draughty, and I fiddled with the heater as it blasted cold air at me. He closed the vents.

'Wait until the engine warms up,' he said.

'Whose van is it?'

'I borrowed it from James.' He indicated and we pulled away into the busy traffic.

'So how come there's a rental slip with your name on it?' I picked up a piece of paper that was on the dashboard.

He smiled. 'Busted. Okay, I rented it.'

'For me?'

'Well, yeah. I wanted to help. I knew this was gonna be a special day for you.'

'My God! How much did it cost? Let me pay you back.'

'Add it to the list,' he said.

I couldn't tell if he was joking or not. The fact that he'd rented it must mean he was hoping to take me home all along. The heater began to blow warmer and I relaxed back into the hard seat, trying to get comfortable. One of the business cards slid out of my pocket and I ran my fingers over the raised surface.

'This was such a nice thing to do. A total surprise. Did you design it?'

'Yeah.'

I turned to look at him and he glanced almost shyly at me briefly before returning his eyes to the road.

'Today wouldn't have been possible if it wasn't for you.'

'Glad to help. Listen, did you have any lunch?'

'Some chocolate and crisps from the vending machine.'

'Eating healthy, huh?'

I shrugged. 'It filled a hole.'

'Are you hungry now? We're not that far from my place. We could get something there if you're not in a hurry to get back.'

I was longing to see where he lived. 'Sounds great.'

When we got to his flat in Fulham, he cursed at the lack of parking places. It was quite a walk back after he finally found one big enough for the van, several streets away. He put his arm around me when he saw me shiver, and I snuggled into him. The streets were lined with beautiful large semis with neat front gardens, interspersed with massive detached houses and rows of beautiful terraces. We stopped outside what must once have been a detached house, now split into flats. It was a beautiful building, made from a pale, stone-coloured brick with massive bay windows. There was a tiny but untidy front garden and a path that led up to the front door. We went through a little gate, up the front steps, and he unlocked the door. The ground-floor flat on the left was his. Once inside, he flicked on the lights. This must be worth a bomb. Everything in it looked top end. I dreaded to think how much the rent was. I stood, turning about me in a full circle. I just thought 'Wow!'.

It was a real bachelor pad, all polished floors, hard edges and boys' toys, yet the original features of the room still shone through. The ceilings were high with wide, deep moulding and what looked like the original ceiling roses, and the whole lot was painted in pristine white. The TV was massive, above what looked like an original stone fireplace, opposite a black leather corner sofa. A large multi-gym dominated the other end of the living room. And the place was immaculate; there was absolutely no mess or clutter anywhere. Lord knows what he must have thought of mine the other day.

'Do you actually live here?' I joked. 'It's like a show home.'

His answer was a shrug. He pulled the blinds down at the front window, turned the thermostat up, even though the flat was warm, then swapped the hard, overhead lighting for wall lights that flooded the space with soft yellow pools. I watched him move about the flat, unable to tear my eyes away from him. Despite his size, he moved with a lithe gracefulness that was almost hypnotic. All the while I stood, feeling awkward and gauche, fiddling with the strap on my handbag. He hung his jacket up near the front door and hung my coat up next to his. A neat line of shoes, boots and trainers were lined up underneath, all with toes facing the wall. There was not a trace of mud or dirt on any of them.

'Drink?'

'Okay. Thanks.'

I followed him into the kitchen and gasped. 'Chris, this is amazing. It's my dream kitchen.'

'Is it?' He looked around him as if seeing it for the first time. The room was beautifully lit with subtle LED lights that were hidden under the cupboards. I felt under the edge and touched them. Even the white floor had lights in the sparkly tiles. The worktops were black, maybe granite or quartz, atop white gloss units, and two stainless steel ovens sat snugly in a housing. I'd always wanted two ovens. I ran my hand over them, jealously. A huge island dominated the centre; the sink and hob were set into it. The tap was one of those designer affairs that spit out boiling water and cost hundreds. None of it looked very used. He held up a bottle of white wine I'd never heard of. Just going by the label, it looked expensive.

'It's a little early, but go on then. It's been a special day.' I laughed.

He poured us both some wine and led me back into the living room, carrying both drinks. After putting the drinks down, he traced the neckline of my dress with a forefinger. His touch was cold from the bottle and I shuddered. He trailed the dress's ties through his fingers, loosening them slightly.

His eyes darkened. 'Do you ever do anything reckless, Sexy Sarah?' His voice was low and quiet, and I leaned forward, straining to hear him. He let go of the ties and trailed one finger lightly down the front, right between my breasts and down to my navel.

I shook my head and caught my bottom lip between my teeth. My heart was beating so fast and loud it was a wonder he couldn't hear it. 'No. Not really.'

'Would you like to? For once?'

'Yes.'

He walked around me in a slow circle, his eyes never leaving my body. 'How much?'

'A lot.'

He picked up my wine and handed it to me, letting his fingers brush over mine.

I put it straight back down on a nearby side table. His eyes locked onto mine.

He put his beer beside it, and I took a step towards him, so our toes were touching. He tugged at the ties holding the edges of my dress together and it fell apart, exposing my lacy underwear.

I heard him breathe in. 'Perfect.'

He removed my clothes slowly while I removed his, trying to stop my hands shaking. I savoured the moment where he was revealed to me. I couldn't get enough of him. His naked body was honed, unyielding and totally beautiful, and my fingers caressed every bit of his olive-toned skin. His lips were all over me, and we did it on the sofa, the floor, in the shower and in his bed while the drinks grew warm. It was visceral and primal, like him. It was chemistry. And I'd never felt anything like it with anyone else.

Later, much later, in his king-size bed with snowy-white bedding, he trailed a finger around my mouth, and my eyes closed at the sensation. He was propped on his side on one elbow, his face above mine, with his massive bulk dwarfing me.

'Do you want me to fuck you again?' he whispered, slipping the tip of his finger into my mouth.

A ripple of excitement ran through me at the thought. 'Yes.'

He rolled on top of me and I lost myself in him once more.

When it was over, he asked me, 'Have you ever had sex that good with anyone else?'

'No,' I said. 'Never. Have you?'

He shook his head. 'No.'

I never wanted to let him go.

24

2005

IN MY FIRST WEEK at Bristol uni, I met Alex at a Fresher's party for students on my Computer Science course. I was on my own at the bar and he came to stand next to me. He looked at my can of Dr Pepper and ordered the same.

'Alright?' I said.

He grimaced, rubbing his hand over old acne scars that covered his face. It was like a lunar landscape. 'Ah, man. My head. I really should have gone to bed tonight instead of coming out again.'

'Yeah, I know what you mean. I haven't got to bed this side of four all week,' I said.

He wasn't with anyone and seemed content just to stand there.

'Want to sit down?' I asked, pointing at a couple of empty seats in a dark corner.

'Yeah, okay.'

'So where are you from?' I asked him when we were slumped into the chairs.

'A little village in Cornwall no one's ever heard of. What about you?'

'Leeds.'

'At least I've heard of that,' he said.

We talked about computer games and the course, me avoiding giving any information about my family and the fact that I got here on a bursary. I never went back home after I'd moved into the flat above Simon's shop. After I'd started to apply myself at school, I did well in *my final exams, went to college and did my A' levels, supporting myself on money from the computer shop and the glass-collecting job in the pub. Simon was great, like the big brother I never had. He often took pity on me and I went home with him for meals, showers and such like. Not having to pay any bills for the flat was a turning point for me. Independence and self-sufficiency would have been too high a price if I'd not had that.*

Alex, as it turned out, was staying in the same halls as me, a couple of floors up from my room, which was tiny and stark, like a prison. Maybe my old man's cell was more luxurious than this. Funny how I rarely thought of him, of any of them, these days.

Alex told me as much about his background as I told him about mine: precisely zilch. I didn't pry, and neither did he. By some unspoken agreement, we palled up and started to go around together. My interest in computers had gone stratospheric after Frankie, and then Simon, started teaching me about them. It was a natural progression that if I managed somehow to get to uni, I'd choose a career in IT. Also, it turned out I was shit hot at anything to do with computers; that was how I'd got a bursary through college to get here. For outstanding achievement and ability they said, although the piss-poor parents that didn't give a shit part was a major factor too, I think.

Alex was a quiet, guarded person, often preferring to stay in and mess with his computer on an evening after lectures. One Wednesday evening, two months after the course started, I jogged the four flights of stairs up to his floor and banged on his door.

'Everyone's going to Kaliber. Fancy coming?' I asked when he opened his door. His body was shielding the rest of the room from view, but I could see there was no one in there. So he wasn't holed up with some girl then.

'Nah. I'm not one for clubbing,' he said.

'What you up to?'

He pulled the door tighter behind him.

'Nothing much. Just, like, some coding and stuff.'

I held up a six-pack. 'I'm not bothered about clubbing either. We can stay here and drink these, if you like.'

He glanced at the beer, then back at me, studying me. As if deciding whether to let me in on something or not. After a while, he stepped back and opened the door wider.

'Okay. Come in.'

Inside the tiny room, I put the beer down on the desk and sat on the single bed, the only other place to sit being the chair in front of the desk. I passed him a beer and opened one for myself. Everyone here seemed to assume that drink was key to having a good time at uni, but I actually drank very little. With parents like mine, it held no fascination for me. It was for losers, and I was never going to be one of them.

Alex took the chair, still studying me, not speaking.

'What?' I asked him. 'How come you keep looking at me?'

I got an unpleasant shiver as his eyes fixed on mine. Aw fuck, he wasn't gay, was he? Had I been palling round with him all this time and not noticed? I shifted uneasily, getting ready to spring up off his bed if he tried anything. I'd knock his head off if he came near me with his crater face.

'Just trying to work out if I can trust you,' he said.

'You what? How do you mean?'

He nodded. 'I think we're the same, you and me.'

Fuck! He was gay. I was just about to tell him I didn't swing that way when he spoke.

'So, can I trust you?' he asked.

'About what?'

'Something not strictly legal.'

Mystified, I nodded, as much out of relief as anything. 'Course.'

'Look at this,' he said, nodding, as if he'd come to a decision that I could be trusted after all.

He pointed to something on his computer screen. It was some sort of code, but I didn't know what. I'd never seen it before.

'What is it?'

'A virus. Trojan Horse.'

I knew what that was, of course. I sat, thinking. Next to him, on his desk, was what looked to be a list of email addresses. Two sheets of A4 stapled together. I picked it up slowly.

'Whose are these? Where d'you get them from?'

'You don't need to know that.' He grabbed it and placed it at the other side of his computer.

'Is mine in there?'

'Is it hell! What do you take me for? You're my mate.'

'So, you're sending emails with viruses in, to infect their computers?'

He said nothing. I knew he was wondering if he'd done the right thing in telling me. A little anticipatory shiver ran through me at the prospect of what he was doing and the possibilities it threw up.

I burst out laughing. 'Man, that's fuckin' brilliant. How long have you been doing stuff like this?'

'Ages. Since I was at school.'

'Are you running scams and making money?'

'Some,' he said. His eyes had a glint in them, and he searched my face, more intently this time.

I leaned closer to him. 'What sort of stuff do you do?'

'Get bank details, personal information, IDs, hack phones, that sort of thing.'

Wow! This was huge. I scooted forward on the bed until I was right next to his chair. Our shoulders were touching, and our faces were lit up in the glow from the screen.

'Have you actually been in people's bank accounts then and moved money out?'

He looked shifty. Once he admitted to this, he could never take it back.

'You have, haven't you?'

He didn't answer.

'Can we make money out of it?' I asked.

'We?'

'Yeah. You and me.'

He paused. Then, 'Yeah.'

'How much.'

He opened the desk drawer. It was stuffed with cash. 'More than that. If we don't get caught,' he added.

'Have you ever been caught?'

'No.'

'Why do you do it? Assuming you don't always do it for money.'

He stared into the screen. I wondered what he was seeing. 'I like the way machines do what I tell them. It's addictive. Know what I mean?'

'Yeah. If the machine doesn't do what you ask, it's you that's at fault, not the computer. I like the control.'

'Exactly.' He turned to look at me.

'Why are you telling me now?' I asked.

He was quiet. Then he said, 'Because you're good.'

'As good as you?'

He nodded.

'Show me.'

25

LEE HAD STAYED AT her parents' after work the night of the wedding fair, so she was unaware I hadn't come home. She hadn't said as much, but I didn't think she liked being in the flat alone, after the flowers from Craig turned up. There had been nothing since, but where the hell was he? It was unnerving her, and watching her so jittery was getting to me.

By the time I got back on Sunday, after calling at the supermarket, she was in. It was a good job; my keys weren't in my bag or my coat pocket. I had got a horrible feeling I might have dropped them at the venue yesterday. I'd have to call tomorrow to see if anyone had found them.

Lee had gone to work before I left for the wedding fair yesterday morning, so she wouldn't know what clothes I'd gone in, and that they were the same ones I was still wearing now. My long coat covered my dress so she wouldn't really notice it and wonder why I was dressed up on a Sunday morning. She let me in when I rang the bell, carrier bags in both my hands. She eyed them as I dumped them on the floor.

'Oh, good,' she said. 'You've been to the shop. We're almost out of milk.'

I nipped into my bedroom to get changed into jeans and a hoodie.

'So how was yesterday?' she asked as I came back out.

'Absolutely brilliant. I can't wait to do another one.'

'Tell me all about it,' she said, so I did. Except the bits about Chris.

Just then, I remembered Adam's text from yesterday. I'd forgotten to answer him. I checked the time.

'Adam's popping round in half an hour.'

She raised her eyebrows at me. I changed the subject.

'Oh, I forgot to tell you. I went past the vintage shop earlier and guess what? There's a sign in the window. They want staff. More specifically, a buyer.'

Her mouth dropped open. 'Really?'

'And I thought of something else as well. There were a couple of wedding dress stalls doing original designs yesterday, but they were quite expensive. I wondered if there was a way you could buy second-hand dresses and make new ones out of them, then sell them for reasonable prices. Or is it a crap idea?'

She went very still for an awfully long time before speaking, first stroking her hair then twirling strands of it around her fingers. 'Sarah, that's a great idea. I can't believe I've never thought of it. Do you think it could work?'

'Yeah, definitely, looking at what was on offer yesterday.'

She wandered off into her bedroom and closed the door. I smiled to myself. She was probably Googling second-hand wedding dresses already.

Adam rang the bell early and I let him up. He'd been so busy with work I'd barely seen him lately.

'You can tell me all about yesterday,' he said as he came through the door. 'I can't wait to hear what happened. And how that business meeting went.'

Oh God! 'Alright. I'll make some coffee first. Or tea. Whatever you want.'

'Either. Got any biscuits?' he asked. 'I'm starving.'

'Red tin over there. Plates are in that cupboard.'

Adam arranged digestives on a plate as I watched. A feeling of dread filled the pit of my stomach. I needed to be honest with him. Yesterday, with Chris, it was as if it was meant to be. It was all I could think about. I'd been stirring the coffee for way too long and Adam nudged me.

'Penny for them?'

'Oh! Nothing. Sorry.'

'Spill, then,' he said as we went into the living room. 'And don't leave anything out.'

I told him about the wedding fair. Adam was interested and fired questions at me while eating half a packet of biscuits. Of course, I missed out the part where Chris turned up, took me home to bed, and we shagged all night. And again the next morning. Twice. I was still aching. Thankfully, he didn't mention my dad picking me up, so I glossed over how I got home and when.

'What's that noise?' he asked, as a mechanical humming started up.

I grinned. 'Ha! It's Lee. She's got her sewing machine out. First time in ages.'

'What's she sewing?'

'I don't know, but just the fact that she is means she's seriously considering my idea.'

'What idea?'

'Making new wedding dresses from second-hand ones and selling them at wedding fairs and such like. Like my cakes.'

'Sounds good.' He took a piece of paper out of his jacket pocket and handed it to me.

I peered at the picture on it. 'What is it?'

'A smoke alarm. But not *just* a smoke alarm. This one has a hidden camera in it.' He sounded smug.

'Really? How clever!' I conjured up some fake enthusiasm. Why would you want one of those?

'You could have one outside your door here and be able to see who's there. We're selling loads of them. I could fit one for you, if you like.'

'But no one gets in without me buzzing them up.'

'Sarah, someone could just hang around and grab the door when it's open. People do it all the time. You're way too naïve.'

I grinned and held up my hands. 'What can I say? I'm just too nice.'

'You should be more suspicious, that's for sure. So, do you want one?'

I pictured Craig sneaking in through the door downstairs. 'How much are they? I'm stony, at the moment. I had to get a lot of stuff for the wedding fair cakes. That and Christmas cleaned me out.'

'Don't be daft, I wouldn't charge you. It's what friends are for. I could fit it next week if you like. Maybe Friday. Straight after work.'

'Friday? Erm...'

'Okay, that's fixed, then. Oh, I forgot to tell you, my sister wants to meet you to see about doing her wedding cake. When shall I tell her?'

'Do you want to give her my number and we can sort something out?'

'Okay, yeah.'

For the next hour, we made small talk and I fended off his hints at another date, saying how busy I was going to be with the orders from the wedding fair. He accepted it but didn't look happy. When he went, I found Leanne at her sewing machine. I showed her the picture of the smoke alarm and she was all for it, just like I knew she would be.

'He's fitting it next Friday.'

'Great. I'm away, remember? The spa weekend for Mum's birthday?'

Shit! I'd forgotten. That meant it would just be me and him. I could hardly tell him I didn't want to go out with him when he was coming to do me a favour. I looked at the piece of fabric in her hands.

'What're you sewing?'

'Just an old scrap. Seeing if I've still got the touch.'

'Course you will have. Listen, we could go looking for second-hand clothes shops if you like, see if any of them are open on a Sunday?'

She jumped up like a little kid. 'Okay, yeah. Let's go past the vintage shop and I can read the job advert. Tonight, I can brush up my CV. Do you really think I could get the job?'

'I think they'd be stupid to not take you on.'

It was freezing out, with snow flurries stopping and starting. We hurried to the vintage shop and Leanne took a photo of the advert on her phone after scrutinising every word. On our way back, Lee stopped dead as we turned into our road.

'Who's that?' She clutched my arm.

There was some bloke standing outside our flat, looking up at it. I couldn't see who it was. I was too far away.

'It could be anybody,' I said. 'Are any of the downstairs flats empty? Could be a prospective tenant.'

'It's him,' she said. 'I'd know him anywhere, just from the way he's standing.'

'What? Craig?'

She nodded then suddenly marched off down the road with me trailing after her. When she reached him, she went right up to him and pushed him so hard in the chest he stumbled back.

'What are you doing here?' she yelled.

He held his hands up. 'I just want to talk to you.'

'Well, I don't want to talk to you. And don't send me any more flowers. You can shove them up your arse instead!'

'But—,' he said, his mouth flapping open.

'You're not supposed to come near me. I have an injunction out on you. Do you want to go back inside?'

I stood watching her, mesmerised. Where had all this come from? She was like a raging bull. He took a step towards her, holding his hands out.

'Leave me alone, you cheating bag of shit!' she snarled. 'Get out of here.' She pushed him again.

'Please,' he said. 'Just listen to me.'

I gasped when Leanne pulled her arm back, balled her fist and let it fly straight into his face, busting his nose. Blood sprayed down the front of his coat.

'Never speak to me again. I hate you! Do you understand?' she snapped.

He nodded, holding his nose. A dark look clouded his features and I resisted the urge to step back. Instead, I moved closer to Leanne. He looked at her a moment longer, then at me, then said, 'Okay. Fine. I get it.' He walked unsteadily back off up the street without looking back.

'God, Lee! You were amazing. What did that feel like?' I asked her, when I found my voice.

'Awesome. Although my hand is killing me.' She flexed her fingers. 'Nothing broken, thank God.' Her knuckles had blood on them. Whether it was his or hers, I wasn't sure. I hoped it was his.

'Bloody hell! Where did all that come from?'

'I don't know. Just the sight of him, I think. Just as long as I don't get done for GBH or assault or something, I think it'll be alright,' she said.

'Weren't you scared?'

'Of him? Funnily enough, no. I wasn't.' She turned on her heel and headed towards the door. 'Well, come on. Are we going to get dinner on or what?'

26

I'M HALFWAY UP THE M1 to Leeds. My sister, Shay, has done nothing but ring me for days. 'You need to come home, it's serious,' is all she will say. I'd have carried on ignoring her, but she's set a thought off in my head. What if Dad has found out what I did? What if he's out of prison and none of them have told me? She won't tell me over the phone what the crisis is, and I can't make her.

If Dad has been released and he's found out the truth, I'm a dead man. He's the nastiest bastard I've ever met, the only person I've ever truly been scared of. Even though I'm no longer the little boy hiding behind the sofa as Dad rages around the flat, looking for something or someone to hurt, the fear is still there. I know the old drunken bastard can't hurt me anymore, but it doesn't stop my guts from twisting and churning. Another memory is battling to get out, one I've kept down for so long. A scream. A screech of tyres. A dirty, rusting, tan Cavalier. I can smell the fusty interior and feel the grease on the seat where my dad used to sit.

I concentrate hard on the miles of tarmac being eaten up under the car wheels and shut the memory out, squeeze it back down where it belongs. Two more hours and then I'll be there, should find out what the big mystery is.

I stop at the next services on the M1. While I'm filling the car up, I run my hand over her roof. She's beautiful, my pride and joy, a Mazda MX-5 soft top. It's the first time I've had her out of London and she's easily living up to my expectations on the motorway. Twenty grand of sheer beauty, power and perfection and worth every penny.

I wolf down a sandwich and some coffee, and shoot back onto the motorway. Roadworks and the obligatory congestion around Sheffield don't help, and I'm stiff and aching when I finally pull up in front of the shitty, disgusting block that my mother and sister still call home. Is it safe to leave the car here? She might be on bricks when I get back. I park in a space directly under Ma's window, where I can keep an eye on her. If any little bastards touch it, they'll be sorry.

I lock up and set off up the concrete entranceway. It's dingy and depressing and two teens, one tall and one short, are skulking about in the shadows doing fuck knows what. I glance back to see the car about to be descended on by a swarm of grubby-looking lads on bikes who look about ten. The teens don't seem to be doing much other than smoking and hanging out.

'Watch my car and I'll give you twenty quid when I come back out. Don't let them little bastards touch it, okay? I won't be long,' I say to them.

They peel themselves off the wall in unison, in a fluid movement, interested now, their skinny jeans hanging off their skinny arses.

'Thirty,' says the tallest one, dragging on his cig.

I pull my shoulders back. 'Don't fuckin' push it, okay? Twenty's good for a few minutes of your time.'

They look at each other. The taller one shrugs, nods. 'Yeah, okay.'

They go outside and sit on the low wall that runs round the parking area, separating the grass from the tarmac.

One of them shouts at the kids, 'Oi, you little twats, touch that car, any of you, and you're dead.'

The kids are riding round the car in fast circles, mouthing off but keeping a safe distance and eyeing the older boys warily. They won't touch her. I start up the stairs to flat 326. The lift still doesn't work, and the stairs still stink of piss. Nice to see nothing changes around here. I smile grimly at the sense of continuity.

I don't breathe in while I climb the stairs to the landing. The concrete walkway is as dim and ugly as ever, with graffiti and obscenities plastered all over the walls. I remember when, for a whole year, crude pictures of cocks and balls were spray-painted in bright red right opposite our door. Finally, the council painted over it, but it bled through. The outline was still visible if you looked closely enough. I don't look closely now.

I bang my fist on the door, and my sister opens up. She looks like an emaciated tramp, and I step back with a grimace.

'About time,' she says with a fierce look. 'I've lost count of the number of times I've rung you and left messages. This is serious.'

'Yeah, well, I'm here now, aren't I? God, Sis, you look dog rough.'

Niceties over, I push past her into the short corridor that leads straight down to the living room. Even if the old man has been released, he wouldn't be here. I follow the smell of fag smoke to find my mother propped up on the same sofa I used to cower behind. She's covered in a grubby brown blanket. A one-bar electric fire glows in the corner. With the amount of dust on it, I'm surprised the place isn't on fire. With the curtains closed, it's so dark in here I can only just make her out. Sparse strands of hair are scattered over her scalp and she looks frail but still manages to suck down the smoke from a cig as if her life depends on it. An empty bottle of vodka lies beside her on the floor. I feel nothing when I see her; well, nothing good. The memories of her throughout most of my childhood are of her lying on this couch, swigging whatever she could get her hands on. She'd have necked down lighter fuel if that's all there was. Although, she did have more hair then, even if she rarely washed it.

'Alright Ma?' I step across to the window and pull the grimy curtain back on the thin wire with the tip of my forefinger. A weak beam of light struggles to get through the dirty nets and the glass beyond is covered in greasy streaks. It makes my skin crawl. I can hardly believe I used to live here. She groans at the light and shields her eyes with her hand. Shay has followed me into the room. She too has a fag smouldering between her yellow fingers. Her fingernails have a layer of grime underneath them.

'You taken up gardening or summat?' I ask her.

'You what?' she asks, frowning.

I put a hand over my nose, making sure the finger that touched the curtain doesn't touch any part of my face. 'It fuckin stinks in here. Don't you ever clean up? It's disgusting.'

Shay takes a drag before answering. 'That's okay for you to say. You're not the one coping here twenty-four-seven. She can't make it to

the toilet now. She hasn't got long left.' She pauses for dramatic effect.
'She's got cancer.'

Ma's been ill for so long now that it's like that boy crying wolf thing.
It falls on deaf ears. She's been drinking since the old man fucked off
when we were little. The miracle is that she's still here. I wish, not for
the first time, that she'd hurry up and get on with it so we can all move
on. But this time it's different. I take in the wizened face and body and
crusty scalp. It's then the realisation hits me that Shay's announcement
is the reason I'm here—it's got nothing to do with the old man. Despite
the relief, I suck in a breath and suppress the urge to hit something.
Something like them. I've been dragged all the way up here for nothing
but some game Shay's playing.

Shay is still going on. 'She was diagnosed three months ago with it,
at late stage. She's had some chemo, but it's too late.'

Ma swivels her head towards me as if seeing me for the first time.
'Colin, is that you?'

When she calls me by my birth name I actually shudder. I'd almost
forgotten I was ever Colin. Now I can see her better in the light, she
does look bad. I'd kneel down, but there's no way my jeans are touching
this carpet. I crouch down, balancing on the balls of my feet, determined
not to touch the sofa.

'No, it's the Queen of fuckin Sheba. Yeah, course it's me. Who
d'you think it is?' I hold up the empty vodka bottle in front of her eyes.
'Still drinkin' yourself to death then, Ma?' Her eyes fix on it. I swing
it from side to side and she follows the movement like a cat with a torch
beam.

I turn back to Shay. 'So why did you insist I come? Nothing much
has changed other than she's gonna die earlier of summat else than
drink.'

'You heartless bastard.' She drags deep and coughs as the smoke
hits her eyes. 'I need some fuckin help with her.'

'What sort of help? I live fuckin miles away, if you hadn't noticed.
Plus, you could have told me she had cancer on the phone. You didn't
have to be so mysterious and drag me all the way up here to tell me.'

'I can't manage her anymore. It's too much for me,' she whines.

'She should be in a hospice by the look of her. Why's she still here?'

'She won't go in one, will she?'

I look at Shay and remember the teenager she used to be. She was good looking when she was younger, and it's a shame to see what she's become. She looks like an old hag. Am I really from the same gene pool as this lot? Tears glimmer in her eyes and I turn away.

'*You think you're so much better than us, don't you, with your fancy job and posh cars and shit!*'

The car! I pick my way through the rubbish on the floor and use the same finger to pull the curtain aside more. It's difficult to see through the filthy glass, but the Mazda is just visible. The two teens are doing a grand job of guarding her and the kids on bikes have gone. She's fine. I turn back to my family; my loving mother, and my sister with the scars of needle marks in her arms from shooting up.

'*Yeah, I am better than you. I wouldn't live like this if you paid me. It's a fuckin shit tip. I can't help you. So, I'm off. Unless there's owt else.*'

Shay looks outraged and needs a hefty drag to calm herself.

'*You bastard! What am I supposed to do? I've just told you our mother's got cancer and you're off?*'

'*I'm sure you'll manage.*' *I nod at the burning cig.* '*Carry on like that, you'll be next. Bye Ma, I've got to go now. I've got more important things to do.*'

The figure on the sofa turns her head in my direction; she doesn't even know what day it is. A coughing spasm overtakes her; whether it's the cancer or the fags, I can't be sure. I drop the vodka bottle on the brown blanket next to her and her fingers creep out to touch it.

Shay lunges at me and grabs my sleeve, screaming. '*You can't leave me like this. I don't know what to do. She's your mother as well, you know. Take some fuckin responsibility.*'

I flick her to one side, and she stumbles. It's like swatting a fly.

'*What do you want me to do? I'm not a fuckin doctor. If you want to help her, phone one. Tell them she needs a hospice. Or put a pillow over her face and put her out of her misery.*' *I can feel her touch lingering on my sleeve and I brush at it desperately, trying to remove it.*

Shay sinks onto the nearest chair, a tatty mushroom-coloured velour thing with stains I wouldn't even like to hazard a guess as to the origins of. My mother disgusts me even more; even with the cancer ravaging every cell in her body, all she cares about are the fags and booze that most likely put it there. It's totally sickening. I have to get out before it infects me as well.

'Let me know when she croaks.' I stride out, desperate to leave the stink behind. 'And fuckin clean up once in a while.' The door shakes in the frame when I slam it after me.

Outside, I gasp lungfuls of air and march over to the car. The teens get up from the wall. Maybe I could not pay the lads their twenty quid, but there's plenty of bricks lying around to lob at the car if I don't. Even if they did it and I hammered them, the car would still be damaged and need fixing. Besides, a deal's a deal.

'Here.' I fish two tens out of my wallet and hand them over. 'Cheers lads.'

They snatch the notes greedily. The tall one's cigs are protruding from his jeans pocket and I grab them, toss them in a nearby puddle and grind them under my boot.

'Them things'll kill you. Pack 'em in or you'll end up like her up there.'

Their faces twist in anger, but they look me over and decide, wisely, it's not worth it. Instead, their shoulders droop and they slink off back to their lair in the entranceway.

'A word of advice, lads,' I call after them. 'Work harder at school and get yourselves out of this shithole. Best thing I ever did.'

I can see them considering my words as their eyes slide back to the Mazda. I hope they have the sense to really listen.

'There's more to life than this place,' I add, getting in the car. Before I start her up, I pull out a bottle of hand sanitising gel from the glove box and apply it liberally over my face and hands. They watch me leave in a streak of burning rubber. Fresh air comes in as I crank the windows down to get rid of the smell of fag smoke. The stink pisses me off. The car's gonna have to be valeted. I can't have her reeking like this.

Four hours tops and I should be back. I can't wait to have a shower and scrub off my history. It's amazed me how quickly the accent came back. I'll have to get rid of that again, too. It's the last time I'll ever come back here.

27

THANK HEAVEN IT'S FRIDAY,' I said to Pauline when I arrived at work exhausted after being up late again baking for the delis. They now wanted things two or three times a week. Plus, I'd started doing the desserts for Porters too. But I wasn't complaining. I loved it.

'What are you doing this weekend?' she asked.

'Remember Kristen, that model from the wedding fair? She's picking her cake up, so I've just got to finish it off.'

'Aw, your first one. That's great, Sarah, love.'

My phone rang, and so began another day. I couldn't stop yawning and the time dragged endlessly until five, when I could escape. Chris had left so there were no more flirty emails, with me knowing he was only one floor up, no more walks in the park or lunches at the café. It was horrible.

Pauline stood up at four fifty. 'I've had enough,' she said.

I got up, too. 'So have I.'

We walked over to the coat racks, got wrapped up, then went down in the lift together.

'I'll see you on Monday. Have a good weekend,' she said and walked away quickly, hunching her shoulders up against the cold.

I rushed to St Paul's tube station, threading my way through the Friday rush hour commuters, only to find the bloody train was delayed. Adam was coming to fit the smoke alarm camera tonight and Lee wasn't going to be there. The spa break was another Groupon deal she'd found. She was always finding bargains on it. Whenever I looked at the deals, there was never anything good. I don't know how she did it.

I'd tried to get out of Adam coming tonight, texting him this morning to tell him he didn't have to do it today if he was busy, but he insisted. I wasn't looking forward to it. I'd rehearsed a speech about us just being friends, it's not him, it's me, etc. Maybe I wouldn't mention Chris at all.

With the delay, I ended up hurtling down the road, forty-five minutes late. Luckily, Adam wasn't waiting outside. I raced up the stairs and dug out the spare key from my bag. My keys hadn't turned up anywhere. They weren't handed in at the wedding fair. I thought they must have been at Chris's but they weren't there either.

While I waited for Adam, I sorted through some clothes. I'd decided to sell the stuff I don't wear on eBay and put the proceeds towards the business. My bed was covered in piles of clothes, shoes and bags when he arrived, holding a box and a stepladder.

'Sorry I'm late. Got held up on a job. Right, I'll just take this one down,' he said, pointing up at the old smoke alarm.

He removed his leather jacket and dropped it on the floor, climbed up the stepladder and unscrewed it. His hands were stretched above his head and his polo shirt rode up, revealing a wide line of hair from his navel that disappeared into the waistband of his loose trousers, which looked like they were in danger of falling down any minute. His stomach was very flat, and his hip bones jutted out.

'Do you want a coffee or anything?' I asked, looking away.

'Yeah, go on then.'

I disappeared into the flat to make them. When I got back, he was just screwing the new smoke alarm into place. I put the coffees on the shelf near the door. He climbed down and handed me the old smoke alarm.

'That still works. Might as well keep it.'

'Where's the camera thing?'

He climbed back up the ladder and pointed to where the camera was located. I couldn't see a thing.

'You'll be able to see everything on your computer and your phone. You can check it remotely when you're out as well. I'll explain the whole set up when I've finished.'

He clipped the cover into place and came back down.

'Don't forget to check the batteries every so often and replace them when they need it. They should last a long time though.'

'Okay. Will it beep like a normal one when they're running low?'

'Yeah, should do.'

He folded up the stepladders, picked up his jacket and followed me into the flat.

'Well, that's the outside bit done. Where's your computer?' He picked up his coffee.

'In my bedroom through here.'

I hoped he wouldn't get the wrong idea. It felt weird him being in here. The bedroom was as messy as the living room had been when Chris came round, even more so with all the clothes on the bed.

'Just sorting out some things to put on eBay,' I explained, kicking some shoes under the bed, as if it made a difference.

If he thought it was messy, he kept it to himself. I pulled out the stool for him and noticed I had a new email from Leanne. He sat down at my little desk, on the pine stool, looking like an adult on the nursery chairs at school, and picked up a square black box thing. It had cables sticking out of it which he connected to the back of my laptop. For the next few minutes he was busy clicking keys and plugging stuff in, totally absorbed in what he was doing. None of it made the slightest sense to me, so I kept sorting clothes into separate piles. The pile for selling was far bigger than the pile I wanted to keep.

Eventually, he looked up and swivelled the laptop a couple of inches towards me so I could see the screen, which displayed the hallway outside my door.

'So,' he said, 'As you can see, it covers a fairly wide angle so anyone out there is fully in the frame, head to toe. You can zoom in or out as well. This demo shows how you use it.' He clicked a few keys and the picture changed to a mock-up interior, with boxes down the side containing still-shots of figures. 'If someone comes to your door, a motion sensor will start the camera recording onto this box here. It will store the image on the screen with the date and time so you don't have to go through endless footage to find anything. If you click on it, it'll start to play. Of course, it'll record everyone who comes and goes, so it's best to delete unwanted ones at the end of every day. Just right-click and press delete.'

He did that, and the image disappeared.

'It's weird, isn't it? Watching people. All these hidden cameras and things. Makes you wonder who's watching you.'

Adam looked at me and shrugged. 'It's the way, now. Anyway, that's all there is to it. I'll link it to your phone now so you can watch your door from anywhere and you're good to go.'

I passed him my phone and he did something on it.

'Right, I'll let you have a play around with it and make sure you're okay with how it works and everything.' He handed it back to me.

It was simple to use and easy to get the hang of. Idiotproof. His stomach gave a loud rumble, reminding me that he'd come straight from work. To do this nice thing for me. I felt worse than ever.

'Thanks, Adam, this is great. Look, have you eaten yet? I could make us something if you like.' It was the least I could do.

'Are you sure? That would be great. If it's no trouble. I'm starving, actually.'

'What do you fancy to eat? There's pizza in the freezer.'

'Great.'

While the pizza was in the oven and Adam was busy clearing his tools away, I read the email Lee sent earlier. It said 'Bingo!!' and there was a link. I couldn't believe what I saw when I opened it.

'Adam! Quick!' I shouted.

I heard hurried footsteps. 'What?' He poked his head around the door, and I beckoned him in.

'Read this.'

He bent over my shoulder, and we read it together. There, on the screen, was a photo of Ben. It was a clear shot and without the beard, he looked like he did when he got out of our shower.

'He's on a missing persons' website?' Adam said.

'Yes. He's a registered missing person. Oh, my God. If someone reported him missing...' I swivelled round to look at Adam.

'He has a family somewhere,' Adam finished. 'Looking for him.'

SARAH APPEARS IN FRONT of her laptop, peering at something on the screen. I settle back, scanning her lovely face. Now I've slept with her, it's even better. Although, the state of her bedroom. God! It's a tip. There are clothes all over the place. I'll have to try and make sure some of my ways rub off on her.

Hang on a minute. There's a bloke in her bedroom. Who's he? He looks like he's making himself comfortable. I switch the mic on so I can hear them. Something about a smoke alarm he's putting in? Soon, I get the gist. I stand up, leave the bedroom and grab my jacket.

Time to pay a visit and find out what's really going on. And I have the perfect excuse.

'THAT WAS GREAT. JUST what I needed.' Adam pushed his plate away and tried to cover up a light burp.

'It was only a frozen pizza.'

'Yeah, well. I've burnt loads of them in my time.'

I glanced at Kristen's cake on the side, waiting to be finished off. Adam raised his eyebrows at the amount of pizza still on my plate.

'Weren't you hungry?'

'Yeah, but I've had enough.' Go on, tell him. Now. *I've met someone else... there's something I need to tell you... I think we should just be friends...* none of those seemed right.

I took a breath in and paused. Then went for it. 'Adam,' I said, hoping instinct would guide me to the rest.

We both jumped when someone hammered on my door. Not the bell downstairs, but my actual flat door. I knocked the fork right off my plate, and it clattered onto the floor.

'Who's that at this time of night? It's gone nine.'

Adam looked excited. 'Let's go see who it is. Try the camera out.'

I grabbed my phone and did parrot-fashion what he told me. Chris was standing outside with his arms folded and his legs apart, looking bullish. My heart plummeted at the sight of him, although I was relieved it wasn't Craig.

'Who is it?' Adam asked.

'Someone from work. I'd better let him in.'

'Hi,' I said with forced brightness, as I opened the door for him. 'I didn't know you were coming. I didn't hear the bell downstairs.' *Please don't kiss me.* I kept a good distance between us.

He held up my keys. 'The van hire place rang me. They found them when they valeted the van and have been trying to find who lost them ever since. You must have dropped them. I know you've been worried about them, so I thought you'd want them back pronto. I picked them up earlier.'

'Ah! Brilliant. Thanks.' I held my hand out for them.

His eyes fixed on something behind me and I knew he'd seen Adam. He bent down and picked up a laptop bag and a large black case I hadn't noticed.

'What's that?' I asked.

He strode past me, straight towards Adam, dropping the keys on the shelf, next to the spare. As if he owned the place. 'Alright, mate?'

'Adam, this is Chris, from work.'

Adam's eyes widened momentarily as he cast an eye over Chris's physique. I'd be damned if he didn't pull his shoulders back. This was all I needed. When he stood up straighter, he was the tallest but nowhere near as wide. I placed myself in between them. The testosterone was practically coming off the pair of them like stink lines, and my scalp prickled with unease.

'Adam has his own security firm. Look what he's got me. He's just installed it for me. It's great.' I scurried back out onto the landing and pointed up. 'There's a camera in it so I can see who's outside. Isn't it good? I knew it was you before I opened the door.' Unfortunately, I was babbling to myself as they were both still inside, neither paying any attention to me. More than likely they were still sizing each other up. It was bloody annoying—I wasn't some prize to be won and dragged off by the hair, back to the victor's cave.

'Great, yeah.' Chris called with a quick backward glance. He took off his jacket and hung it up. 'Your website's ready. Want to see? And I have another surprise.'

Out of the corner of my eye I saw Adam hovering uncertainly in the passageway.

'I'll put the kettle on. Who's for coffee?' I asked. God, this was just awful.

'I'll have one,' said Chris.

Adam was silent. 'Adam?' I asked.

His eyes slid from me to Chris and back again. 'What van?' he asked.

'Chris gave me a lift home after the wedding fair,' I said, praying it wouldn't prompt more questions.

Tension showed in his downturned mouth and the narrowing of his eyes. Then his shoulders slumped ever so slightly. He wasn't going to pursue it now, thank God.

'No, I'm done,' he said. Chris had stolen his thunder and I felt for him. He looked like he'd just been run over by a steamroller.

'I'll see you soon,' Adam said, going to the door.

'Thanks again. I do appreciate it.' I took a tiny step back. Maybe he saw the pleading in my eyes. I felt something pass between us.

'Okay. Well... see you,' he said.

Chris just wandered into the living room without looking back. He shouted me to come and look.

'In a sec. I'll just get the coffee.'

Adam must have been feeling awful, but the relief that he'd gone was overwhelming. I slumped against the worktop. That could have been even worse. But my heart skittered at the thought that Chris was here in my flat and we were alone. When I went into the living room, he was standing there with a broad smile on his face.

'Ta da,' he said, turning his laptop to me with a flourish.

'Wow!' was all I could manage. My new website was totally brilliant. Chris had done an amazing job. In front of me was a striking web page, with a black background with lettering that matched the cards he made me. *'Sarah's Cakes'* was emblazoned across the top in a slanting gold font, and some of the pictures from my blog were on the title page, arranged into categories in a grid, each one taking you to another page when you clicked on it. There were wedding cakes, celebration cakes, family bakes, stuff I made for the deli, recipes from my blog and more besides. There was a link to the blog itself and a box with 'contact me' in it with my phone number and email address. There was also a picture of me from my blog and links to some of my YouTube videos.

'Chris, I don't know what to say. This is so good. How much do I owe you?'

'Shut up about that, woman,' he said, kissing me.

'What's in there?' I pointed to the large black case. Like a model would have a portfolio in.

'Just a little something extra I thought you could use. I couldn't wait any longer for you to see it.'

He bent down, unzipped it and pulled out a white folder with *Sarah's Cakes* in the same font as the website, handing it to me. It was a portfolio. A beautiful cake was displayed on each page. The photos were sharp and clear, and it looked amazing; you could see all the fine detail. There must have been twenty pages in it. I didn't know what to say. For a moment, I couldn't speak. He'd done all this for me. It was making me tearful.

'This is just fantastic,' I said when I found my voice. 'Why are you doing all this for me? I don't deserve it.'

'Course you do. I'm just trying to help you get your business noticed. Do you think this might help get work in?'

'Yes, I do. Absolutely. I can take it when I go to see new clients. I can also add to it, can't I, when I do new cakes?'

'Yeah, you can add new pages in, easy.' He picked up his coffee. 'It's worth it just to see your face.'

'I don't know what to say, honestly. I'm just blown away.'

'Oh, I have something else for you as well, but it's not half so exciting.' He reached into the laptop case and brought out three white four-way extensions. 'To do something about your cabling and plug problem.'

I burst out laughing. That was so practical, something only a man would think to get as a surprise present.

'You saved the best 'til last, I see. Well, knock yourself out,' I said, settling myself on the sofa to watch. 'I shall observe and take notes.' *And watch your fantastic body while you work. And marvel that you're here alone, with me in my flat right now.*

He went over to the TV and pulled it out on its stand. After studying what all the wires were for, he spent the next few minutes plugging stuff in.

Halfway through, he twisted round to look at me. 'That Adam, is he the one you said at the Christmas party you'd had a few dates with?' I couldn't read his expression.

Shit! I'd hoped he'd forgotten that.

'Erm, yeah. It is actually. But we're friends is all. Haven't really been out since.'

'Mmm.' He turned back, carrying on sorting cables out. He covered the cables in some white plastic tubing. It was really neat when he'd finished, but Lee and I would probably never notice it again. I had to say, though, it had improved that area of the room no end. The same couldn't be said for the rest of it. I hadn't exactly got round to tidying up yet.

'That looks great. Ta. But where are the others for?'

'Anywhere you want. How about the kitchen and your bedroom?'

'Okay.' I followed him to the kitchen, and he unplugged the fridge and put the four-way in instead, then plugged the fridge into that. And the kettle and the microwave. He tucked it neatly behind the fridge. It had a space left on it when he'd done.

He held up the remaining four-way, his eyes sparkling. 'Your bedroom, did you say?'

'I may have done.'

He followed me in, and I could feel the heat coming off him, he was so close behind me. Damn, the bed was covered in a clothes mountain.

'Just a minute while I put these somewhere. I need to keep them in separate piles, but it's actually messy in here for a reason.' I started to scoop up the clothes on my bed. 'These are going to fetch me a tidy sum when I flog them on eBay. It's all good stuff.'

I piled them into a corner. It might look a jumbled mess, but I knew what they were. Then I made myself comfy on the bed, leaning back on the pillows in what I hoped was an alluring and seductive manner. Images of us ripping each other's clothes off crowded my mind.

'What would madam require plugging in here?' He held up the extension and gave me a look that could melt the polar ice caps.

'Well... let's see; er, computer stuff, printer, phone charger, iPod charger.'

He looked so happy sorting stuff out. Maybe he had got some mild form of OCD. When he finished, he stood up and surveyed me, lounging on the bed.

'Job done. What should we do now?'

I pulled a face. 'I have to carry on working. Kristen's collecting her cake tomorrow and I need to finish it.'

'Bo–ring.' He took a step towards me, filling my small room with his massive frame. 'Where's your mate? Quiet as a little mouse in her bedroom?'

'Away for the weekend.'

'Really?' He raised his eyebrows and lay down next to me on his side.

'So… we've got the place to ourselves then?'

'Maybe,' I said.

'Has anyone ever told you you're a ten out of ten?' he said, gazing into my eyes.

'No.'

'Well, you are.'

He trailed a line of kisses down my neck, laughing softly at how it made me shiver. I was still in my work clothes and he unbuttoned my shirt, slipping it off my shoulders. He made an appreciative noise at the way my skirt had ridden right up my thighs.

'Can I stay over then and shag you all night?' He tangled his fingers in my hair and slid a hand under my skirt until I gasped. There was no way my body would let me say no.

'Alright,' I said. 'If you insist.'

'I insist,' he said.

It was much later when I finally finished the cake.

30

MY PHONE RANG AT eight the next morning, jerking me awake.

'Hello?'

'Sarah, it's Jenny. Sorry for phoning you at this hour on a Saturday. I wanted to catch you in. I know it's short notice, but could you pop into the deli today about four, if you're free? Sandra and I want to talk to you about something.'

'Yes, of course. See you later.'

I put the phone down. What was that about? I hoped they weren't going to tell me they didn't want any more of my baking. Chris was fast asleep next to me; the phone obviously hadn't disturbed him. I settled back into my pillow, but I was wide awake now. Kristen was coming in two hours to pick up her wedding cake, so I might as well get up and see if it needed tweaking. Chris didn't stir as I got out of bed and got dressed.

Ten minutes before Kristen arrived, Chris made an appearance fully dressed.

'I'm gonna go. I've got some work to do,' he said, kissing me. 'I'll ring you later.'

'What about breakfast?' I called after him, disappointed that he'd gone. I'd imagined crawling back into bed with him and demanding he do rude things to me.

'No time,' he called back. 'I'll ring you later.'

Kristen was thrilled to bits with her cake. She brought her fiancé, Jason, with her, a tall, athletic bloke whose scalp was starting to show through his hair.

'I can't believe how gorgeous this cake is. Do you like it?' she asked Jason.

He nodded. 'Yeah.'

'Will you send me some pictures for my new website?' I asked.

'Course I will.' She gushed over her upcoming wedding and I felt excited for her. It was going to be in a castle in Scotland somewhere with three hundred guests, followed by a honeymoon in the Maldives. When she handed over the cash, the biggest sum so far, it felt amazing. My first wedding cake sale. Six hundred quid. She would have paid much more than that from some wedding cake suppliers. I was just glad she chose me. It more than covered the cost of the stall.

The flat was quiet without Lee. Everything had been leading up to getting this first cake done and now it was over, I wandered around the flat at a loose end. The afternoon was spent catching up on some serious cleaning, having being shamed into it by Chris's tidying spree. With one eye on the clock, I tackled the kitchen, bathroom and my bedroom, and by the time I'd finished, it was almost time to meet Jenny and Sandra. Chris hadn't been in touch, so I texted him, telling him I'd got a meeting at the deli. I got one back. *OK* was all it said.

***

'Sorry?' I stared stupidly at Jenny. 'Did you just offer me a full-time job?

She laughed. 'Yes.'

'What do you think?' asked Sandra.

I did a quick calculation—the money was less than at the office, but only by fifty pounds a month. I could still make the rent okay. My heart sped up and I couldn't stop smiling.

'I think I'm going to say when can I start?'

'You'll be in charge of desserts at both shops while we concentrate on getting the café side of things up and running.'

'It's a bit sudden, isn't it? Are you sure?' I was suddenly scared of packing my job in and this not working out.

'Perfectly. Opening cafes at both delis will take us in a whole new direction and we need you to be able to do it. You've more than proved yourself capable. Your stuff sells out straight away.'

I bit my lip hard to stop from screeching in delight. The urge to run around the shop whooping was strong. *Be professional.* I could spend all day doing what I truly loved. I couldn't wait to tell Mum and Dad.

'Sounds amazing. I can't wait.'

'How much notice do you have to give at work?'

'A month. And then I'm all yours.'

***

On the way back home, I remembered the email from Leanne and swung by the Tube station to see if Ben was there. I usually saw him a couple of times a week and gave him a sandwich and a drink, and we'd chat about nothing in particular. He was there, huddled on the pavement, as usual, being ignored, as usual.

'Hi,' I said.

He smiled. His beard was back. 'Hey. How are you?'

I jerked my thumb towards the café over the road. 'At a loose end. Want a bite to eat? If you've got time!'

He laughed. 'I think I can fit you in. Thanks.' He upended his cup and about three quid fell out.

'I'm buying. I've just sold my first wedding cake so I'm flush.'

'Fair enough. Congratulations.' He struggled to his feet and we walked over the road. He was still limping badly. A blast of welcome hot air greeted us as we opened the door.

It wasn't busy and I picked a table furthest from the door while he went to the toilets to wash.

He said a sandwich would do, but I ordered us both a full roast dinner instead. He must be starving. Part of me wanted to invite him back to mine again to have a shower and a sleep, but I was alone in the flat and what did I know about him, really?

More than he thought I did.

As we waited for our food, I wondered how far I could push him. Couldn't hurt to try.

'So, Ben, what's your story?'

He looked startled. 'Um, what?'

'I know you were a soldier. What happened?' I kept my voice gentle and low, like he was a frightened animal that could bolt. Which he was, really.

His (now clean) fingers tapped on the table top. Then he sighed.

'You want to know why I left?'

'Yes.'

He gave a tiny nod. 'I was on tour in Afghanistan. It was horrendous. It wasn't my first tour. I'd done loads. We went out on patrol one day. There were six of us.' He paused, swallowed, and gazed out of the window. How much was this costing him? But maybe getting it out there was what he needed to do. 'The short story is that we were targeted in a town we'd gone to, to help some civilians, and my mate was blown up by an IED.'

I closed my eyes and my hands, under the table, clenched into fists.

'He was right next to me. I'm talking to him then next thing I know, I'm wearing bits of him.' He smiled a grim, humourless smile at me.

I didn't know what to say. My chest felt tight.

'After that, I couldn't hack it,' he said. 'I got out, came back, couldn't seem to get any help and ended up here.'

He cleared his throat and gazed down at the table.

'You poor man,' I whispered, blinking back tears. 'And there's no one to help you back home?'

He shook his head. I recognised the expression on his face. It was shame. If he did have a family, he'd run from them for his own reasons. Should we interfere at all?

By the time our food arrived, I'd lost my appetite, so Ben ate both.

31

I'M AMAZED WHEN I look at the clock and see it's lunchtime. I feel like I've only been working for ten minutes. I love my new job. I had to laugh when I got it: I'm working as an ethical hacker! And I'm good at it. I was headhunted by a previous company who I worked for as a security consultant. They were impressed at how easy I found it to break into systems. They said they knew I'd be good at it. Damn right.

When Sarah had asked me about my new job, I was deliberately vague. 'Same old stuff, really, you know, but I'll be working from home more.'

She'd nodded, not particularly interested. 'That's nice,' she'd said, her attention on her currant buns or whatever the hell she was pratting about with.

I spend the next couple of hours working on a security test for a new client. By the time I've finished, I've identified four different ways of getting through their security. After a quick lunch, I take a couple of hours off. There's something I've been meaning to do.

I grab my jacket, slam the door on my way out and run straight into minging Luisa, who's skulking about in the passageway. God! Not now. Why can't I have a neighbour I never see?

'Oh, hi. Are you working from home today? I saw your car outside earlier,' she says as her eyes roam over my biceps. She looks like she wants to take a bite out of me, and her eyes linger over my chest. Is this what women feel like when men talk to their tits? My jacket's in my hand and I put it on.

'Look, I'm just on my way out. I'm in a rush, actually.' I move to step around her and she moves the same way, blocking the door.

'Going anywhere nice?' she purrs. She must think she sounds sexy, but she doesn't. She sounds like a desperate, stupid cow. She looks like one as well, with her too-tight jeans and jumper clinging to the roll of fat around her middle. She must be around forty, but she's trying to pass herself off as younger, by the look of it. Her hair is a horrible shaggy mess of blonde and dark streaky bits. Lines like a spider's web fan out from her mouth, drawing attention to the fact she must have smoked for years. Plus I can see the fag packet sticking out of her jean's pocket. As if I'd want anyone who smokes, for fuck's sake. She's looking quite tanned. Come to think of it, I haven't seen her for a couple of weeks. She must have been away.

She trails a hand through her hair. 'What do you think? I've just had it done. It's ombre.'

I blink. What the fuck is she going on about?

'Right. Er, yeah,' I say, hoping she'll shift out of my way.

'Listen, do you fancy a coffee sometime?' she asks, standing up straighter and sticking out her chest. After all this time, she's actually asking me out? 'I've just come back from Florida. I could show you my holiday snaps.'

Thank Christ she didn't say 'white bits.' I make a point of checking her out slowly, as she tosses her hair back over one shoulder. I smile as if I'm appraising her and it's favourable. She's no more than a three at best. Maybe she was a three and a half when she was in her twenties. I stifle an urge to laugh. I'm awarding half points now? What's next—quarters? I go for the sucker punch.

'I don't think my fiancée would like it.'

Her face falls. I take advantage of the moment and slide nearer the door.

'Oh, I didn't know you were seeing anybody, let alone engaged.' Her eyes dart to my left hand. A look of suspicion creeps over her face. 'Are you sure? I haven't seen anyone here.'

I go one way, then quickly change direction and dodge past her.

'I think I'd know,' I laugh and lean in closer, so I'm right in her face. 'What would you know about me, anyway? Nowt. Let's keep it that way, eh?' My words are harsh and her face crumples. She can hardly admit that she lies in wait to ambush me at every opportunity. 'Bye then.' Smile and finger-wave.

I walk quickly outside and leave her standing there. Maybe I was kind of cruel, but now she might leave me alone. She once told me she's a freelance journalist and photographer who works from home a lot. I don't know if it's true. She must get her money from somewhere. Perhaps Mummy and Daddy died and left her a nice big inheritance, although she doesn't seem posh to me.

I jog down the road to the Tube, adrenalin coursing through me at the thought of what I'm about to do. All the way there, my excitement grows. I can hardly wait.

And now I'm in their flat. I've let myself in. I'm not bothered about the camera in the smoke alarm recording me. I can delete the images of me entering and leaving the flat from Sarah's computer later, using my own. Sarah won't notice a thing. While she was asleep in my bed after the wedding fair, I swiped her keys out of her bag. She never lost them. I've now got my own set. I put a bug on her phone at the same time so I can now listen in to her calls and voicemails and read her texts and emails. Using this, I can locate the phone, therefore, her.

They're both at work and I have all the time I need to nose around. I take my time in her room, looking through drawers, cupboards and wardrobes, especially the underwear drawer. I wouldn't even have to be that careful to replace everything exactly as I find it; she's so slapdash I doubt she'd notice. But I am, just to be on the safe side. It's the little details that can give you away. I'm scrupulously careful. On the desk next to her laptop is brown paper, string and Sellotape and a pile of clothes. Stuff she's sold presumably and has to package up. The small room is looking tidier, possibly because she hasn't as much stuff left. Or she's taking a leaf out of my book. Am I rubbing off on her? The bed is made, and the curtains tied back. The picture above her bed, a beach scene, is crooked. It takes all my effort not to straighten it.

The bag I got her from ASOS is on her dressing table. When I stayed over the other night, I'd spotted it and picked it up. 'This is nice,' I'd said. 'It's the one you took to Porter's, isn't it? Is it new?'

She'd taken it from me, stared hard at it, and nodded. 'Yes, but I didn't buy it. It just got delivered here, with my name on. And some other stuff has come since, clothes and things. It doesn't make sense.'

'Stuff like that happens all the time,' I'd said. 'The other day, I got a Tesco delivery. It had Tampax in it. I definitely didn't order them.'

She'd said, 'This is different, though. It's all things I've liked online. It's weird.'

'Could it be that Adam bloke?' I'd asked.

'No. I doubt it. He hasn't said anything and how would he know?'

'Life's weird,' I'd told her. 'It's just coincidence.' I'd pulled her on top of me and kissed her. By the time I was through, she'd forgotten all about it. She didn't mention it again.

The flatmate's room is unfamiliar. But—bingo! There's another laptop. Another webcam. I haven't had this much fun in ages. Not one to pass up an opportunity, I get her email address from Sarah's computer and send an email to it from my phone. The computer doesn't even have a password. It doesn't go into hibernation mode by the look of it, so, unless it's done an update, it's permanently on. I'm straight into her emails. She saves her passwords on the machine, so she doesn't have to enter them all the time. Although, if it had needed a password, it wouldn't have been a problem. I listen when people talk. And I ask the right questions: surnames, maiden names, pets, birthdays, etc. You never know when it'll come in handy. The ones most people use are so obvious, and their birthdays are all over Facebook. Twenty-four today? Easy to work out the date of birth then. Why are people so stupid?

I get rid of the email when the virus is in. I don't need to go through it now when I can do it from home and take my time. I have a quick rummage through the drawers, which, as expected, don't turn up anything exciting. There's just one more thing to check—the four-ways I plugged cables into all over the flat. They're all exactly as I left them, thank God, tucked in and out of the way. Keeping things tidy. But there's more to them. These little things are ingenious. Each one contains a listening device and a sim card I can dial from my mobile, allowing me to listen to conversations that have taken place, either real-time or recorded. It's through these little beauties that I know Leanne, Little Miss High and Mighty, doesn't like me. I heard her say so to Sarah. She didn't take to me that time she met me. There's something about me, I give her a bad feeling. Well, the feeling's mutual. I don't like her either. She's too skinny and ginger. Not to mention judgemental.

I leave the flat with a light, jaunty step. There's only one thing I didn't plan on, which is bothering me, and I don't like surprises. The whole thing started out as a game: see beautiful woman, work with beautiful woman, hack her and have some fun. But I really like Sarah. I mean, really like her. Like I've never liked any other girl before. I didn't like that Adam guy being around her. I've been getting a funny, tight feeling in my chest when I look at her. Yesterday, I googled it and it said the weirdest thing. When I put my symptoms in, it said it was love. Okay, it was a jokey-type website, but it made me think; I wouldn't know. I've never loved anyone. I'm unaccustomed to the feeling. But I think I like it.

32

SINCE I HANDED IN my notice, every day at work had dragged. All I could think about was how different my day would be when I was working at Delish. I was in the kitchen making coffee when the door opened behind me and Chris appeared, dressed in a sharp black suit with a white shirt and red tie. My stomach clenched at the sight.

'Er, what are you doing here? You don't work here anymore, remember?'

He strode straight into my space after kicking the door shut behind him, grabbed me tightly and started to kiss me.

'Come to mine, straight from work,' he murmured. 'I want you so bad.'

'I can't. I'm meeting a client about a wedding cake.' Adam had confirmed earlier by text that Debbie could make it tonight.

He groaned and pulled a face. 'You're joking.'

'I'm sorry. I'm clocking off early. I've got to get to the Post Office before it shuts.'

He stared at me. 'What client?'

'Oh, no one you know.'

'Where?' he asked.

'At a pub near mine.'

'Can't I come? I can sit quietly in the corner. No one will know I'm there.'

God! No. What if Adam was there? 'No. Look, I'll ring you when I'm done. It shouldn't be too late. Come over.'

He rolled his eyes and muttered, 'Okay. Fine.'

'I'm really sorry." I kissed him again and picked up the drinks I'd made. 'What are you doing round here anyway, all dressed up?'

'I had a meeting.'

'How'd it go?'

'Good. So, I'll see you later then, yeah.' He left, still grumbling about tonight.

'Thanks,' said Pauline as I put her drink in front of her. Chris was almost at the door. I was still watching him from the corner of my eye when he stopped abruptly, spun round, then marched back over to my desk. He bent down, tilted my chin up and kissed me properly on the mouth. Not just a peck either. Pauline was leaning back in her chair, looking flustered and hot. For all I knew, she could be hoping she was next. From the heat in my cheeks, though, I was probably redder than her.

'She already knew,' he said to me, his hands palm upwards. Then he flashed me a cheeky grin and left.

I turned to Pauline, who was looking smug.

'I've known for ages,' she said.

'Since when?'

'Since I saw you two snogging at the Christmas party. I mentioned it to Chris ages ago and he admitted it. I've been waiting for you to tell me. I think you make a lovely couple, by the way.' Then she turned back to her work and calmly got on with it.

At four o'clock, I dashed home to change before my meeting, which was set for five thirty. I rifled through what was left of my wardrobe and selected a short, fitted, scoop-necked tunic dress with a bold purple, pink and black print, thick black tights and a black work jacket. The addition of some high black stiletto boots that ended just below my knee gave me the look I was going for; young, funky and go-getting. Someone who knew about trends. I wore my hair loose, and subtle make-up created a soft, smoky eye that completed the look. After a good squirt of perfume, I picked up my bag and grabbed my portfolio. Time for its first test.

I had four packages to take to the Post Office on the way, the latest batch of eBay sales, and I rammed them into a carrier bag. It was a good job the Post Office was only two minutes away. After dropping them off, I walked to the bar. It took longer than normal as my boots were so high. At least with them on, I was almost up to the same height as most other people if they had no shoes on. Confidence-heels, I called them. And it was funny, but after getting some orders at the wedding fair, I felt much more positive.

I arrived bang on five thirty. It was Friday and the pub was was busy. Off to my left, Adam was sitting at a table with what must be his sister and her bloke. I made my way over.

'Hi,' I said.

'Hi,' he said. His smile was tight and didn't reach his eyes.

The woman spoke. 'Hi, Sarah, I'm Debbie and this is Andy. Don't introduce us, will you, Adam!' She rolled her eyes.

'Sorry,' Adam muttered.

Andy shook my hand vigorously. He had blonde floppy hair and a devilish smile. I liked him. 'Hiya,' he said.

'Drink?' Adam asked.

'Prosecco, please. Just a small one,' I said, and he went off to get it while Debbie seated herself opposite me. She eyed up the folder.

'Ooh—may I?'

'Of course.'

I slid it over to her and she started leafing through it.

'Oh, wow, these look gorgeous. Adam said you were good.'

They bent over it and started oohing and aahing. Adam came back with my drink and passed it over as he sat down next to me. He was all angles, elbows and knees, sitting stiffly in his chair. He was unusually quiet and didn't look at me. I knew what this was about. I hadn't seen him since Chris turned up. Other than texting me about tonight, I hadn't heard from him. Had he guessed? I really should tell him. I tuned back into what Debbie was saying.

'These are amazing. We're never going to be able to decide, are we?' Debbie looked at Andy.

'You can have whichever one you want,' he said. 'They all look nice to me.'

'Mmm, they do.'

'What sort of thing were you looking for?' I asked. 'Do you have any ideas?'

'Well, I thought something traditional until I saw these, but now I like the more modern ones.'

'I like this one.' Andy pointed to the one I did for the wedding fair with the black painted design.

'What colour are the bridesmaids' dresses and your flowers?' I asked.

'They're wearing purple, similar to your dress,' said Debbie. 'And the main flowers in the bouquet are freesias. With white lilies.'

'I could paint the flower design in different shades of purple; that would look good. And a hint of pink to contrast but blend. Maybe paint freesias on it.'

'Mmm. I like this chocolate one as well, that's really different. God, I'm never going to be able to decide.'

'Do you want to take the book away?'

'Can we?'

'Keep it as long as you like. The wedding's not until next September, right?

'Yes.'

We sat and chatted about the wedding for a while until it was time for me to go. Adam didn't offer to walk me home, just sat there ripping a beer mat into tiny shreds.

I guessed that was my cue to leave then. So I did.

***

Back home, I tried to sketch out some designs for Debbie's wedding cake, but I couldn't get the freesias to look right. I googled pictures of them, but I wasn't really in the mood. I tried Chris's phone several times, but there was no answer.

'Sarah!' Leanne shouted suddenly. 'Come quick.'

I leaped off the bed and ran into her room. 'What?'

She was sitting on her bed, her laptop in front of her, open on Facebook.

'Read this.'

I sat down on her bed. It was a photo of a newspaper story, but it was too small to read. There was a picture of Craig.

'He's gone back to prison,' she said. 'Nothing to do with breaking his injunction and turning up here, either. He tried to slip Rohypnol into some girl's drink, and she caught him doing it. He was going to rape her.' We stared at each other in horror. 'I can't believe it. But he's back inside, thank God,' she said.

We both sagged with relief. I pictured the pathetic creature on our street. It didn't seem like the same person.

'Well, good,' I said. 'Best place for him.'

She nodded. There was nothing more to say, and I went back to my room, still thinking about Craig. Looked like Leanne really had had a lucky escape. I tried to write a blog, but the words wouldn't come. What I really wanted was to talk to Chris. I rang his phone several times more and eventually he answered. He didn't sound quite right; he was kind of hyper and giddy, and there were voices in the background.

'Hey,' he yelled into the phone. 'Wotcha doin?'

Someone was clearly laughing, and I could hear music, maybe a TV or something.

'Where are you? I've been ringing you all evening. I thought you were coming over.' I hated the needy tone in my voice.

'I was. Change of plan. I'm missing you though.' He made smoochy kissing noises into the phone.

Was he drunk or taking the piss? A male voice laughed in the background, followed by more kissy noises further away.

'Where are you?'

'At home.'

'Well, who else is there? I can hear other people.'

'My mates, Danny and Harry. The footie's on.'

A cheer went up in the background, and it sounded as if they were watching a game. The music must have been an ad break.

'Come on, Chris. Charlie's here,' yelled a voice. Charlie? Harry? Danny? Exactly who was there? I didn't know any of these people.

'Alright. I'll come round in the morning, if you like, after I've dropped an order off at the deli.'

'Okay. Yeah.'

'Come on, mate. Get a load of this,' someone shouted. Bottles and glasses clinked, voices murmured, and then the phone went dead. At least one of us was having a good time.

I went into the kitchen to get a glass of water and Lee followed me in.

'Want one?' I held up the glass.

'No thanks. Who were you yelling at just now?'

'I just rang Chris. He's got some mates round, and they were making a real racket.'

Her face took on a guarded look. It was the same whenever I mentioned him. 'Is it serious then, you two?'

'I don't know, it's early days. But I really like him, Lee. He's so sexy and funny and...'

'Mmm,' she said.

'Don't you think he's good looking?'

'He obviously is. But people are about more than that, aren't they?'

'Yes, course they are. You'd like him if you got to know him.'

'Maybe. But I thought he was full of himself, if you want to know.'

'You barely spoke to him. He's not like that, at all.'

'Yeah, well. I just don't want you to get hurt, that's all.'

'Listen, I know you're looking out for me, and I appreciate it. But he's fine, really.'

'Alright,' she said, looking unconvinced. 'Well, I'm off to bed. Oh, I forgot to tell you earlier, what with all that stuff about *him*, I've got an interview, for the vintage shop.'

'That's great. When is it?'

'Next Tuesday. Night.'

She went back to her bedroom, closing the door quietly. I wished she'd at least give Chris a chance. The point of him coming round tonight had been to make her face the truth: we were together. If that was the truth. A ripple of excitement ran through me when I thought of him turning up at work today to announce that we were together. And maybe I didn't need to tell Adam anything after how he was today. Maybe he'd gone off me.

33

I PACKED THE CHERRY mallow cupcakes and the skinny lemon drizzle traybake into the last two boxes and closed the lids. It was seven thirty in the morning and I had five boxes to deliver to the deli. They'd lent me a new wheeled trolley, which made it much easier if I avoided as many bumps and kerbs as possible.

Jenny was thrilled with the delivery and I left happy, having made some more cash. With the money coming in from Delish, Porters and the odd wedding cake, plus the extra from selling my clothes on eBay, I'd never had so much to spare. Normally I'd have gone straight out and blown it on more clothes and nights out, but I didn't want to anymore. I wanted to save it, maybe for a car, or a small van.

It was nine o'clock when I arrived at Chris's, after a detour for croissants at a bakery I passed on the way. I was early, but I never told him what time I'd be round. When he eventually let me in, after I'd been ringing the bell for ages, he looked like hell. His hair stuck up at all angles, black stubble shadowed his face, and the only thing blacker were the circles under his eyes.

'My God. You look like shit. What happened?'

He actually groaned when he saw me, which wasn't the welcome I'd been hoping for. He shuffled into the living room and sank onto the sofa, one hand placed over his closed eyes.

'Heavy night?' I said.

He grunted.

'It's a good job I didn't come round for hot sex,' I said.

He opened one bloodshot eye. 'I could try.'

'Urgh! No way. I wish I'd stayed at home.'

He just groaned again and hauled himself back up. 'I need a shower. A long one.'

I watched him stagger off to the bathroom and contemplated, for a second, whether to join him but decided instead, judging by the state of him, to stay out here and have breakfast. I opened the bag of croissants and ate one, while Chris banged and clattered around in his bathroom. By the time the water eventually stopped running, I'd had another and was watching Saturday Kitchen on the sofa. A few minutes later he shuffled out, still looking rough.

'Better?' I asked, flicking the crumbs off my lap onto the floor and hoping he hadn't seen. I hid them under my shoe.

'Yeah.' He eyed the croissants and picked one up. 'These look nice. Did you make them?'

'Nope. What exactly did you do last night?'

'Watched footie and drank too much.'

'And who are Harry and Danny?'

He groaned. 'Harry moved in here a while back. Irish banker, older than me. He's a good laugh. I've known Danny for years. He's a knobhead.'

I looked around the place. It was actually quite a mess, not up to its usual show home standard. I felt a stab of glee; not so perfect after all, then. 'So, who's Charlie?'

Chris rubbed his forehead as if trying to erase a headache. 'Erm, a mate of Harry's.'

'You still feeling rough?'

'God, yeah.'

'Well, I suppose you can always punish yourself on your home gym later. What do you fancy doing this weekend?'

'I haven't even thought about it. I need some coffee. Can you make it?' he begged.

As soon as I got up, he crawled onto the sofa and nicked my place. In the kitchen, the coffee jar was empty and there was a total of two tea bags. Two teas coming up, then. I had to clear empty beer bottles and crisp packets out of the way to make them.

'Bring some plates,' he called from the sofa.

When I gave him his tea, he sniffed it. 'What the hell's this?'

I shrugged. 'It's all there was. Go shopping, for God's sake. And it's a tip in here,' I said with a big grin.

He grunted but drank the tea anyway, and after two croissants declared he felt much better. He sat back on the sofa and curled an arm around me, pulling me closer to him.

'Erm, Chris?'

'What?'

I twined my fingers through his, examining his nails. It felt so intimate. 'That little display of affection in the office? In front of Pauline yesterday.'

'What about it?'

I swallowed. I realised how badly I wanted us to be together. I'd never really met anyone like him before, super-charged and exciting, and the sex was awesome. And I loved being with him. Did I love him?

'Did you mean it? I mean, are we together? Properly?'

He looked at me. 'Do you want us to be?'

'I think I do.'

'And so do I. So, yeah.' He kissed the tip of my nose. 'I've fancied you since I first saw you.'

'Have you really?'

'Yeah. You're so sexy it hurts to look at you.' His voice had dropped, soft and low. 'You're a ten out of ten, remember? I've never said that before. Never met one. No one's got higher than a nine point five.'

I shook my head at his corny words, but inside, my heart jumped. It was as if something big had changed, like it was a game before but now it was different.

'How was your meeting? The wedding cake client,' he asked.

'Oh, really good. She's taken the portfolio to look at. I think she's going to order a cake from me.'

'Who did you say the client was again?'

'I didn't. Um, you remember Adam, who fitted my new smoke alarm? His sister, Debbie, is getting married. Adam gave her my number.'

He nodded slowly. 'Right.' He was silent for a while. Then he said, 'It's no good. I still need coffee.'

'Then you'll have to go and get some.'

'Will you go? Please.'

'No. I made the tea. Anyway, the fresh air will do you good.'

He grumbled and got up slowly from the sofa. 'Anything else?'

'I don't know what you've got in. It's not like you ever cook anything.'

'I do!'

'Like what?' Everything in your kitchen is brand new. Most of your utensils still have the labels on.'

'I have used it occasionally. I'm gonna cook you dinner for that.'

'You don't need to. Why don't we go out? Or I can cook.' He can't cook. He'd told me often enough. When he was bulking up and exercising loads, he only ever ate chicken, steak and eggs.

'I said I'll cook. What, you think I can't make a meal?' He fixed me with a stare. It would be fun to make him do it.

Yeah, actually, I know you can't. I shrugged. 'Okay. It's up to you.'

'I'll be a while longer, then. I'll have to go and get some stuff for dinner.'

He grabbed a coat and his wallet and went out, slamming the door behind him. I looked around properly this time. The flat really was a mess. It must have been quite a bender last night by the look of it. There were dirty glasses and sticky rings on the coffee table, and bits of foil and plastic bags scrunched up. The smell of stale beer tainted the air. I bet it wouldn't look like this by the end of the day. Maybe I could clear up, but it seemed cruel to deprive him of the pleasure, what with his OCD and stuff.

A phone started ringing nearby and I followed the sound of it. It was tucked down the back of a cushion. Chris's iPhone. It must have fallen out of his pocket when he stood up.

'Hello,' I said, snatching it up.

'Is Chris there?' The voice was gruff and raspy, and 'there' was pronounce 'thi-er'. I thought it was a woman, but I wouldn't put money on it.

'Oh, sorry, no. Can I pass on a message?

A loud sigh came over the phone followed by a tut. She (?) sounded irritated. 'Who's that?

'Erm, it's Sarah. Who's this?'

'His sister. Where is he?'

I didn't even know he had a sister. 'He's just nipped out. He'll be back soon. I'll tell him you phoned, shall I?' Silence. I could almost hear the cogs turning. 'Hello? Are you still there?'

'Yeah. Give him a message. In fact, give him two. Tell him he's a wanker.'

What? Bloody hell! Bit strong.

'Er, right. And the second message?'

'Tell him his mum's just died.' Beep, beep, beep. She'd hung up.

Oh, Christ! I had to tell Chris that? My insides churned at the prospect. Before the screen went black and locked me out, I scribbled her number down and put it in my bag. I wasn't sure why, but I was so starved of information about his background that any connection was better than nothing.

He came back twenty minutes later and pushed the door shut with his boot. He had one carrier bag in his hand, and it didn't look very full. I rose slowly from the sofa, watching him, trying to discern what mood he'd come back in. He pulled out a bottle of wine, a family-size bar of Galaxy, frozen oven chips and some fish fingers. And a bag of washed spinach. Was that the healthy bit? Fish fingers, chips and spinach. Yuck!

He held up the Galaxy. 'Ta-da! Your favourite pudding.' He stopped and looked at me closely. 'What? What's happened?'

Better to just come out with it. 'Your sister called. You forgot your phone.' I held up his mobile. 'You left it here.'

He paused, his face unreadable. 'What did she want?'

'She said your mum's died. I'm so sorry.'

I didn't bother with the other message. He was completely still. 'Mmm,' he said, as if to himself. Then he picked up the chocolate, unwrapped one end, and started to eat it.

'Did you hear what I just said?'

His eyes narrowed. 'Yeah.'

He handed me the chocolate, took the phone from me and left the room, while I just stood there. I heard him open the fridge and freezer, putting the shopping away. When he returned, he acted as if nothing had happened. To avoid putting my foot in it, I remained silent. He showed absolutely nothing, like he felt absolutely nothing. That couldn't be right, could it?

SHAY DIDN'T WASTE ANY time telling me the old cow is dead. Well, that's one funeral I won't be going to. Hopefully, it'll be the last I hear from my darling sister. Pity Sarah had to speak to her, though. I'd rather that hadn't happened.

I need to be careful about something else, as well. Danny, a dickhead of a friend I rarely see other than for piss ups, shouting, while Sarah was on the phone, that Charlie was waiting. Now Sarah thinks Charlie is a person. But Danny meant cocaine. The other night was the first time I've taken the stuff since THE INCIDENT all those years ago. I needed it. I can't sleep properly lately, not since my sister raked it all up for me by dragging me back to Leeds. Now it's back, haunting me in my dreams and when I'm awake. But, the other night, I liked the feeling the coke gave me. I'm older now; this time I can handle it. It's under control. And maybe, all those years ago, what happened may have had nothing to do with the coke. Perhaps I'd have done it, anyway. But I need to be careful. Sarah wouldn't approve of recreational drugs. Says her drug is cake. And she's not joking either.

'WHAT DID HE SAY?' Leanne asked as we walked to the supermarket.

'He said he was an open book and that I could ask him anything. I asked about his childhood and he said he was from Leeds, had a shitty family, both parents were drinkers, his dad left when he was a kid and his mum's dead.'

'Just like that? Kind of, a list?'

'Well, yeah. He said he doesn't have anything to do with his family, and his sister rang out of the blue. So, he's not keeping deep, dark secrets from me, like you think.'

Lee shrugged and turned away. 'Good.' She sniffed.

'Can I borrow your phone? I've left mine at home on charge.'

'Yeah.' She handed it over.

'Thanks. I'll be in in a minute.'

She went into the shop, leaving me standing outside the entrance. I didn't know why, but I didn't want to tell her what I was about to do. Before I could talk myself out of it, I got the piece of paper with Shay's number on out of my bag and rang it from Lee's phone. She answered straight away but sounded drunk.

'Ello?'

'Is that Shay? It's Sarah. Chris's girlfriend. Is this a bad time?'

'Who? Oh, right. Yeah. What do you want? Has he told yer to ring me?' She sounded suspicious.

'No. I... I was just wondering if you were okay. With your mum and everything, you know. I wanted to tell you how sorry I was to hear she'd passed away and we didn't get a chance to talk last time.' *Before you hung up on me.*

She sounded surprised. 'I'm alright.' She paused then said, 'Listen, can you come to Leeds? I need to talk to you.'

'Oh, um… I'm not sure. I mean—'

'As soon as you can. There are some things you should know. And see. Have you got a pen? I'll give you the address.'

'Er, okay. I'll write it down. Just give me a second.'

I found a pen and a scrap of paper in my bag and scribbled down the address.

'ASAP', she said. 'It's important. It's for your own good.'

'Oh, but this isn't my number,' I said, but she'd bloody hung up again. She was one weird person. Why did she want me to go to Leeds? I didn't feel like going behind Chris's back, but she said it was important. And Chris wasn't helping her with anything to do with their mum. If I wanted to find anything out, I'd have to go.

After dinner, I decided to go for a walk to get away from the incessant sound of Lee's sewing machine. She'd been hard at it lately and the noise was doing my head in. When I got outside, Adam was sitting on the wall at the front. I hadn't heard from him at all for the last few days. I thought he wasn't speaking to me.

'Oh, hello,' I said. 'What are you doing?'

'I was about to ring your bell.' He stood up slowly.

'I was just going for a walk.'

'I never see you these days. Not avoiding me, are you?'

'Course not.' Even though I suppose I had been.

'You haven't answered any of my texts.'

'What texts? I haven't received any.'

He frowned. 'Well, that's odd. I've sent loads.'

'Really? I haven't got a single one. I thought you'd fallen out with me or something. What have you been up to, then?' I asked.

'Working flat out.' There were dark circles under his eyes. 'You look tired.'

'I am, actually. I've been on call every night. Nathan's on holiday for two weeks. Lanzarote. Anyway, what have *you* been up to?'

'Just busy with the baking thing.' *Tell him about Chris.* 'But there is one good thing that's happened.'

'Oh? Like what?' He sat back down on the wall. I sat too.

'I've been offered a job at the delis. Full-time.'

'Oh. That's brilliant. Well done.'

'And Craig turned up, Lee whacked him one, and he's back inside for attempted rape.'

'Bloody hell!' he said. He looked at me and reached for my hand. 'So, are we going out again? It's been ages since we went out. Properly, I mean. I know you've been busy and all but...'

Now was my chance. I had to do it now.

'I know. I'm sorry. It might be better if we were just friends for now. I'm going to be busier than ever when I start at the delis and it's not fair to you, Adam, for me to keep cancelling on you all the time. It's not the right time for me to have a relationship, with everything else that's going on.'

When he looked at me, there was such disappointment in his eyes. It killed me. I hated doing this to him. There was no need for him to know about Chris and make it worse.

'Is there someone else? Is that why you're giving me the brush-off?' His voice had a slight edge to it, and he dropped my hand as he stood up.

'No, Adam. It's just a bad time. You know I like you, but there's too much else going on right now. Like I said, it's not fair to you. You're a really great guy. We can still see each other as friends. You can still come round.' God, why was I saying this? In trying to soften the blow, I was probably making it worse for both of us.

'So, maybe later, when you have more time, we can go out again?' He looked hopeful.

This was awful. 'Maybe. Who knows how these things turn out?'

He looked happier now. 'I can wait. If there's no one else. Look, I'm on call again tonight so I really need to go. I'll see you soon.'

I watched as he walked away, whistling. It was as if I hadn't said what I'd just said. I should have told him properly, been more forceful. I'd have to do it eventually, before he found out some other way. I walked slowly down the street, feeling the yellow stripe of cowardice burning into my back.

36

TWO DAYS LATER, I got off the train at Leeds, after phoning in sick at work. I was leaving anyway so what did it matter? And this was more important. I had no idea where I was going. I left the station and looked for the nearest taxi rank. The driver took the address Shay had sent me to Lee's phone and nodded.

As he drove from the station away from the city centre, I knew I'd never have found this place without a taxi. It was worth the twenty quid fare. I asked the driver for his firm's number so I could ring them later. As we pulled up outside the address, I wondered if we'd ended up in Beirut by mistake. I didn't want the driver to abandon me here. Surely this place couldn't be safe. The driver turned and looked at me when I didn't move.

I paid him and slowly got out. The car door gave an ominous *thunk* when I closed it. I looked up at Granford Towers and didn't want to go in, but the taxi was already pulling away. I couldn't imagine Chris living here as a boy. In fact, I couldn't really imagine him as a boy at all. The building was like a towering concrete prison, painted a dirty cream colour with black spray-painted graffiti on it, mainly swear words, people's names and rude drawings. There were about six or seven similar towers, all at right angles to each other. Dogs roamed and little kids sat on steps. Some of them looked like they should have been at school. Others looked far too young to be out alone. Maybe their parents were watching from inside. A small square of grass, more a patch of dirt, was littered with cans and wrappers of all kinds. And mounds of dog mess. My own upbringing was modest, but it was a thousand times better than this. The thought of wandering around on my own trying to find the flat terrified me, so I found the scrap of paper with Shay's number on and rang her.

'I'll come down,' she said and hung up. 'Come' pronounced 'cum.'

I waited nervously, imagining gangs of hooded youths or drug dealers about to burst round every corner, and I didn't make eye contact with a girl in an unzipped shiny silver puffa jacket and black leggings who was pushing a buggy towards me. Wearing proper Ugg boots, too, by the look of it. Her hair was piled up into a dangerously high beehive that looked like it might topple over at any minute. A lit cigarette was clamped between her lips and a child that might have been four at most was behind her, dragging her feet and sucking on a lolly.

'Come on, Nirvana,' the girl snapped, turning back to the child. A pregnant belly stuck out in front of her and the cigarette wobbled dangerously but didn't fall. 'I aint got all fuckin day,' she added.

The child saw me looking and ran to catch up to the girl, presumably her mother. The girl took out a phone and started talking to someone. I jumped when I felt a tap on my shoulder.

I turned to see an unkempt, skinny woman with lank, greasy hair and creased, baggy clothes that hung off her. She had Chris's dark colouring and bore a vague resemblance to him. She could be his mother.

'Shay?'

She nodded and looked me up and down non-committally then said, 'Let's go.'

She strode away and I turned my phone off. I didn't want Chris ringing me while I was here. I trailed after her, through a concrete foyer and up some stairs that reeked. I wouldn't even like to hazard a guess as to what of. Piles of rubbish had blown in and it looked like nobody ever bothered to clean it up. She opened the door and I followed her along a passageway and into a tiny living room. There was something sticky coating the carpet and my shoes felt welded to it. My stomach flipped at the smell that hit me; years of smoke and cooking fat had coagulated in layers, and coated the walls, carpets and furnishings. Everything was brown and dingy, and the place was filthy.

'Do you want a drink of owt?' she asked.

'Oh, no, I'm fine, thanks. I've just had one,' I lied.

She sniffed, as if she knew what I was thinking. 'You're Sarah then.'

'Yes.'

'*Chris* never mentioned you.' She seemed to imbue 'Chris' with sarcasm and a sneer.

'When?'

'Few weeks ago. When he came up here, when our mam was still alive.'

'He was up here the other week?'

Shay sniffed again. 'Yeah. Something else you didn't know, then? Well, that's no surprise. Anyway, I'll tell you what you've come to find out, if that's what you want.'

'It is,' I said.

'Are you living with him?'

'No, we don't live together.'

'Well, that's good, at least.'

'Why?'

'Cos your boyfriend's not who you think he is.' There was no warmth in her raspy voice but there was a slightly triumphant look on her face. 'Sit down.'

I sat on the tatty, stained sofa, trying to minimise the bits of me in contact with it.

She flashed a humourless smile. 'You're about to find out all *Chris's* secrets.' Again with the emphasis.

I just looked at her, wordlessly.

'I need a fag first,' she said and went through another doorway into a kitchen.

From what I could see of it, it wasn't in a better state than the rest of the flat. The cupboards were straight out of the seventies, a bright yellow Formica, with dark, greasy drips running down the front of the doors, and brown worktops piled high with dirty crockery. A dingy net curtain over the sink did little to let daylight in. Her slippers scraped on the torn lino as she moved about.

From next door, muted shouts periodically bled through; a man and a woman, followed by a child crying and screaming. Shay didn't bat an eyelid as she came back, holding a can of lager and a lit cigarette. The smell of this place was disgusting. My skin crawled where the sofa touched my clothes, but I didn't think my legs would support me if I stood up. I eyed the can of lager. It was barely midday. She saw me looking and glared at me. I looked away.

I tried to think back to what little Chris had told me of his family. He said his parents were alkies. I waited for Shay to speak, but she was more bothered about sucking as much smoke into her lungs as she could. Her cheeks caved in when she inhaled, giving her face a skeletal, sunken look, and twin plumes of smoke spiralled from her nostrils. She threw a folded piece of paper across the ring-stained coffee table towards me. I blinked at it stupidly, as it landed in the overspill from the ashtray.

'Pick... it... up,' she enunciated, as if I was an idiot.

'What is it?'

Her eyes never left me as I reached for it with two fingers and shook the ash off. It was a badly creased and stained birth certificate for someone called Colin Gillespie. Did Chris have a brother I didn't know about?

'Er... I don't...'

She snatched it from me and jabbed her finger on the name. 'Look at the birth date.'

I did. The day and year Chris was born. 'He had a twin?'

'What? Fuck, no! That's him.'

'Chris is actually Colin? You mean he's changed his name or something?'

'Ah, at last. The penny drops. You're not too bright, are you, love?'

I bristled at her sarcasm. 'Look, you've got me up here. Why don't you just tell me what you want to tell me instead of playing stupid games?'

She laughed, a phlegmy, rasping rattle, and clamped her lips around the cigarette to hold it, while she plucked a heavy photo album from the table and flicked through it, stopping near the end. She swivelled it round to show a photo of Chris in his school uniform. He was maybe thirteen or fourteen. There was no mistaking it was him. On the opposing page, under clear plastic film, was a yellowed newspaper clipping of three boys and a man holding a rugby ball, all in sports gear. Under the picture were the words *Goal Scorers: Philip Capaldi, Colin Gillespie and James Porter.* The boys were flanking their rugby coach and looked the same age as Chris did in the other photo. The afro on one of the boys was so big it half obscured the boy next to him. It was definitely James Porter, but a tenth of the weight. Chris, or Colin, was on the other side. I'd have recognised him anywhere, even though it was half his lifetime ago.

'When did he change his name?'

'After uni. Or maybe during. I dunno. Sometime after he left here, anyway. What's it matter?'

I ran my hand over the cover of the heavy book. It was blue with gold trim, torn down the spine, and layers of peeling card showed through at the corners. Darker patches of what could be ink dotted the front and back, and I half expected my fingers to be blue when I pulled them away. Inside the front cover, Chris had written '*COLINS BOOK OF ASSPIRATIONS*'. I recognised the handwriting.

Opening the album from the beginning, I saw photos documenting Chris's life from newborn to fifteen or sixteen. School reports and more newspaper clippings of rugby games, with more pictures of Chris, were all pasted in there, with handwritten dates and locations underneath. A loose newspaper cutting fell out and landed on my lap. It was a local newspaper report from fifteen years ago.

Leeds man, Joe Gillespie, 46, was sentenced to eight years' imprisonment for dangerous driving and unlawful killing. Father-of-two Gillespie's car mounted the pavement and killed nine-year-old Shawnee Thomson and seriously injured her eleven-year-old brother, Jed Thomson. Gillespie was nine times over the drink driving limit. Sharon Brailey, Shawnee's mother, said, 'This man has wrecked our lives. Eight years is a joke. We have lost our angel and, although our son has survived, he will have problems for the rest of his life and needs to undergo countless operations on his spine. Joe Gillespie should never get out. He's a menace to society and decent people everywhere.'

So that was it. Chris's dad ran over a girl and killed her while drunk and went to prison for it.

I jumped when someone knocked loudly on the door. Shay got up and went to the front door, pulling the living room door to behind her.

'You're early,' I heard her say, then she spoke in hushed tones I could no longer hear. When she returned, she was carrying a small package, and seemed brighter, verging on giddy. It was as if I was no longer there. When I spoke, she barely paid me any attention. She sat down, unwrapped the package, and she took a needle and some brown stuff out of it. Oh my God. Oh no. Oh no. She slipped a shoe off and I knew what she was going to do. She concentrated on the grimy spaces between her toes. I couldn't watch this.

I stood up to go, still clutching the book, with my stomach in knots.

'Keep it. Give it him back,' she said, with a horrid cackle. She was caressing the needle and doing something with the brown stuff. I thought I might be sick.

She reached into her pocket and pulled out a brown envelope. 'You need to read that. Now fuck off.'

I grabbed it, stuffed it in my pocket and scrambled for the door, trying to drown out the noises of anticipation she made: a horrid, expectant sigh. I'd seen enough programmes about heroin addicts to not want to see it for real. I jerked the door open, rushed from the flat and down the stairs. Out on the estate, I didn't feel safe, and sprinted to the corner to a nearby bus stop. I didn't want to wait for a taxi. There were a few people about, but no one bothered me and the bus came just minutes later. 'City Centre' was displayed on the front. My head was spinning as I jumped on it and asked to be dropped off at the bus station in Leeds. I never wanted to see this vile place, or her, again. I would never forget the smell of the flat. My backside and the backs of my thighs burned at the thought of the jeans that touched the sofa in contact with my skin. I felt contaminated. I scrabbled around for the envelope in my pocket, desperate to see what was in it, but I couldn't find it. It must have fallen out of my pocket. There was no way I was going back there to find it.

It took ages for my breathing to slow down, but I couldn't stop shaking. Once off the estate, the area improved and there were some lovely bits to Leeds. I finally calmed down. I had an hour and a half before my train, so I walked around the city centre in a daze, trying to process what I'd learned. I wasn't in the mood for shopping, even though there was a Harvey Nicks, but the centre was lovely, vibrant and bustling with street entertainers and buskers, and I could easily have fallen in love with it. I only wished I were visiting it under better circumstances. I sat on a bench on Briggate, watching a young man playing the guitar and singing. He was good, and I threw a couple of pound coins in the hat at his feet.

In Boots, I picked up a bottle of perfume and sprayed myself with it liberally, all over my hair and clothes, much to the astonishment of the heavily made-up girl behind the counter. I bought new jeans and left my old ones screwed up in the dressing room. I spent ages scrubbing my hands and face with the liquid soap in some public toilets. Then I got new shoes and dumped the old ones that walked on that carpet in a litter bin. I still felt contaminated, and I had to go all the way back to London coated in the grime of what I'd learned.

On the train, I leafed through the album again. In every photo, there was just him. I could see the wobbly line where he'd cut other people out.

Nothing that Shay told me meant that Chris was a bad person. I needed to confess where I'd been and give him the book, if we were going to be totally honest with each other. The other day, he'd said honesty was the only way and that I should never lie to him, and that he'd do the same. As we began to approach London, my frayed nerves got worse. I couldn't put off confronting him. He was going to be so mad that I'd been poking around into his background. It may be better to go straight to his and get it over with.

37

IT WAS GONE SIX by the time I got to Chris's. The first thing I saw was a man and woman standing outside on the steps, both smoking. I stopped at the gate and the woman looked me up and down. She blocked the doorway and pulled her cardigan tighter around her body. Her multi-coloured hair was pulled back into a ponytail that flipped as she turned her head, revealing dark roots badly in need of a touch-up. It was one of the worst dye jobs I'd ever seen. She must have done it herself.

'Hello,' I said.

'Hi,' said the man behind her, shifting on the step. He moved in a kind of gangly and floppy way, like a puppet with the strings cut. His face was pitted and scarred, as if from old acne, and his close-cropped hair was dark grey. He was maybe mid-forties.

'Who are you?' the woman said, blowing smoke out of the side of her mouth. Her lipstick had bled into the tiny creases that fanned out from her lips.

'I'm Sarah, Chris's girlfriend. From Flat Two...'

Her lips stretched into a thin, hard line. 'Are you, now? I live at number one.'

I felt naked under her scrutiny, and what was with the way her lips pressed tighter together, as if she didn't like what she saw? It was weird. She didn't even know me.

'I'm Harry. I live upstairs,' the man said. His accent was a soft Irish brogue and his smile wide and friendly. The opposite of her.

The banker. 'Yes, Chris has mentioned you. Nice to meet you,' I said.

'It's good to meet you. I've heard a lot about you.'

The woman's nose wrinkled at that, like she'd just smelled something nasty. Me, perhaps?

'It sounded like you had a good time at his place the other night,' I said, to make conversation. 'You were having quite a party when I rang.'

'Yeah. We were a bit hammered.'

'It did sound a bit wild. With Danny and Charlie.'

He frowned. 'Charlie?'

'Your friend. He was here that night, with you and Danny.'

He looked like he was wracking his brain. 'Oh, right, yeah,' he said slowly. 'That Charlie. Um, yeah, he was Danny's friend, I think.'

'Chris said he was your friend. Oh, never mind. It doesn't matter, anyway.'

He looked at his watch. 'God, is that the time? I'd better go. Nice meeting you, Sarah.' He dropped his cigarette on the ground, ground it out, and kicked it into some weeds.

'Oh, yes, you too. I'll see you again, probably.'

'Yes, hopefully. Bye.'

He hurried back inside and disappeared up the stairs. The woman's eyes were still on me. I felt like a butterfly pinned to a board. Just as I was about to squeeze past her, she spread herself out on the step.

'Excuse me,' I said.

She eyed me a fraction too long and shifted slightly out of my way, so I had to brush against her.

'Are you and Chris engaged then?'

'Pardon?'

'Simple enough question. Are you his fiancée?' She was staring at my ringless left hand.

What was she on about? I turned back to find she'd followed me inside. Maybe she wasn't right in the head.

'Why do you want to know?' Had Chris told her we were? I rang his bell. *Please, please be in.* I could hear footsteps inside coming nearer. The door opened and I went in. 'Look, it's been lovely talking to you. We must do it again.' I said sarcastically.

Just before I shut the door behind me, I heard her mutter 'Nice ring'. Silly cow. She must be unhinged.

Chris was standing near the window with his arms folded. He didn't look happy.

'Who's the weird woman outside? Lives at number one.'

He scowled. 'Oh God, Luisa. You haven't run into her, have you? She's a psycho. She fancies me. She's jealous of you.'

'What? Seriously? You know that for a fact?'

'Yeah. She asked me out.'

'Really? Did you tell her we were engaged?'

He scratched his head in an absent fashion. 'Er, yeah, actually. I'd forgotten about that. I said it to stop her coming onto me. Just ignore her. Anyway, I've rung you loads of times today. Where've you been?'

Shit, my phone was still turned off. What with everything, I'd never given it a thought.

'Sorry.' I grabbed it out of my bag and turned it on. 'It's been off all day.'

He was silent, waiting. Ten missed calls, all from him. Damn it! 'Sorry. Er, I've been...'

He cut me off, his eyes fixed on the carrier bag with the photo album in it. 'What's that?' It was almost as if he knew. The top corner of the album was sticking out.

'Er... I've been to see your sister.'

A muscle in his jaw clenched, but he didn't seem that surprised.

'Why?'

'She asked me to.'

'How did she know your number?'

I went through it all, right from the beginning, and he stood there, saying nothing, just curling his hands into fists at his sides. He took the album out of the bag, sat down and put it on the coffee table, unopened. I sat next to him.

'You're being very calm about this. I thought you'd be mad.' I twined my fingers together, twisting them round and round.

He looked at me, his chin coming up high. 'What, did you think I'd shout at you? Hit you or something?'

'No, of course not. I know you'd never hit me. Don't be daft.'

I jumped when he knocked the album onto the floor with a vicious swipe. Loose scraps of paper spilled out, along with some stray photos.

'I'm not happy about you digging around in my past. You had no right.'

'I'm sorry. I know that. But I've asked about your past before. You're so closed off about it.'

He was on his feet now, pacing up and down. 'Because it's nobody's business,' he roared. 'I'm not *him* anymore. Can't you see that? I'm not that kid.'

I recoiled back against the sofa with the force of his rage. Then I was up, holding him and kissing him, trapping his face between my hands and forcing him to look at me. He was rigid, unbending. Betrayed.

'I know you're not. Honestly, I understand why you had to get out of there. I do. And I applaud you for doing it. There's nothing to be ashamed of about where you came from. You were just a kid.'

He relaxed against me, his heaving chest rising more slowly now with each breath. His head slowly came up, his face inches from mine. Then he stepped away from me and sat down again.

'Any other dark secrets of mine come to light while you were up there poking around?' His voice was dangerously quiet. 'Like I'm an axe murderer or anything?'

I blinked at the sarcasm. I didn't know what to say. When I sat down next to him, he moved away from me slightly.

'Look. We have to be honest with each other for this to work. You said it yourself the other day.' I hated the wheedling tone in my voice.

'Yet you couldn't be honest before the event. Only after. What sort of honesty is that, Sarah?'

God, this was bad. 'I don't get what you're so ashamed about. You had a bad start, you got out and now you're a different person. It's not unlike thousands of other peoples' stories, is it, really? Like a rags to riches thing.'

'Oh, is that what it is? Some romantic notion? I see.'

I reached for his hands, but he pulled them away.

'I'll tell you what this is, Sarah. It's a betrayal. And I think you should go.' He turned his face away and stared resolutely out of the window.

He was kicking me out? 'Chris, please. I'm sorry. We need to talk about this.' I reached for him again, but he stood up and my hands skimmed his body as he stepped away.

'There's nothing more to say. I want you to go.'

'I said I'm sorry. And I really am.'

'I want to be on my own,' he snapped, then walked into his bedroom and slammed the door.

He didn't reply when I shouted him. So that was it then. I'd screwed everything up through my own nosiness. I couldn't blame him for being angry. If he'd done that to me, I'd be absolutely fuming. I left quietly; I hadn't even taken my coat off. Thankfully, that horrible woman outside was nowhere to be seen.

38

SO THAT'S IT. SHE went behind my back and found out everything about me. I thought I could trust her, but obviously I was wrong. It wasn't a total shock. The GPS on her phone told me where she was before she turned it off. I'd known all day. What I hadn't known was why. I must admit, it was a nifty move of Shay's to get her to go up there to get back at me. Checkmate this time, Shay. When pressed for more detail, she told me she used Leanne's phone to ring Shay, in a spur of the moment kind of thing. That explains it then, why I didn't see the call in the log.

After she's gone, I do a hard session on the gym to destress, lifting more weights, doing more reps, then some cardio, skipping. Maybe I'll get a running machine. Always fancied running, but not up and down the streets, dodging winos and dog shit. While I shower, I think back to the coke I had the other day. It lifted me, invigorated me. I could do with some now, to make me feel better.

'Danny?'

'Alright, Chris? Wassup?'

'Got any more of that shit from the other day?'

'No. I can get some though. You want some?'

'Yeah. I'll pick it up later.'

'No probs. It'll be here.'

I ring off, my mind still on the betrayal. She betrayed me so I'll betray her.

'Anita, it's Chris. How you fixed?'

'For you, hun? Anytime.'

'See you in an hour.'

'Right.'

Sorted. Some would say I'm no better than my old man, shagging prossies. But Anita's not like the slappers he used to pay. She's not a druggie, for a start. No needle marks on her arms or between her toes.

I once asked Anita why she did it.

'I enjoy it. I like sex. I'm discerning about my clients and it pays well,' was her answer. Can't argue with that.

Over the next few days, Sarah is sorry, ringing and texting me all the time. I don't answer. I love her and she's hurt me. To be honest, I don't know what to do. It's such a betrayal. It won't do her any harm to stew for a few days. Let her realise what she's lost and then I'll let her come crawling back. And it's not like I won't see her or know what she's doing. I'll still be watching. And listening.

Adam is proving to be more of a problem than I thought. He texts her all the time. Good job I can intercept them on her phone. I've deleted so many. He's almost begging to see her, even if it's just as friends. Some people have no pride or self-respect. It's sickening.

39

SO HE WASN'T SPEAKING to me and had practically thrown me out. I felt like total crap. Of all the ways it could have gone, I never expected Chris to tell me to go when I'd told him I'd seen Shay. But I should have seen it coming. I'd betrayed his trust and gone snooping. Turned out his past was dead and buried for a reason. His father was no stranger to drink driving so prison may be the best place for him. Chris wasn't answering the phone to me, or replying to any texts. Maybe I'd blown it. Or maybe he just needed time to cool off, fingers crossed.

On Tuesday evening, I made the stuff for Porter's for the next day, hoping it would stop me brooding. I'd almost finished when Lee came home.

'Hi,' she called as she closed the door.

'In the kitchen.'

She came in, sniffing the air. 'What are you making?'

'Tarte au citron and salted caramel cheesecake for the restaurant.'

'Sounds nice. So, how's your day been?' She sat down heavily on one of the kitchen chairs and eyed the mess of the kitchen.

I hadn't told her anything about Leeds. I couldn't. It wouldn't exactly win her round to him.

'Okay, yeah.' I looked at her for a moment and pasted a false smile onto my face. Instantly, I knew she was hiding something. She looked far too pleased with herself.

'What?'

She shrugged.

'Oh my God! You got the job, didn't you?' I shrieked.

'Yep.'

'Bloody hell, Lee! That's fantastic.' I threw my arms around her and covered her in flour. 'It's only round the corner. You'll be at work in about three minutes.'

'Two minutes forty-one seconds actually.'

'I'm really happy for you. I bet you can't wait to start.'

'I can't. I'm so excited.'

I started running water in the washing-up bowl to tackle yet another mountain of dirty pots.

'I'll start these if you like, seeing as I'm in such a good mood.' She snapped on rubber gloves and started piling dirty bowls into the water.

'Oh, thanks. You're an angel.' I snipped the corner off the piping bag and began to pipe cream onto the cheesecake.

'Oh,' she said. 'Guess what? I've emailed that missing persons' website about Ben.'

I inhaled sharply. 'Have you? I really hope we're doing the right thing. Do you think we are?'

She chewed at her lip. 'I think so. We have to try.'

'I know.'

She paused with her hands in the water, staring at the bubbles. 'Not seeing lover boy tonight?'

'No. Not tonight.'

Thankfully, she didn't mention him again.

Several times during the evening I rang Chris. His phone was turned off. He never turned his phone off. I texted him instead. Would he read it and would he even care? If only I didn't care so much.

Sorry xxx I sent. He didn't reply and so, too restless to do anything else, I spent an hour googling all my favourite shops. But I was good, and didn't buy anything. This restraint thing was getting easier.

The text I'd been waiting for didn't come until Friday night. *Mine tomorrow? 10am x.* At last we could sort this out.

It had been the worst few days of my life. I thought I'd lost him.

I got to his for ten and stopped off at the bakery for some Danish pastries as a peace offering. My feet started to drag a couple of houses down the road from his flat. What if Luisa Nutjob was around? I crept closer, hoping no one would see me. They'd wonder what the hell was wrong with me. When a man came striding around the corner towards me, I whipped out my phone and pretended to be texting someone. As the front doorstep came into view, I relaxed. *She* wasn't there. I was half-expecting her door to fly open as I stood outside Chris's flat, with my back to her door, knocking softly. I couldn't get in quick enough. Luckily, her door stayed firmly closed.

Chris enveloped me in a big hug, as if the argument had never happened. He also seemed a teeny bit nervous.

'I've got a surprise for you,' he said.

'What is it?' I took my coat off and threw it over the back of the sofa.

He picked it up and hung it on one of the hooks near the door. One sleeve was inside out, and he pulled it the right way round.

'Sorry,' I said.

He held out his hand to me and pulled me into the kitchen. For once, it was a complete mess. And there, on a plate, was the wonkiest, most unappetising, lumpiest, cake I'd ever seen. It was much thicker at one end than the other. I thought it was supposed to be round. I also thought it was supposed to be a chocolate cake. Or maybe carrot. It had burnt bits poking through the yellow buttercream he'd covered it in, and some of the crumbs had come through due to his over-vigorous spreading. But it was the nicest, sweetest thing anyone had ever done for me, and it brought a smile to my face and a huge lump to my throat. It was unique, at least. The inside of my mouth puckered at the thought of eating the black bits. But he'd made such an effort.

'Did you make that for me?'

'Yeah.' I could see from his expression he was immensely proud.

I laughed in delight and put the bag of Danishes down. 'We won't be needing these now. It's fantastic.' I had to say it. 'Can I have some?'

His face dropped. 'That's the worst bit, though. How do you cope with people cutting them up and spoiling them?'

He was serious. He actually thought it would spoil it to cut it up.

'You get used to it. And that's the point, really, to eat it.'

He looked satisfied with that. 'Okay, I suppose. But it's gonna hurt to watch. The others weren't half as good.'

'Others?'

'That's the fourth one. I've been at it since six this morning. The others looked crap. They're in the bin. And I had to go shopping last night for all the stuff.'

I put my hand over my mouth to cover my laugh. 'Shall I cut it? So you don't have to.'

'Well, alright then.' He passed me a knife.

He was looking at it as if it was the best cake he'd ever seen and that was quite insulting seeing as he'd seen loads of mine. I cut two slices, a big one and a tiny one, passing him the large piece. He held the plate up in front of his face, turning it so he could examine it from all angles. Then he nodded, seemingly satisfied.

I took a deep breath, steeled myself, and tasted it. Dear God! My throat seized up and I tried not to splutter as the dry, bitter, burnt concoction welded my jaws together. I didn't think he'd put any sugar in it. To my amazement, he was forking it in by the shovelful, having quickly got over the trauma of seeing it carved up. Then I remembered; he ate anything. I forced in another dry lump and tried to muster up some words, but it stuck to the roof of my mouth, taking away my ability to speak. I looked at him, nodding my approval.

'Mmm,' was all I could manage.

'It's alright, isn't it?' he said, enthusiastically. 'Don't know why you make such a fuss about this baking lark. There's nothing to it.'

***

We curled up on his sofa and it felt right. But I had to bring it up and clear the air. We couldn't keep pretending it hadn't happened.

'Chris, I am sorry. I shouldn't have gone to Leeds behind your back. You were right.'

He stiffened slightly beside me. 'No, you shouldn't have. But I'm trying to understand why you did. And maybe, in the same position, I *might* have done the same. And the cake is my way of saying I'm sorry. For reacting the way I did.'

'I hated it when you wouldn't speak to me.'

'Sorry. I was just licking my wounds. I needed to be alone.'

'I just want to get to know you better, that's all.' I stifled a yawn.

'Tired?' he asked.

'Yeah.'

He kissed me once, then again.

'So, are we good then, you and me?' I asked.

'Yes. More than good.' He swivelled around to face me. His mouth worked but no words came out. He looked helpless.

'What?' I said.

'I want to tell you something.'

Alarm bells started ringing. Was it something bad? He'd just said we were okay.

He tried again, taking my hand first, and breathing out slowly. 'Okay, I... er, I think I love you,' he whispered, brushing his mouth against mine.

My mouth dropped open. I hadn't been expecting that. But at that point, I knew I felt the same. I loved this crazy, sexy, bolshie, sometimes arrogant man.

'I love you too,' I whispered. 'I was so scared I'd lost you.'

He pulled back to look at me. 'Were you? Really?'

I nodded.

'Well, don't be. You haven't.'

He pulled a key out of his pocket and handed it to me. 'I was thinking... take this, so you can get away from Psycho when she's on the prowl.'

'Thanks.' I took it. It felt significant, him giving me a key to his flat.

'Anyway, I've got you a present,' he said. 'Another peace offering. Well, two, actually. To cheer you up.' He went into his bedroom and returned a second later with a carrier bag. He took out a plastic package and handed me it.

'What is it?'

'Open it and see.'

I tore it open and a pink dress slipped out.

'I can't believe it. I was looking at this on the internet last week. I really liked it. How did you know?'

'Were you really? Wow! Well, I saw it in the window in Next when I was walking past and thought it was just so you.'

I looked at the bag. 'But it's packaged from the internet.'

'Yeah. I had to order it. When I went in, they didn't have your size, but they said I could get it online. They gave me the code to put in. It was dead easy.'

'Chris, it's beautiful. I love it. I decided I couldn't afford it.'

'You're worth it to me. I just thought you'd like it. Open this one.'

The second package was gift-wrapped and heavier. I breathed in sharply at the sight of the cream box and black ribbon. I'd know it anywhere. I removed the lid and squealed when a glass jar of Jo Malone body cream dropped into my hands. 'Oh, this is my favourite smell ever. How did you know?'

'You told me.'

I blinked. 'Did I? When?'

'At the Christmas party. You *were* sozzled, though.'

I must have done. It was true I was so drunk that night, I couldn't remember what I'd prattled on about.

'I can't remember much about that night, except kissing you,' I said. 'Anyway, I love it. Thank you. But you shouldn't be spending your money on me.'

'Who else have I got to spend it on? Anyway, I've got an ulterior motive. Try on the frock. Then you can thank me properly by taking it off again. We've got some making up to do.'

40

ADAM COULDN'T ACCEPT WHAT Sarah had told him. He didn't want to be 'just friends'. He wanted her. But he was sure there was more to that big bloke who was in her flat that time. The one who seemed to think he was *it*. Chris somebody-or-other. Apparently, he'd given her a lift home from the wedding fair, and Sarah hadn't denied it. And he'd found her lost keys. He was certainly good-looking, even he could tell that as a bloke. He could see what Sarah might see in him. When he asked her, though, she'd said she wasn't seeing anyone. He didn't know whether to believe her or not, although he wanted to. He didn't want to think she would lie to him.

He put his head in his hands. He needed to find out what was going on—it was driving him mad. He was crazy about Sarah but wasn't prepared to make a fool of himself. He had to know. She still hadn't answered his texts. Maybe it was worth one more shot, to ask her specifically if she was seeing this Chris. If she looked shifty, then he would have his answer.

He decided to go for a walk to think it over some more. It beat pacing up and down his flat. The route to the park took him past Sarah's place. He could pop in, see how she was. She'd said he could still come by. He grabbed his coat and set off at a brisk pace. As he got nearer, his steps started to drag as his courage deserted him and he faltered. It was a stupid idea. He was just harassing her. She didn't want him;

she'd made it plain. He stopped, uncertain what to do. Maybe he should leave it for now.

He was just about to turn around when someone left Sarah's building. It was only him, the bloody ape. Adam ducked into a nearby alley, watching the man. Sarah wasn't with him. Making a snap decision, he decided to follow him. The ape was heading off in the other direction. Adam followed at a safe distance, confident he hadn't been seen. Ten minutes later, they were on the Tube. Central line. Adam was in the same carriage, checking over his shoulder at each stop. When the Tube stopped at Notting Hill Gate, Chris got off. Adam followed suit, squeezing through the doors just before they closed. Chris got on the District line. Adam got in the next carriage. They both got off at a packed Fulham Broadway. For a horrible moment, Adam thought he'd lost him but relocated him halfway up the escalators. Chris turned right out of the station and Adam dropped back, following at a more leisurely pace.

So the ape lived in Fulham, if he was going home. After a fifteen-minute walk, Chris turned down a leafy street, lined with expensive houses. Adam hurried after him. Brookfield Road. Chris went up the steps into an end-terraced property about halfway down. Adam hung around in the shadows on the opposite side of the street. What now? He'd come this far. But which flat was it? He could hardly ring all the doorbells until he found him. A light went on and a figure appeared in the left hand downstairs flat. It was him, pulling the blinds down.

Adam regarded the place. It was proper flash. The rent round here must be astronomical. This guy must earn loads. He might look like an ape, but he couldn't have a brain like one if this place was anything to go by.

He crossed the road at the side of the house and went around the back, into a narrow alley. The house wasn't very deep, so it was a good bet that Chris's place took up the whole side front to back. There was a high wall and gate, but Adam was agile and tall, and vaulted over it in a second, narrowly missing an old metal dustbin as he landed. He remained in a crouch where he hit the floor, breathing hard. At least no snarling guard dogs jumped him. He was in a small back garden with an overgrown lawned area. He stood up and surveyed the windows. Most were lit with blinds or curtains drawn against the cold, damp evening. It was a three-storey brick building with dormers at the top. He crept towards what had to be Chris's back window, keeping close to the wall. The light was on and he could see straight into what looked like a bedroom cum office. The blind was pulled halfway down and Adam crouched to look inside. Someone was sitting in front of a load of monitors with their back to the window. It was the ape. What was he doing? Who needed that many computers? He couldn't make out what some of the stuff on the screens was. He edged closer.

One got his attention straight away. He could see Sarah. She looked grainy, kind of pixelated, but it was definitely her bedroom in the background. Were they Skyping? He'd only just left her. But Sarah wasn't speaking. It was a still image. As he watched, the picture changed and he knew exactly what he was looking at. Webcam pictures. She surely couldn't know about this. The ape had hacked her webcam!

It was like a whack in the solar plexus and he couldn't breathe. He doubled over, sucking in air. It was the lowest, dirtiest trick anyone could play. He straightened up slowly and watched for another few minutes. It got worse. There were loads of photos of Sarah on there. In one, she was sitting up in bed reading. On another monitor, there was what looked like a live link to Sarah's bedroom. The lamp was on, but the room was empty. He recognised the beach picture above her bed and her fancy padded headboard even in the dim glow from the bedside lamp, remembering it from the only time he'd been in there when he'd fitted the smoke alarm with the camera in. He'd seen enough. Sarah was in danger and he had to move fast.

He crept back to the gate and jumped over it, returning to the Tube station, his mind churning over what he'd discovered. When he got home, he rang her, but there was no answer. He left a voicemail, asking her to ring him urgently. He tried twice more then decided to go round there. He leaned on the bell. Again, no answer. Where were they? They must have gone out. He texted her: *Sarah, I need to talk to you about Chris. It's urgent. Please call me. I'm on call tonight so I don't care how late you ring.* In another voicemail, he left more information. He hadn't wanted to tell her what he'd discovered over the phone, wanted to be there to see her face, but he had no choice. She needed to know. He left a message telling her everything.

41

WE'VE MADE UP. EVERYTHING'S alright again. I showed her the cake I made (I won't be doing that ever again—the mess it made of the kitchen), gave her the presents, shagged her senseless, and that was it. I take her home and then do what I should have done ages ago. I locate as many pictures of her as I can that I've posted on websites and remove them. Truth is, I feel bad now about doing it. By taking them down, I can put it right. She'll never know anyway, so there's no harm done. Message to self—the next woman I hack, I won't fall for.

My phone buzzes now. An alert. But it's not my phone that's getting messages, it's Sarah's. For the next half hour, it goes mad, next to me on the desk. I leave it and carry on checking for any missed pictures, then pick it up when I've finished. For Christ's sake, it's Adam again! He just won't give in. He won't stop sniffing round her.

He's left several texts and voicemails this time. I grip the phone tightly, reading his urgent texts and listen to the voicemails, and almost drop the phone in shock. I look behind me at the dark window. All I can see is my own reflection looking back at me. I should have shut the blinds. I've been careless. He's been here. He's telling her what he's seen, what I've been doing! The bastard! I delete all of them. They'll be gone off her phone straight away. Hopefully, she won't have seen them. I remember her plugging her phone in to charge in the kitchen, and she said she and Leanne were going for a walk.

This time, Adam's gone too far. If he sees her face to face, then it's game over for me. What had Sarah said his business was called again? I dredge my memory. Oh, yeah: A & N Solutions. How original! I find the website. Adam's face stares out at me, as does someone called

197

Nathan, the co-owner. Neither of them look like they could punch their way out of a paper bag. There are testimonials on there from several customers, one not too far from here. After some thought, I come up with an idea that might work. I wait until midnight, then change into black jeans and a dark jacket. I shove some woolly gloves into my pocket along with a black woolly hat.

It's below zero out and my breath fogs the air in front of me. Keeping to the smaller side streets, it's about a fifteen-minute walk to the small industrial estate I've picked. The place is deserted at this time, as I expected it would be. I take a look around, noting where any CCTV cameras are, then put on the gloves and hat and force the door of A Cut Above Joinery, who I know Adam does the security for. They gave a glowing testimonial. No alarm sounds, but it should send an alert to Adam's company. According to his voicemails, he's on call tonight. I disappear into the dark shadows at the side of the building, where I can watch the entrance, hoping he won't take too long to arrive. I huddle deeper into my jacket. As my teeth begin to chatter, headlights turn in to the industrial site's entrance and a motorbike comes to a halt in front of the joinery unit.

Adam stops and takes off his motorcycle helmet. He zips up his jacket and jogs up to the door. It's still locked, but I booted it so hard it's loose. Adam rattles it and stands with his hands on his hips. Apart from turning off the alarm, I wouldn't have thought there's much he can do tonight; it'll probably need a new lock or hinges or something. He fiddles with some electronic device, then pulls out his mobile. Now's my chance.

'Oi!' I walk out from the side of the building and Adam looks up in surprise.

He says, 'Who are you?' A nervous tremor in his voice.

When I get closer, he mutters, 'Fuck!'

'Yeah. Fuck!'

'Is this your doing?' He indicates the busted door. Things are dawning fast. 'What d'you want?'

'A word.'

'About?'

'Sarah.'

He's silent. He can't know I've listened to his messages.

I'm caught off guard when Adam suddenly advances with a snarl. Didn't expect that. Before he can touch me, I shove him in the chest, and he goes flying back into the door, slamming into it hard. When he rights himself, we stand silently facing each other off.

'Why don't you leave Sarah alone? You're no good for her, you warped, twisted bastard. I know what you're doing,' he says.

I grab the front of his jacket and pull him around the side, into the shadows. He stumbles when I let him go with another shove. 'I know you know. How much do you want to keep your mouth shut?'

He frowns. 'You what?'

'I said, how much?'

'You're trying to buy me off?'

'It's either that or I hurt you. Bad. Your choice.'

'You're spying on her.'

'Not anymore. I was taking them down, dickbrain. Only you wouldn't know that, would you?'

He blinks twice. 'You just said you knew. How could you know?'

I hold up my phone and waggle it around.

'Shit!' he says as the penny drops. 'You need locking up.' He raises his fists.

'Leave us alone. I'm not telling you again.' I brace myself, putting my weight onto my right leg. 'Just go, walk away. It's your last warning. Forget her. For ten thou. It's my top offer.'

He steps forward and takes a well-aimed, well-timed swing, but he hasn't got the weight to follow through with any advantage or conviction. I dodge back and the blow grazes my sleeve with no effect. It makes me laugh, the nerve of the idiot, going for me not once but twice.

He puts his hands on his hips, breathing hard. 'Why are you such a nasty bastard?'

I shrug. 'Born this way. Like you were born a wanker. So... what's it to be? Fuck off or fight? This is your last warning.'

He lunges again, landing a flurry of punches, but I barely feel a thing. He's tested my patience and now it's finally run out. I warned him. I bend my arm and jab my elbow hard into the side of his head. He crumples to the floor, his legs folding under him like a plane's landing gear. He doesn't get up again. I stand there, waiting, adrenalin raging through me. I'd put my full force behind it and felt something snap in his neck as his head whipped to the side.

'Get up.' I poke him in the side with my foot. He stays slumped on the floor. I put a hand under his nose and a small, warm stream of air hits my skin. Maybe now he knows how much I can hurt him, he'll back off.

I kneel beside him. 'If you don't leave her alone, next time I'll kill you.'

He doesn't move. Maybe it would be better if it looked like a robbery, so I take his wallet then go around the front to find his phone. It lies in the grass, glistening in the fine drizzle that's just started. There are no security cameras here, and an alleyway at the back of the units leads out onto some back streets. I leave that way, running in the shadows until I'm well clear of the place.

42

ON SUNDAY AFTERNOON, WE were snuggled in front of the TV at Chris's when my phone rang. I went to pick it up and he reached across to take it out of my hand.

'Don't answer it. Come to bed again. I want to do dirty things to you.'

I giggled. 'In a minute, I have to get it. It's Debbie. She must have picked what cake she wants for her wedding.'

I snatched it back and answered it, trying not to laugh.

'Hello?' I batted Chris's hand away.

At first, there was just a snivelling noise I couldn't understand.

'Hello? Debbie?'

When she finally spoke, I listened, feeling the blood drain out of my face. I got up and walked over to the window, staring into the road but seeing nothing. Chris was watching me, frowning.

'Not yesterday, no,' I said.

When I hung up, Chris said, 'What is it?'

I turned back to him. 'Adam's been attacked. Last night. He's in a coma on life support at the Chelsea and Westminster. Debbie asked when I last saw him.'

His face went as white with shock as mine.

'Oh no, that's awful,' he said.

***

Debbie met me at the hospital entrance the next morning, after I begged her to let me visit. I dashed in out of the sleeting rain that was bouncing up off the pavement.

'How is he? Any change?' I pulled the hood on my coat down and swept my hair off my face.

She shook her head. Her face was swollen from crying. 'Let's go to the canteen for a drink,' she said.

I walked with her, our shoes squeaking on the grey linoleum floor. The rain was now battering the high windows as if trying to thrash its way in. We sat down and I pushed the revolting coffee to one side after tasting it. Debbie sat opposite me with her head in her hands. Last time I saw her, she had beautiful, long, painted nails. Now they were bitten into raw stumps.

'What have the doctors said?' I asked.

'They're doing tests, but Luke's warned me it doesn't look good.'

I felt like I was falling through the air. *Were they saying Adam might not make it?* It was the first time I'd considered that. I just assumed he'd come out of the coma and be okay.

'We'll know more by the end of today.' She turned to look out of the window, biting her bottom lip. When she turned back to me, her eyes were brimming. 'I can't bear the thought of someone hurting him. Or the thought that he might die. Mum and Dad won't leave his side, only to let me or Luke in, and they only let two people by the bed. I don't think you'll be able to see him. Not today, anyway. I'm sorry for you coming all this way, but Mum's adamant. Family only. I think she's thinking she'll regret every second not spent with him if... you know, they have to…'

She started to cry quietly, and hot tears spilled down my own face. *Lovely, sweet Adam. And you lied to his face.*

'There's massive bleeding in his brain and it's swelling up. They've removed a section of skull to allow for it, but it's not going down. In fact, it's still swelling. The blow to his head must have been massive, they say.' Her voice broke and she sobbed into a tissue.

I shivered with the thoughts of it all. Who could do that to another person? Slamming something into someone's head like that. What if the worst were to happen and I hadn't been able to see him? I lied to him, even though I did it to spare his feelings. I thought I had all the time in the world to put it right.

Debbie returned the tissue to her pocket and shuffled back on the chair. Then she sat up straighter and looked at me, folding her arms across her body and hugging herself. 'He told me he thought he was in love with you, Sarah. He was so happy.'

The words crashed down on me, pinning me to the chair. *What? In love with me? As if I wasn't feeling bad enough already.*

'I liked him. I had no idea he...' I held my face in my hands, hiding my shame from her.

'I don't mean to pry, but I thought you two were serious. According to what he said.'

'Debbie, it was early days. We'd hardly been out.'

'It's okay, I know how full on he can be. And it's none of my business. Anyway, listen, I'm going to have to go back up. I'll let you know of any developments.'

She meant whether he lived or died. She left to go back to her family, and I sat there, overwhelmed and exhausted. All I could do for Adam was hope and pray. I looked up as a man sat down in the chair Debbie had just vacated. I'd never met him before, but I knew who he was by his resemblance to Adam.

'You must be Sarah,' Luke said.

I nodded, and he began to talk.

43

SHE'S AT THE HOSPITAL. *She's just phoned to say she's leaving. I'm pacing up and down outside her flat when she gets home. Her eyes are red and puffy and she's clutching a soggy balled-up tissue. We go upstairs.*

'It was awful,' she says, taking her coat off. 'They're so devastated. He might not make it. I can't believe he might die.'

'I'm sorry.' I pull her into me for a hug, mostly so she can't see my face. And I am sorry. Sorry that the stupid bastard drove me to this with his meddling. Why couldn't he have just stayed out of it?

'The police may have a lead,' she says, her voice muffled against my chest.

'What?'

She pulls away. 'They have a CCTV image of a man in black hurrying away from the area. Luke told me.'

The ground feels like it's just dropped away at a thousand miles an hour, leaving me suspended in thin air. Sweat blooms under my arms and I wipe my clammy hands on my jeans to give me time to think.

'Can they identify him from it?' My voice sounds far away with the blood rushing in my head.

'I don't know. Luke said the police are cleaning up the image and stuff like that, but that's all I know. It seems whoever it was must have known where all the cameras were, except for this one. He managed to avoid the others.'

I feel sick. Where was the camera? The clothes I wore that night are stuffed in the bathroom in the laundry basket. I have to get home and get rid of them. The jacket has a small, coloured logo on the left breast pocket. It's too distinctive. If the image is cleaned up, enhanced… shit! Also, Adam's wallet and phone are still in the jacket pocket. I'd be better off wiping them clean and finding a skip to bury them in. But Sarah wants me to stay. I watch the clock, but every minute seems to take an hour.

When she starts yawning, that's my cue.

'Why don't you go to bed? You've barely slept. I've got a few things to do. I can come back later.'

Thankfully, she agrees and I can go. I sprint up the street to the Tube, run home and shoot through the flat in a panic. It might be best to burn everything rather than dump it somewhere covered in my DNA. Eventually, I find some matches in a kitchen drawer. Where to burn the stuff? There's no fire in the flat and smoke alarms are everywhere. Out of my bedroom window, I see the old metal dustbin rotting in the back garden. That'll do. It's been here so long I never notice it anymore. It's hard to drag it away from the fence as grass has grown through the holes in the bottom and taken root. It takes several sharp tugs to pull it free.

I tip it up and scrape mud out of the bottom with a long stick, then right it again. First, I drop the jacket in, checking the windows behind me. No one's watching. I throw the trousers in, followed by the trainers and drop a lit match on them. It goes out before it hits the bottom. The clothes sit there, mocking me. I could do with some petrol or something, but there's nothing here. Two more matches fizzle out, then another catches the edge of the flammable nylon jacket. Seconds later, the flame whooshes into life and I feel the heat on my skin, so close that it dries the sweat still coating my body. The flames are mesmerising as I watch them eat into the fabric. The trainers don't burn too well, although they're smouldering; red-hot ash glows inside them. Maybe they'll have burnt down in a couple of hours.

I stand shivering in the back garden, thinking of my old man's back garden that night, when I took coke in his shed and killed a kid. This garden's smaller than that one and there's no shed, but there is still the obligatory patch of grass they all seem to have. As the flames die down, I sense movement behind me, and I whirl round to see Luisa standing only a couple of feet away. A small cry escapes me.

'Shit! You scared me to death creeping up on me like that.' I clutch my chest, breathing heavily.

'What are you doing?' Her eyes are flicking over everything, taking it all in.

'Nothing. Just burning some rubbish; paper and stuff. My shredder's broken.' I move to stand between her and the bin so she can't see inside.

I haven't seen her since I was rude to her. She's probably been avoiding me. There's a weird expression on her face; let's just say she isn't smiling. Probably still pissed off with me. She turns without a word and walks back inside, leaving me standing protectively over the dustbin.

When everything is cinders, I go back inside and lean against the door. I have an overwhelming need to block out the rest of the world and everything in it, but I don't have anything that will give me oblivion. Instead, in the bedroom, I open a drawer and find a bit of coke I stashed there, wrapped in silver foil. I've been saving it. I unwrap it with shaking hands, knowing it won't really help. It'll make me hyper, and that's the last thing I need. I take it anyway, then ring Danny to get some more.

44

IT HAD BEEN FOUR days since Adam's attack, and he hadn't improved. If anything, he'd deteriorated. I still hadn't been able to see him, and Debbie's words were a constant loop in my head: 'He thought he was in love with you'. Nothing I did could take my mind off them.

I had a wedding cake to do that was due soon so, even though I didn't feel like it, I made a start on it. Lee came in from work at five, having already started at the vintage shop.

'Any news on Adam?' she asked.

'No. I mean, he's no better. Um, Chris is coming by later.'

She shrugged. 'Well, I'll be in my bedroom, sewing,' she said.

This wasn't getting any better. We were just going round in circles. She wasn't even trying to like him. And whenever he came round, it was clear he didn't like her either.

Lee went back into her room, closing the door, and I carried on with the cake, thinking about Adam. When Chris rang the bell downstairs, I looked round the kitchen. Piles of messy pots were strewn across every single surface, and I was covered in flour and icing sugar as I let him in. He looked tired and hot as he followed me into the kitchen. He stopped with a groan when he saw the mess.

'God, not again!' he said.

'I know. I had this cake to do. I didn't feel like it but...'

He sighed deeply and started to fill the washing-up bowl. 'You know I wouldn't do this for anyone else, don't you?'

He gave me a small smile. 'Sometimes I think you're taking advantage of my super-evolved cleaning gene.' He sniffed.

'I'm not. Really. And I'm grateful for your super-evolved cleaning gene. Are you okay, though? You look a bit rough if you don't mind me saying.'

'Oh. I didn't know you were here already. I didn't hear the door.' We both looked round to see Lee in the doorway.

He didn't answer, just continued to place dirty pots in the sink.

'How are you, Chris?' she said stiffly. I looked at her in surprise. She was making an effort.

'I'm great,' he answered shortly, still not looking at her.

Lee looked at me as if to say *see*. What the hell was wrong with him?

'Well, I only came in for a glass of water,' she said.

Chris moved to one side so she could get to the tap. She quickly filled a glass and hurried out of the kitchen.

'What was that all about?' I said to him.

'What?'

'You were rude to her.'

'I wasn't.'

'You were.'

'I don't know what you're on about.' His shoulders were tense, the muscles showing through his thin shirt bunched and rigid.

'Don't give me that shit. You do.'

'Alright. She doesn't like me, does she?'

'What?'

'I think she thinks you can do better for yourself. That I'm no good for you. Probably Adam might have got the seal of approval—I don't know.'

'What makes you say that?' I couldn't tell him he was wrong. He was practically reciting her exact words.

'So. Am I right?'

'No, course not. She hasn't said anything like that to me.' Lies.

'Is that right?'

He looked me straight in the eye and I tried not to squirm. 'Look, will you try to get on with her? For me? If she makes an effort too. Like she just did then. You might find you have things in common if you talk to each other.'

'What, like sewing?'

I narrowed my eyes at him.

He sighed. 'Okay. I'll try.'

Something on his face caught my eye. A dark red rivulet was tracking down from his nose to his upper lip.

'Oh no, Chris! Your nose. It's bleeding.' I grabbed the kitchen roll and ripped some off.

'What? Shit!' His hands were in the washing-up bowl, so I held the paper under his nose while he dried them.

When he took the paper away, it was covered in blood.

'Shit,' he muttered and went to the bathroom.

He was in there a good ten minutes and came back with a giant wad of toilet paper against his nose.

'Are you okay?'

'Yeah.' When he took the tissue away, it had stopped bleeding.

'Do you get them often?'

'No. I used to get them when I was little sometimes.' He leaned against the worktop. 'I only get them occasionally, now. Anyway, come here.' He held out his arms to me and I went into them, pulling him close.

I was suddenly aware that his heart was racing so fast there was barely a pause between beats. I pulled my head back to look at him; he was sweating, and he didn't look at all well.

'Chris, you look terrible. Go and lie down.'

I propelled him into my bedroom with my hand on his lower back before he could protest, and he sat on the bed.

I touched his forehead. It didn't feel like he had a temperature. I sat down at my laptop.

'What are you doing?' he asked, dabbing a finger under his nose to check for blood. 'I'm not ill.'

'Googling your symptoms.'

He groaned. I wasn't sure whether it was because of how he felt or what I'd just said. I typed in 'excessive sweating, nosebleeds, racing heart' and got 353,000 results. I clicked on the first one and a long list of possibilities came up. At a first glance, none of them helped.

'Well,' I said, 'It could be panic or an anxiety attack, but they wouldn't cause a nosebleed. Um, most of these don't include all three.' I scanned further down the list. 'Narcotic abuse, cocaine abuse, insulin reaction, mini stroke, pulmonary embolism, haemophilia. It's none of these. Unless you're a secret druggie.' I turned to look at him and he smiled weakly at my glib tone. I turned back to the screen and read further down. 'We'll get nowhere this way.' I went to kneel beside him, holding his hand. 'Er, my diagnosis is you need to see a doctor.'

He sat up. 'Maybe I'm coming down with flu or something. I don't want to be ill here. You don't mind if I go, do you? I think I'll be better off at home.'

'No, course not, not if you're not well.'

He got off the bed and pulled his jacket on at the door.

'I'll ring you tomorrow,' he said.

After he'd gone, I popped my head into Lee's room. Three second-hand wedding dresses were on her bed, all unpicked and tossed into piles. It was still tidier than my room. She was sitting at her sewing machine, and mounds of silky white fabric puthered onto her lap. 'Has he gone already?'

'Yeah, he's not too well, actually.'

'What was that all about earlier? I wasn't exaggerating, was I?'

'Honestly? I don't know. Anyway, he says he'll try if you will.'

'I did just try. You heard me. He wasn't interested.'

'I know. But it's really hard for me, Lee, stuck in the middle. Please?'

She didn't look convinced but nodded. 'Alright.'

My phone beeped. It was Debbie. *Turning his life support off in the morning. There's nothing more they can do.*

45

I SIT STARING AT Sarah's phone with mixed feelings. They're turning his life support off. On one hand, that's good. He can't talk. Can't tell people I hit him and can't tell Sarah what he saw me doing. On the other hand, it's now a murder hunt.

I rub my temples, trying to ease the pressure in my head. I need some light relief. For the next hour, at least, there's something I can do as a distraction, something I've been saving as a special treat. I need this. I deserve this. I get a beer, pull the blind down (I've learned my lesson) and turn the lamp on, then scoot my chair under my desk, nice and tight. Loading up the files from Leanne's laptop doesn't take long.

After thirty minutes, the hope inside me is dying and I want to whack my head on my desk in frustration and boredom. Leanne's computer is as dull as she is. There's nothing good on it yet. I've been through every file and document, scrutinised every word and line and picture. Nothing even remotely interesting. No juicy emails either. Complete waste of time.

My shoulders ache from leaning forward for so long, and I roll them back a few times. On another screen, Sarah's webcam shows an empty bedroom. She's left a lamp on and I can see her bed with yet more clothes strewn across it. Honestly, she's incapable of hanging anything up.

Now there's just the Recycle Bin left. I've been meticulous going through everything else. No point rushing things and overlooking something good. You never know what you'll find in the Recycle Bin. That's why I've saved it for last. This one is full of the usual crap, but I still go through each bit methodically. That's the nature of this sort of work—order, method, scrupulousness. There's stuff on here that looks like old coursework notes from college, all with titles that don't make sense to me. Sketches and drawings of clothes from six and seven years ago, from the file dates. Some of them look quite good. Nothing like the way she dresses herself.

One is a folder of Jpegs and I click on it, going through them one by one. Lots of the pictures are duplicates of ones I've seen in her Pictures folder: weddings, family pictures, out with friends. I open a folder that's named '17'. The first picture makes me sit up straighter. My jaw drops. A very young Leanne smiles shyly out from the screen. She's almost naked. She looks about seventeen, probably hence the folder name. Bingo!

In the picture, she has more fat on her than she does now, and it suits her. Everything is curvier and more rounded. She's laying back on a double bed, on a plain white duvet, in black bra and knickers. Soft sunlight is being filtered through a gauzy curtain at the window, giving the room a hazy, flattering glow. With her hair spread all over the pillow like a halo, she looks like a Rubenesque goddess. Whoever's taken the photo has tried to do it in an arty way. Her legs are firmly clamped together, one thigh slightly raised. Despite my dislike of her, it's still a pleasing sight. The only thing spoiling the picture is a teddy bear half in shot in the top right corner. I don't like it. Makes me feel like a paedo.

I click on the next one. It's similar to the first, but she's sitting in an armchair, topless this time, her hands covering her tits. They're nice and round and full. These days, she hardly has any. I lean forward to study the crotch area closely. Her legs aren't clamped together quite as much but there's still nothing really visible in that area, more's the pity. I click on another. She's standing with her back to the wall, in a skimpy bikini this time, with her arms above her head, a knowing smile spreading across her face, along with the curls that tumble over one cheek. Her eyes are half-closed in a dreamy sort of way. Nice. Who'd have thought it of her? A few more pictures are similar, in various skimpy outfits or no outfit at all. In some, she's in skimpy underwear. One in a miniskirt and stockings, nothing else, shot from the back, with the skirt riding up to show a tiny bit of arse. I like that one—it's as if I could reach into the screen and flip the skirt up, see what's underneath. In another, she's shot from the side, in underwear, leaning *over and pulling a stocking up over her thigh, her foot resting on the bed. Only two more left to go. Sweat slicks my top lip. Come on, show us some more. Stop teasing. Click! Wow! I sit bolt upright.*

This time she's totally naked. She has no hair anywhere. She's flat on the bed, legs together but, thank fuck, minus the teddy. Then I click on the last picture. She's standing, wearing only a pair of very high-heeled shoes, and staring right into the camera. The earlier traces of shyness in her eyes is gone. She was obviously feeling much bolder by the end of the shoot. I go back to the one on the bed again, savouring the feeling of excitement mingled with triumph. You don't feel like this every day.

What a result! She's obviously got rid of the photos by putting them in the Recycle Bin but they're still there for someone like me to find and enjoy. Oh, you silly girl! You silly, silly girl! When will you ever learn?

46

IT FELT SO WRONG to be burying someone as young as Adam. I'd been dreading this day for the past two weeks, since they turned his life support off, and now it was finally here I just wanted it to be over. I wanted to do something to help in some way, so I suggested the delis for the catering. When Jenny and Sandra saw how upset I was about what had happened, they said they wouldn't charge, other than for what the food cost them. They'd been great, considering I was supposed to be starting work for them this week.

'Start when you feel up to it,' they'd said when I told them a close friend had died.

Debbie and Andy were having the wake at their house, and Jenny and I went round there earlier to set the food out. Having that to do at least focused my mind for a few hours, and it was the last thing I could do for Adam.

Now, I sat on the end of my bed, dressed and ready to go. Adam's Facebook page was open on my laptop. The last update was three days before the attack and now it was frozen in time, accentuating the fact that his life had been cut short in the worst, most violent way possible. There were photos of him with various friends from school and uni, most of whom I never knew. In every one, he was smiling or laughing. That's how I used to think of him, and that's how I wanted to remember him. There was a photo of me on there, with him, taken at our flat by Lee. He'd asked her to take one of us with his phone. I didn't even know it was on there until just now. Strange how a social media addict like me rarely went on it anymore. I hadn't had time lately; I'd been too busy getting a life while Adam was losing his. I reached out and touched Adam's image just as the door opened, and Lee came in.

'Are you about ready?' She sat beside me on the bed.

'Yeah. Can you fasten this for me?' I picked up the silver necklace with the tiny butterfly that Adam had given me. I didn't know if I would ever wear it again.

She fastened it around my neck then put her arm around me. 'Come on. Let's get this over with.'

It was a short bus ride to the church and as we neared the gates, there was a sea of umbrellas, mainly black, as people huddled together in the drizzle, waiting to get through the bottleneck of the heavy wooden doors. I put my arm through my friend's and we joined the line, following black-clad backs into a gloomy, cold, stone interior, where an organist played a sombre piece. My heart seemed to lodge higher up, almost in my throat, and was so tightly constricted it felt like a tourniquet wrapped around me.

Twenty minutes after the service was due to start, the double doors opened wide, and the organist stopped briefly before starting up again. I looked back through the doors and just before everyone stood up, I caught a glimpse of a black carriage and two black horses outside. They had tall red plumes on their heads and a woman in some sort of dark livery was beside them, holding the reins. One of the horses tossed its head as the woman put her hand on its nose. My heart stuttered at the next sight, poignant and devastating, as four figures came into view holding the coffin aloft on broad shoulders. The top was awash with blood red and pure white flowers spelling out ADAM and SON. Somehow, it was confirmation that this terrible, devastating thing had really happened. My vision blurred quickly and hot tears spilled down my face. Lee turned at the sound I made and reached for my hand, gripping it tightly.

I couldn't stop thinking how bad it must be for his parents as I watched them walk past, his father's back ramrod-straight and his mother's bent forward as if her spine had melted. Adam had clearly been an amalgamation of them both, with his mother's honey-gold colouring and his father's tall, slim build. The sight of their white faces as they walked to the front of the church would haunt me forever. Adam's parents had him for a quarter of a century, and now his future had been wiped out. There would be no children or grandchildren of his to get to know and love.

When I saw Luke carrying the coffin at one back corner, his face resolute and his shoulders set, my tears came faster. The service passed in a haze of prayers, readings and hymns, and it was a relief to get out of the church. Then there was the horror of the crematorium with the dreaded moment when the curtains drew to a damning close after the coffin was shunted through. Finality. The sound of sobbing intensified at that point. No matter how hard I tried, my mind was filled with visions of Adam's burning body being reduced to ashes. An image of him up the stepladder replacing the smoke alarm and smiling down at me came unbidden into my mind, but the burning image was stronger and his smiling face faded into the flames. Then it was onto the wake.

Debbie's modest-sized house was packed, and we had to push our way inside out of the rain. Adam's parents were in the living room with Luke and Debbie. They obviously had no idea who I was. Luke was standing with the man who had carried the coffin at opposite side to him, and he saw me looking. They both came over and Luke introduced the man as Nathan, Adam's business partner. Nathan was short and fair, in a suit too big for him. The sleeves came halfway down the backs of his hands. I wondered if he'd borrowed it. He nodded at me, his hand wrapped around a cup of tea, and seemed to lapse into a world of his own. Luke looked tired, his hair was all over the place and his tie was askew. He looked so similar to Adam it hurt to see.

'Hello,' he said, clutching a cup of tea.

'Hi. How are your parents doing?' I asked, my eyes sliding back to them. His mum and dad were gripping each other's hands.

He shood his head. 'Not good. They're inconsolable. I didn't know a person could cry as much as my mum, and my dad's not far behind. We're all walking round in a daze, to tell the truth.' Tears glittered in his eyes and he looked back at his parents. I tried to imagine how it felt to lose your twin. I couldn't even come close.

Debbie appeared at Luke's elbow, with Andy not far behind. She looked like she'd been hollowed out. Her eyes brimmed when they met mine, and her lower lip trembled.

'I'm so sorry,' I said, reaching for her hands.

'I can't believe this day. I never thought we'd be burying Adam, never in a million years. I thought he'd be okay, you know. Come out of the coma, sit up and grin that grin of his...'

She was sobbing hard now, and Andy put his arm around her. I had no idea what to say to her, what to say to any of them. We stood in a sad little circle, everyone in their own world with conversation at a halt, and they soon drifted away. Lee squeezed my hand.

I thought about asking Chris to come today, but decided against it. It would surely have been disrespectful to Adam. On reflection, it was the right decision. I think he'd had too much of death lately. He still never spoke about losing his mum, but I was positive it was affecting him more than he let on. He barely slept and had terrible nightmares. He didn't look well, and I was worried about his nosebleeds, which were growing more frequent, but whenever I brought it up, he just got irritable. It was better not to mention it.

After the funeral, Lee and I went home. Chris was coming round later and I'd yet to tell Lee.

'Do you mind?' I asked her as we hung our coats up. 'I don't feel like going to his. I'd rather be here. We can stay in my bedroom, out of your way.'

'No need. I'm going out.' She turned away from me and pulled her boots off.

'Where?'

'Just fancied a walk.' Her face glowed as she stood back up.

I glanced out of the window at the rain hammering on the glass. 'Well, don't forget to take a brolly for your *walk*.'

I went to my bedroom to change, pulling on sloppy jogging pants and a thick baggy jumper. Lee had disappeared into the bathroom and I heard the bath running, along with the soft sound of her humming. She was still in there when Chris arrived.

'Was it awful?' he asked, enveloping me in a big hug.

'Yeah. Terrible.' My eyes stung and I blinked quickly.

'I can imagine.'

Chris looked tired and pale, and I traced my finger over his brow bone. 'Not slept again? You're looking awfully peaky.'

'No. I was up half the night feeling queasy. I'm alright, though. Let's have a drink.'

I made coffee and we sat at the table, listening to the noises coming from the bathroom, then Lee's bedroom. When she appeared, she was wearing skinny jeans, new boots I'd never seen before, and a chunky jumper. Plus, more make-up than normal. Her ringlets had been defined and were almost as glossy as her lips. She flushed slightly when she saw us, whether from my appraisal or Chris's presence, I wasn't sure.

'Hi Chris.' She sounded slightly nervous.

'Hello. You look nice,' he said in a stilted fashion.

Her eyebrows shot up. 'Oh. Thanks. See you later.' She grabbed her coat and left.

I turned to Chris with a smile. 'See, now, that didn't hurt, did it?'

'What?' He raised his eyebrows, all innocent.

'You know what. And thank you.'

He chuckled to himself and kissed me.

'Where's she gone anyway, all dolled up?'

'I don't know. A walk, she said. I'm suspecting some bloke, though. At long last.'

'Right. Well, let's hope so. It might remove the stick from up her arse.'

I elbowed him in the ribs. 'Oi! You're being nice, remember.'

'Oh yeah.' He eyed my comfortable clothes. 'At least she's dressed up for her man.'

'Hey! It's cold! It's not as if we're going anywhere.'

He laughed. 'We've got the place to ourselves then?'

My horribly unsexy clothes clearly hadn't put him off. 'I've just come back from a funeral. You can't seriously expect me to be in the mood.'

He pulled a face. 'Suppose not.'

Instead, we sat close together on the sofa. I didn't want to talk about the funeral, and he seemed happy with that. We watched a crappy made-for-TV film, both of us dozing off more than once. Later, we were flicking around the TV channels when a Crimestoppers ad came on, one of those where they appealed to the public for information. I froze and couldn't breathe when I realised it was about Adam. I didn't want to watch it but couldn't tear my eyes away. There was some grainy footage of someone in black leaving the scene, but they were so covered up it could have been anyone. Chris had gone completely rigid next to me. He leaned forward, studying the image. The only bit of colour seemed to be some logo on the front of the jacket, but it was just a blurry mix of colours.

'They'll never catch him based on that,' I said. 'It's not clear enough.'

Chris said nothing. He was squeezing my hand too tight.

'Ow!' I said, extracting it and flexing my fingers.

'Sorry,' he muttered, still gazing at the screen.

I knew how he felt. Those ads were so different when it was someone you knew.

When the ad went off, we sat in silence. It had really shocked me. I'd thought this day couldn't get any worse, but the appeal put you right at the scene of the crime and it was just horrible. Chris looked dreadful. He was white as a sheet.

'Have you been to see the doctor yet?' I asked him.

'No. But I will. Honest.'

'Why don't we have an early night? You could stay here.'

He hadn't stayed over while Lee had been here yet. She must know it was going to happen.

'No, I'd be better off going home. And maybe it's better if I don't stay over until Leanne's more used to me. See—consideration!'

I didn't want him to go but it made sense. She would be uncomfortable with him being here in the morning. I didn't get much sleep, in the end. All night, the images of Adam's funeral, mingled with the Crimestoppers appeal, played through my head on a constant spool, over and over.

47

MY FIRST DAY AT the deli was absolutely manic. Jenny had said I could put off starting for a few days but I wasn't going to sit at home brooding after the funeral all day. It would only make me feel worse.

So instead, I started as planned at the deli round the corner from my flat, losing myself in the bliss of making a selection of different cheesecakes and Danish pastries. It was just what I needed to take my mind off Adam. By eleven o'clock I was ready to take half of them round to the South Bank Delish in a tiny van that belonged to the company.

I loaded the boxes in and stood looking at the van, gathering the courage to drive the bloody thing. I was petrified as I set off for the South Bank shop. My first drive in years was as awful as I'd thought it would be. I was shaking so much I could barely get it in gear. There was so much traffic and I stalled three times, trying to pull away too quickly at traffic lights, to a cacophony of horns behind me. When had everyone become so aggressive and impatient all the time? Maybe, if I borrowed the van one weekend, Chris would come with me for some practice. It would be better knowing there was someone experienced next to me, and he was such a self-assured and accomplished driver. I let my mind drift a tiny bit while still concentrating on the driving, remembering Chris's vulnerability when he had told me his sad story about his childhood. It made me realise he wasn't so self-assured after all. He'd really worked at how he came across. Maybe I should take control of how I appeared to other people too. If you convinced others you were confident, you could convince yourself. It was funny though, but since I'd found out more about his background, his accent seemed more pronounced from time to time, like he just slipped back. I'd never really noticed it before. Maybe it was because I'd heard his sister speak.

After a near miss when a van shot through a red light and narrowly missed my front bumper, I pulled up at the back of the shop, trembling all over. I turned the engine off and sat there, hyperventilating. It was a massive relief to get there in one piece. I wasn't sure my legs would hold me up when I got out.

I stayed there until mid-afternoon, helping with the lunchtime rush, and my feet barely touched the ground. The time whizzed by and at the end of it, we had sold out of everything in both shops. It was almost four o'clock. We shut up when there was nothing left to sell. Each shop employed two part-timers, who both left to do school runs. Brenda, the one at this shop, had already left to pick up her granddaughter.

'Is it like this every day?' I asked Jenny, slumping in the nearest chair.

'Pretty much, yes, now we have such a good reputation. Once the cafes are up and running properly, we'll be even busier. You get used to it, honest.'

I tried and failed to stifle a yawn.

She smiled. 'You look done in, Sarah. Why don't you get off? I'll finish here. Well done on a great first day. You were just brilliant. Take the van if you like.'

I shuddered at the thought. 'No, it's okay. I'll get the Tube. See you tomorrow.'

I wanted to go home to change before I went to Chris's. The flat was empty when I got there, and I had no idea where Lee was. She was usually home by this time. If she'd gone to her mum's, she'd have left a note. I texted her. *Are you okay? Where are you? xx*

She texted straight back. *I'm fine. Just with a friend xx*
What's his name?

This time there was a ten-minute wait before she answered. *Don't know what you mean lol xx*

She was such a bad liar. I was glad for her though. If he could help Lee heal, then I was all for it. I took a long shower to get the smells of cooking off me. I'd have liked to use the body cream from Jo Malone Chris got me, but I kept it at his flat. After I'd got dressed and dried my hair, I set off on the Tube, where I wrote a blog post about my first day that I could post later.

Once I got to Chris's street, I slowed down, hoping Luisa wasn't around. I hadn't seen her since that time with Harry, but I didn't want to run into her. Chris maintained that she fancied him, and that was why she was funny with me. I didn't know if that was true (I knew how full of himself he could be) but I still didn't like her. When I got near his flat, I caught a glimpse of movement outside. *Shit!* She was there, smoking again, lit up in the glow from a streetlight. Now I had to get past her. Hopefully this time she wouldn't be as weird. *Yeah, right!*

She blew out smoke when she saw me. 'I've got something to ask you,' she said, out of the blue. No hello, no nothing.

I didn't answer.

'Why was Chris burning clothes in that metal dustbin out the back?'

'What?' I rummaged around in my pocket for my key and squeezed past her. 'I have no idea what you're talking about.'

She flicked the cigarette onto the tiny front garden, where it joined a dozen others. Chris wouldn't like that, but at least it was on her side of the building. She followed me in, not done yet.

'He said he was burning paper, but it was clothes. Looked like decent stuff to me. Wait there. I want to show you something.'

She disappeared into her flat, leaving me no choice but to wait for her. Within seconds she was back, clutching two photographs which she thrust under my nose. Under the dim light in the passageway, I squinted at the first one, grabbing it out of her hand so I could see it properly. There was a reflection, as if the pictures had been taken through the window. It was Chris, sure enough, standing in front of that metal dustbin in the back garden. Smoke was curling up from it and he was holding something that looked like a black rag, bunched up, about to drop it in. The second photo showed much the same thing but from a slightly different angle.

'Well?' she demanded.

'I don't know. It's his business. Why are you going around taking pictures of him, anyway? Is that normal?' That got the desired response.

She bristled. 'I'm a freelance journalist. Investigative reporter. I notice things. It's my job. This was odd.'

'He says you follow him about all the time. Like a stalker. Like you fancy him.' The words were out before I realised, and I wasn't sorry. By the way her face flushed, it was the truth. 'He says you asked him out a few weeks ago. Even though he has a girlfriend.'

She pressed her lips tight together. 'That has nothing to do with this.'

'Oh, really?' I folded my arms and tried to look taller.

'No.' She pointed at the photos. 'So…this…Why would he do it?'

'Have you tried asking him?' I gave an exaggerated sigh.

'Yes, actually. I asked him that day in the garden. He was rude, but then he often is. He jumped a mile when he saw me, as if he was up to something. Struck me as odd. Watch!'

She played a short video on her phone, of the same thing: Chris dropping black cloth into the dustbin and setting it on fire. Again, there was some glare on it and it was hard to make out. When it ended, she waggled the phone aggressively right in my face, causing me to step back.

'Odd!' she said again.

She was really starting to wind me up now, but if she was mentally unstable, I needed to be careful. I frightened myself by imagining a blade flashing in her hand before she plunged it deep into me.

'Sorry, but I can't help you. I don't know anything. Nice talking to you. We must do it again soon,' I said, unable to stop the sarcasm. I made sure she saw me with my own key to Chris's flat, just for spite. I gripped the key tightly, making sure I didn't drop or fumble with it, and slammed the door behind me. That woman was toxic. And I bet Chris didn't know she was going around taking pictures of him. He'd go mental.

'Sarah?' Chris called from somewhere in the flat.

He walked from the bedroom rubbing his wet hair on a towel and wearing just his boxers, droplets of water from a shower glistening amongst the hairs on his chest. My stomach muscles tightened at the sight.

'I'd have stayed in the shower if I knew you were here. You could have joined me,' he said, kissing me.

'I would have, but I've just had one at mine. I stank of cooking and sweat. That kitchen is hotter than hell.'

'Nice!'

'I've just seen the psycho out there. She collared me.'

'God! What did she want?' He stepped away from me.

'Something weird about you burning clothes the other week. Even had photos and a video of it. She *filmed* you.'

He exploded. 'God! The nosy bitch! It's got nothing to do with her.' His face was bright red and the good mood he was in moments ago evaporated. I wished I'd never mentioned her.

'What *were* you doing, anyway?'

'Just burning some papers and old rags that were lying around. The landlord left some of that black weed membrane rotting in the garden and I got sick of looking at it. You know me, making the place presentable.'

I smiled. 'That's your OCD kicking in again. Tidying up the garden now? Even though it's not yours.'

His shoulders relaxed a little, and he smiled, obviously seeing the funny side. 'Ah, well. That's me. So, anyway, how was your first day?'

'Brilliant. I loved it. Can't wait to do it all again tomorrow.' I told him about my day, everything I made, every last detail, while he listened. 'I didn't like the driving part. Will you go out with me in the van, so I can get some confidence back?'

'Yeah, course. I want you to be safe.' He took a step closer and brushed his gorgeous body up against me, nuzzling my neck. 'What do you say we go into the bedroom? I've lit one of those expensive candles you like,' he whispered.

I breathed in deeply. I could smell it wafting through the flat now he'd mentioned it. He started to take off my shirt.

'In that case, how could I refuse? Although I might fall asleep within seconds of my head hitting the pillow.'

He shook his head, the last remaining water droplets on his hair falling onto my face. 'Believe me. For what I've got planned, sleep will be the last thing on your mind.'

48

I ROLL OFF SARAH, onto the mattress. We're both panting and coated in a sweaty sheen. It takes a while to get my breath back before I can move. The reek of that fucking candle doesn't help; it's making my eyes water and my throat close up. Then I turn onto my side, prop myself up on my elbow and watch her. Her eyes are closed, and a faint smile is turning her mouth up at the corners. I kiss the smattering of freckles on her nose.

'God, I love you so much,' I tell her. I know now, after Googling it, without a doubt it's what I'm feeling. Anxiety at being apart: check. Thinking about her all the time: check. The tightness in my chest when I look at her: check. The way I can't imagine my life without her in it: double check.

The thickly-lashed green eyes spring open and the smile gets wider. 'I love you too.'

I'm tracing circles on her stomach and she shivers, rubbing her tummy.

'It's tickling,' she says, laughing and moving my hand. She inhales sharply. 'Ow! Probably indigestion.' She relaxes again.

'Have you ever thought about kids?' I ask, clearing my throat.

Her eyes fix on mine, assessing whether I'm serious. 'As in, do I want them?'

I nod.

'Yeah. At some point, I suppose. Why? Do you?'

'I didn't at one time, but I do now. Two, maybe three. For sure.'

'Wow!' She laughs. 'You're way ahead of me. I've never thought how many I might want.'

I lean over her and blow the candle out, then rest my hand on her hip. Her skin is creamy smooth and soft. 'I want to give them everything I never had, being brought up in that shit hole. Mine will have the best of everything.'

She traces a hand down the side of my face. 'Where's all this come from?'

'Just thinking out loud. Does it bother you?'

'No. I like it.'

'Do you think we're going too fast?'

'No. I think if it feels right, do it. What else can you do? Besides, there are enough miserable people about. Why not be happy?'

We both fall silent and snuggle up. Soon, her breathing slows, and she's asleep. I slide out of bed and sit naked in the chair at the side. Her phone is in the living room. Mine is on the bedside table and I pick it up to check the texts and messages on hers. Apart from one from the friend who went to America saying she's coming home next month for a flying visit, there's nothing of any interest.

Luisa comes, unbidden, into my mind. I can't believe what Sarah told me earlier. That cow told her about me burning clothes in the back garden! And apparently, she's taken pictures of me doing it. How is that normal? She's insane! Certi-fuckin-fiable. I'd suspected it before, but now it's confirmed, it's different. This needs sorting. She needs sorting. And fast.

At least Sarah didn't dwell on it too much. She was too full of her new job; cake this and bake that. I tried to be interested, but I couldn't stop thinking about Luisa. Sarah believed my explanation, thank God. People believe what they want to believe, don't they? But Luisa could really stir up trouble for me. I haven't seen her for a while. She's probably avoiding me again.

'Ooh, guess what?' Sarah says. I thought she was asleep. 'Leanne is seeing someone.' She sits up in bed, the sheet slipping from the top half of her body, and looks accusingly at my hand. 'Are you on your phone again?'

No, I'm actually on yours. I put it down. 'Are you staying tonight?' I ask her.

She pulls a face. 'No. Can't. Got some things to do for James.'

'You're going to wear yourself out, what with the deli, the restaurant and the wedding cake business.'

'No, I'm fine. I do need to get back though.'

'Alright. I'll drive you, if you like. I don't like you going home in the dark.'

'Would you? Thanks.'

It takes ages to get from mine to hers. Every light is on red and every roundabout and junction is backed up. I park near her flat and as she climbs out, she bends over sharply and cries out, grabbing the car door for support.

'Ow!'

'What's the matter?' I'm out of the car and around it in seconds. She holds her hand up to me, panting. 'Just give me a sec.'

'Sarah? What is it?'

She breathes out. 'It's okay. I had a pain, but it's easing off now.' She stands up carefully, stretching her shoulders back. 'Wow, that hurt.'

'What was it? Didn't look like indigestion to me.'

'I don't know. Hope it's not appendicitis.'

'Could it be?'

'I suppose. Could be anything.'

'Maybe it's wind!'

'Thanks! Maybe.'

'Come on. I'll help you up the stairs.'

She waves me off. 'I'm fine, really. It's gone now. You'd better get off before the 'wind' starts leaving me!'

I laugh and watch the door close behind her. On the way back, I think about Luisa again. The rage that surfaces makes me drive too fast and I have to slow down. No need to take it out on the car. Better to hit the home gym and my new running machine to work it off instead.

Back home, I strip off and study my naked body in the mirror. I look good, better than ever. Turning from side to side, my torso is probably the most ripped it's ever been. Maybe to do with eating less overall the last few weeks; it's exposed the muscle tone. No wonder Sarah can't keep her hands off me. I'm sleeping a bit better, but not much. The police haven't called round and clapped me in leg irons yet, so maybe the Crimestoppers appeal didn't throw up any new leads.

I put my exercise gear on, along with some music, and do a quick warm up, some stretching and bending. After a session with lighter weights and more reps, I go on my new running machine, going hard at it for forty minutes. I like the feeling of exhilaration I get from it. I'm drenched in sweat after and my heart is thumping hard. After a shower, I go down the street to the takeaway to get a Chinese chicken meal for dinner.

Wacky Luisa is nowhere to be seen. The windows of her flat look dark. She's probably hiding inside, keeping a low profile. She must know I'm not going to stand for it, what she said to Sarah, the interfering bitch. It's unacceptable. I'm tempted to hammer on her door. Maybe she'll be around when I get back.

She's not. I eat straight from the containers to minimise washing up. I've never done so much washing up since meeting Sarah. That woman hits a kitchen like a hurricane, leaving a trail of devastation behind. It's unbelievable. I'm beginning to think my ways won't rub off on her as easily as I thought. At least hers won't rub off on me. I could never be as messy as her in a million years.

I sit in front of the computers, staring down at a little package of coke on my desk. I want to take it but the nosebleeds are becoming a real nuisance. Instead, I drink some coffee, ignoring the slight shake in my hands when I see the coke sitting there, waiting.

Sod it! I grab it and snort it fast. If my nose bleeds, so be it. I sniff hard, shake my head and turn my attention to my evening entertainment. I'm going to have some fun with Leanne's photos. Even though I've been nice to her for Sarah's sake, I'm not passing this opportunity up. She's still said all those things about me. I look at all the photos of her again. She certainly looks hot in them, too young for my taste, but it's turning me on looking at them again. I linger over the nude ones. I still can't get over the shock at her posing for them. I never would have thought she'd do that, not in a million years. She acts like Goody-Two-Shoes all the time, which sticks in my throat. I've enjoyed the past few weeks though, nursing the secret of what I've found. I've barely been able to keep a straight face. I wonder if even Sarah doesn't know what she did.

And who took the pictures? An old boyfriend? I can just imagine some young spotty punk talking her into it as I save them on my own computer, for my own private use. I wouldn't have too much trouble getting off on them, even though I don't like her. It's the illicit kick that's the real turn on. She must be ashamed of them, or why would she have dumped them in the Recycle Bin? Like Sarah, she could do with some lessons on how to use a computer properly if you want something erased for good.

I discard the ones where she's wearing something; they're too tame. I upload the naked ones and send them off to various sites. From there, they could go anywhere, to be enjoyed by anyone who knows where to look and, even if she could get them taken down from one site, they'll just pop up somewhere else. She'd never find them all, anyway. Serves her right for trying to come between me and Sarah. She's just jealous.

Whilst I'm at it, I search again for any stray photos of Sarah. None turn up.

Satisfied now, I lean back and think about Sarah again. One of the things I find fascinating about her is how impulsive she can be (except for the time she ran off to Leeds behind my back). Maybe I should let loose once in a while instead of thinking everything through all the time, go and do something without analysing it first, just to prove I can. I'd intended to post Leanne's pictures and leave it at that, but it'd be more fun to make sure she knows someone's got them. I'll make sure no one will be able to trace it back to me.

Excited now, I decide to take the leap and see how it feels to relinquish control for once. My hands shake as I get the email ready. All I have to do is email her a link to one of her own photos on a website. I wish I could be there when she gets the email, to see the smile wiped off her face.

I make it look like it's come from somewhere in America. The first person she'll suspect is whoever took the photos. How funny would it be if Sarah suggests she comes to me for help, with me being the computer expert and all? To be on the safe side, I remove the photos from my machine onto a flash drive and delete the histories of the websites I've been on today. A pro like me could recover the information, but they'd have to be good and I don't know anyone as good as me. Except Alex.

My finger hovers over the send button. Instead, I save the email in drafts. I won't send it tonight. I'll do it when I'm good and ready.

49

'I'M SAM. GOOD TO *meet you.*'

'*Chris. Likewise.*' *As if. I've been dragged here.*

Who would have thought it? A double date! We're meeting the flatmate's new man. Not my idea of a great night, spending it with Leanne. It's not my thing, but I couldn't get out of it. Sarah insisted, saying it might 'bring us all together'. Plus, she's excited about meeting him for some reason. She wanted me to get us in at Porters. No way. I don't want Leanne on my territory, sullying it. I told her he was booked up so we're at some skanky Italian around the corner from theirs. Red and white checked tablecloths and candles stuck in bottles—are you kidding me? We've just got there and joined Leanne and Sam at the bar, and I'm wishing the evening was over already.

I look him up and down as he gets up off the stool and take his outstretched hand. This guy is big. His grip is firm, and he pumps my arm up and down before letting go. The guy looks like he could bench press 300 pounds easy. Well, I'll be damned, if Leanne hasn't gone out and got herself a guy like, well, me. A blond version. Holy shit! I wonder if she secretly has the hots for me and is in denial. Maybe I should cut her some slack. Perhaps she can't help slagging me off to Sarah but she's doing it to convince herself I'm no good.

'*Hey Leanne! How are you? You're looking lovely tonight,*' *I say in a grossly exaggerated fashion. My eyes flick over her: the bony chest, the barely-there tits, the sensible shoes. She wouldn't know sexy if it bit her in the arse. Then again, I think of the photos and picture what's underneath the shapeless woolly-type dress thing she's wearing. She's such a dark horse.*

'Thanks,' she says, her smile slipping slightly. 'It's nice to see you again.'

Apparently, Sam's a junior doctor in some hospital. I was expecting a weedy bloke when I heard that. I thought doctors wouldn't have time to shit, never mind work out, but he obviously knows how to take care of himself. If we had a bench press competition, I genuinely don't know for sure that I'd win.

'Would you like to order drinks? Your table will just be five minutes,' the waiter says.

I order Stella. Sam orders a shandy. Fuckin shandy! What a dick! Apparently, he's working tomorrow. He could have one proper beer, surely.

'What do you drive?' I ask Sam when the drinks arrive.

'I don't,' he says.

Fuck me! I nearly choke on my beer. He can't even drive yet, just gets the Tube everywhere. Been too busy studying and working to do menial things like learn to drive. He doesn't ask me what I drive.

The waiter shows us to our table. Me and Sam are left to 'chat', as the girls look over the menu. They're talking amongst themselves, about shopping or some other girly shit. 'Ooh, Emma's coming back next month for three days. She's going to drop by,' Sarah says. I tune them out and try to concentrate on Sam.

After five minutes, I have one overriding impression of him. He's bland, as pale and uninteresting as his hair. He's not really got anything important to say. We've got nothing in common other than lifting weights, and when it comes down to it, he's not that serious about it. He has a naturally good physique, but a couple of times a week is his limit. It seems he's one of those lucky bastards who's just built that way. I definitely could press more than him then. I sniff and turn to look out of the window at the dark street.

Sarah touches my arm. 'What are you having? Are we having starters?'

I open the menu. 'Dunno. Pizza maybe.'

I go for Loaded Skins to start and a large deep pan Hot and Spicy BBQ Chicken for main. At least while I'm eating, I don't have to engage so much with Sam. He's training to be a GP, doing hospital *rotations at the minute. He's done a stint at a local surgery near Sarah's.*

'Is that where you two met? Did Leanne come to you with period pain or something?' I ask, waving a piece of pizza about on the end of my fork.

Leanne colours up and stops chewing. Sarah punches me in the arm.

'Chris! Don't be crude!'

'Only asking. She could have.'

Sam laughs, taking it in the jokey spirit I meant it in. He can't be embarrassed talking about that stuff. He's a doctor, for God's sake!

'No. We met in the park. Got chatting,' he says.

Leanne is looking daggers at me. Maybe they haven't slept together yet and I've brought up her monthlies. Christ! Or maybe perfect people like Leanne don't have such base bodily functions.

The evening drags, despite the jovial atmosphere. The frostiness my comment brings on doesn't last long. I'm forgiven, it seems. Why do women have to be so touchy? I join in the conversation even though it bores me stupid. It's mainly about new jobs: Sarah's at the deli and Leanne at some clothes shop or other.

'Chris started a new job recently too, didn't you?' Sarah announces.

'Doing what?' asks Sam.

'IT stuff...'

Noting their glazed expressions, I steer the conversation back to medical matters so Sam can hold the floor, which he does quite well. I tune out, nodding when the others do and saying, 'Mmm,' when it seems appropriate.

'Well, I've had a lovely evening. It's been great to meet you, Sam,' says Sarah. 'Do drop round the flat. Don't be a stranger.'

'You can help with the washing up she generates,' I say. 'I've never seen anything like it.'

Sarah laughs politely but shoots me a dirty look.

What's her problem? Tonight, I've been friendly, genial, approachable, a good laugh. Everything she wanted me to be. Maybe all my effort's gone unnoticed. I stand up.

'I'd better be getting back. There's a few things for work I need to do before I turn in.' Tomorrow is an important day for me. I've got a meeting to decide what I'm going to be working on for the next six months. There are several things in the offing and I can pick which most appeals.

'Me too,' says Sam.

We all walk to the door and say our goodbyes. Sarah is stopping at her flat tonight, so I'm going home alone. As I drive away, I think about how boring Sam is. It seems he and Leanne are well-suited. My phone rings. I press the button on the steering wheel.

'Hey Danny. Wassup?'

'Just checking you're still coming over tomorrow night?'

'For what?'

'My birthday! Aw, you hadn't forgotten you were coming over, had you? I've got the drink in ready.'

'Er, yeah. I had, actually. Did I say I was?'

'Yes! Don't let me down, man. I was counting on you.'

'Yeah, alright. But I don't want a late one. I'll drop my car home and come straight there.'

At least tomorrow night should be better than tonight.

50

'GOOD LUCK,' SAID LEE, as I went back out of the door.

I'd just walked past the Tube station five minutes ago and seen Ben sitting there. I'd snuck past him without him seeing me, and my job now was to try and lure him back to ours. I walked quickly back to where he'd been. Failure wasn't an option, but there was loads that could go wrong. No messing about, I decided. If I had to resort to bullying, I would.

He was still there.

'Hi,' I said, stopping in front of him.

'Hey.' He looked up at me, his eyes red-ringed. He looked exhausted.

'Come on! You're coming with me.'

'Er, what? Where?'

'My flat. It's about time you had another clean up.'

'It's okay. I'm fine, really,' he said. Then he smiled and sniffed an armpit. 'I can't smell me anymore.'

'I'm not taking no for an answer. The dinner is on and there's enough for three.'

'Well, if you're sure,' he said. He struggled to his feet. 'Why are you so nice to me?' he asked, as we set off.

'I was born this way,' I said, trying to hurry him as he limped along. It seemed to take us ages to get there. He had a hard time with the stairs at our flat but managed to get up them in the end. Once inside, I started to relax.

'We're here,' I called out.

'Hi Ben,' said Leanne, in a too-loud, jovial way, stepping from the kitchen into the hallway. She was way too giddy.

Ben looked bewildered. 'Hi.'

I placed myself between Ben and the front door, and nodded at Leanne, who slipped into the living room. A second later, she came out again, followed by Ben's wife, Kate, who was holding the hand of a small girl, who was the image of her. The girl's blonde hair was caught up in high bunches on both sides, and wispy tendrils were sticking out all over. She was dressed head to toe in purple, clutching a hideous troll doll with purple hair and a blue face.

Ben staggered back against the door at the same time Sofia, his daughter, started to cry at the sight of him.

'Mummy?' she said, sounding scared.

'It's okay,' said Kate. 'Daddy just grew a beard, that's all. That's why he looks different.'

Sofia gazed up at him, the tears stopped. 'You look all dirty. Daddy, you are smelly.' She trapped the doll under her arm and nipped her nose shut with her fingers.

Ben still hadn't spoken or moved, and my heart started knocking against my ribs, hard. He looked from Kate to Sofia and back again.

'This is Catalina. She's new,' Sofia said, thrusting her doll out to Ben. He had no option but to take it.

'She's beautiful. I like her purple hair,' he whispered.'

Sofia reached up and snatched it back, clasping it to her chest with both arms. 'She's mine!'

'Hello darling,' said Kate. 'We've come to take you home.' She stepped forward and embraced him, filth and all. Then she was crying softly. 'We've been so worried about you.'

Painfully slowly, Ben's arms tightened around her waist. Lee caught my eye.

'You can go in the living room. We'll be in the kitchen,' I said. 'Take all the time you want.'

We left them, went into the kitchen and closed the door.

'What do you think is going to happen?' I asked, clutching at my chest, daring to believe we'd done the right thing.

'I hope they're going to take him home. That's what Kate said. Might as well leave them to it without us gawping at them.'

We sat at the table. I could hear distant voices but couldn't make out many words.

'Do you want a drink?' asked Lee.

'No.'

'Should we offer them one?'

'No. Let them sort things out.'

I heard Kate say, 'Look at your daughter, Ben. She's changed so much since you've been gone,' in a raised voice, followed by something indiscernible in Ben's low rumble. We sat in silence for half an hour, Lee tapping the table with her fingers. I sat completely still, leafing through the same magazine over and over and seeing none of it. The living room door finally opened with its familiar scrape across the carpet.

'Hello?' called Kate.

She was carrying Sofia and holding Ben's hand. Her eyes were red and puffy from crying but she still managed to look delicate and pretty. Ben met my eyes. He looked like he'd been run over by a bus.

'Thank you,' he said, bowing his head.

'We're taking him home,' said Kate. 'Back to the hotel tonight then Inverness tomorrow.'

'Daddy's going to have a bath,' said Sofia. 'Grandma and Grandad are at the hotel. They're waiting for Daddy.'

'Will you keep in touch?' Kate asked us.

I stepped forward and touched her arm. 'Yes, of course we will. Won't we?'

I looked at Lee, who nodded and said, 'I hope things work out for you.'

'Thank you,' Kate said. 'We're going to get him the best treatment we can find. And now we've found him, we're never letting him go. We'll never be able to thank you enough for this. Both of you.'

Ben nodded, but his face was inscrutable. We ushered them out and the flat seemed empty when they'd all gone.

'I hope we did the right thing,' Lee said.

I hope we did, too.

51

THE PAIN IN MY stomach that started the other day was back again. Jenny could see I wasn't comfortable and sent me home early. I went straight to bed when I got in. At first, I thought it was just indigestion from all the stuff I'd been tasting at work, but it got steadily worse. Thanks to some painkillers and a hot water bottle, it eased off, but I couldn't sleep. After an hour, I gave it up as a bad job.

I got my laptop off the desk and sat up in bed with it on my knees. Typing *abdominal pain* into Google threw up over 24 million results. Great! A scan through them revealed I could have bowel cancer, ovarian cancer, wind, irritable bowel, Crohn's Disease, gallstones or a hernia, among a million other things. Was I vomiting blood? No. Did I have black, bloody or tarry bowel movements? *What? Urgh, no!* Was my skin yellow? No. Apparently, if the answer to all these was no, then it was a good sign. I repositioned my hot water bottle and checked my emails; there was one from Ben.

Dear Sarah,

I just wanted to write and let you know what's going on. First of all, another big thank you for everything you did for me. I know you don't like me to go on about it, but you really have saved my life. (I can't believe how much easier it is to write this stuff down than to say it face to face, so here goes; everything I wanted to tell you but couldn't).

First, I'm sorry for not telling you about my family. I had good reason. They are good people and the truth was that I felt I didn't deserve them, and to stay with them would make them unhappy. I thought me being there would hurt them more than if I left. I convinced myself that after a time they would get on with their lives without me and would be happier in the long run. I can see now how stupid that was, not to mention selfish. I've put my wife and my parents through hell. Sofia not so much, as she barely remembers me. We've had to start from scratch, me and her. It's early days, but we're doing okay. People keep telling me how resilient and adaptable kids are. I hope it's true.

I can't really explain what was going on in my head when I came back from Afghanistan. I didn't understand it myself, so how could I expect anyone else to? Depression is a terrible thing. Couple that with the things soldiers see and what they have to do sometimes in their day job and it's a great big melting pot of shit. Not that I'm complaining; I signed up for it. No one put a gun to my head (no pun intended) and it's wrong that I didn't get the help I needed, but I gave up too soon, too easily. I didn't fight for me. It was easier to just run away, then even harder to go back.

There were many times living rough that I hoped I just wouldn't wake up in the morning, but somehow I always did. I lacked the courage to make the final decision to do the job myself. Big bad soldier, but deep down—gigantic coward.

I stopped reading and swiped away the tears that were streaming down my face. Poor Ben. Once I could see, I started reading again.

Thank Christ I did lack the balls. I realise now that it wouldn't have been fair to my family if I'd taken the coward's way out. I've fought for my country, but I never thought myself worth fighting for until now. My wife is a wonderful person who sees only good in me. She often sees things in me that I can't. Sitting here now, I can't believe I stayed away from her for so long. It's only been a few days since she came to bring me home, but my whole world has changed since she did. She believes in me, always has, and that has never faltered. I don't deserve her, and I know I'm lucky to have her. I never completely let them go, you know. Every few days I checked her Facebook page to see her face and find out what she was doing. Her page was dedicated to finding me.

I now believe her when she says she loves and needs me. Before, I thought she was just paying lip service and spewing out empty words, again because of what was going on in my own head. My daughter is a total joy and every day with her is a revelation. She is teaching me what the world looks like through her eyes. I know all this might sound over-sentimental and slushy, but it needs to be said.

If you were sitting here now, I wouldn't have been able to tell you any of this, but when I read back what I've written it's all true. I've got a long way to go, I know, but I'm daring to think I just might make it.

So, thank you, Sarah, for stopping that day, for feeding me cake, giving me money you couldn't really afford (I know that now) and for seeing the real person sitting outside the Tube station that day. I owe you so much. No one in my life has ever shown me the kindness you have. You are a wonderful person.

Please, please stay in touch. Friends like you don't come along very often. I want you to get to know my wife and my little girl. They'll love you; I just know it.

I owe you a huge debt of gratitude and if there is anything I can ever do for you, don't hesitate to ask.

Speak soon

Love Ben xx

P.S. Inverness is lovely, especially in summer. If we're lucky and it stops raining, the sun can even come out! You and Lee come any time you want. You'll always be welcome x

I sniffed and wiped my eyes. That was the best email I think I'd ever received. I'd been so worried that we'd done the wrong thing, that he didn't want to go back. It was a great relief to learn that we hadn't and that he was on the mend. I leaned over and put my laptop on the floor, then lay back down.

The pain in my abdomen started up again, and I turned over, pulling my knees up. It was one in the morning. I was going to be so tired tomorrow. Suddenly, there was a loud scream from Leanne's room. Before I realised, I'd shot out of bed and was running into her room, expecting someone to have a knife at her throat or something. Instead, she was sitting, facing me, on the bed with her laptop on her knee and her hands covering her eyes.

'What the hell?' I yelled, doubling over as the pain gripped, then started to subside. 'What's wrong?' My first thought was Craig.

I scanned the room for signs of an intruder and flipped back the curtains to check there was no one there. The window was firmly shut. At least she'd stopped screaming now. Instead, she was sobbing, and rocking back and forth.

'Leanne, what's the matter? Jesus, I thought someone was murdering you.' My heart was banging so fast I could barely breathe, and I clutched at the doorframe to steady myself.

She closed the lid down on the laptop and leaned on it with her elbows. Now I was confused. She had her head in her hands. *What was on the laptop?*

'I can't believe it,' she said. 'How could this happen?'

'What? What's happened? Tell me.' My breath was coming in shallow pants now.

'This email. I clicked on it and… oh my God. I don't know who else has seen it.'

I tried to take the laptop from her, and her hands shot out at lightning speed to snatch it back.

What could be on there that was that bad? I waited for her to speak. Eventually, she looked up at me with swollen red eyes and raised the laptop lid. I still couldn't see what was on it.

'I got this email from a name I don't recognise. When I opened it, there was a link to a picture of me. One I deleted from this computer ages ago. It wasn't on here anymore. How could someone send it to me? I don't understand.'

'What picture?'

She swallowed hard, trembling all over. 'You remember Will, don't you, my first boyfriend?'

'The spotty one?'

She tutted and raised her eyebrows. 'He had a few pimples, that was all. Anyway, he talked me into posing for some photos. No, actually that's not fair; I was willing. We were messing about and it ended with me, well... naked. I was young, and we were experimenting and all that. It was a giggle at the time. He was my boyfriend, after all.' She sounded defensive but swallowed again and took a deep breath .

I tried not to let her see how surprised I was. She'd always been so straight-laced.

'When we split up, he was great about it. He didn't keep any copies or anything like that. I watched him delete them from the camera and the card thing. The only copies were mine, we made sure of it. They were on my previous laptop and when I got this one, I had everything copied over from my old one. I forgot all about them and found them a few months ago, in a folder that I couldn't remember what was in it. I hate them, so I deleted them. Now, someone's got one and they've sent it to me. God, what if Craig's got them somehow? And if it's not him, who is it? How did they get it?' Her voice was rising, and she was one step away from hysteria again.

'I don't know.' Something icy was gripping my guts and coiling around inside me, a growing fear that was taking over. 'It must be Will. Let me see.'

She looked at me for the longest time, fear and uncertainty played across her face.

'I don't want anyone to see,' she whispered. 'I thought the pictures were gone for good once I'd deleted them.'

I would have thought the same. 'I understand if you don't want me to see, but you've only got the same as me, after all.'

She shook her head. 'I know I might be being silly but, no. I am a prude, I know I am. I can't help it.'

It was true; all the time we'd lived together, I'd never seen her undressed. She'd seen me, loads of times, getting out of the shower or getting dressed. I even walked around naked. It didn't bother me. But she's not me.

'Okay, alright. Show me the email then.'

She turned her laptop round to show an ordinary-looking email with a link and nothing else.

'Could someone have your old computer somewhere? Or maybe it's still on this one somehow.'

She paused. 'I don't know. I've heard of people being able to get things off hard drives that you think have been deleted. But why would anyone want to? And how is it done? No one has access to my computer. And my old one wasn't working. In fact, my dad smashed it up and took the hard drive out. Smashed that up too. He said you can't be too careful.'

We looked at each other. I had a plummeting feeling in my stomach. Were we talking about computer hacking? I needed her to say it.

'What are you thinking?' I said.

'That my laptop might have been hacked. It can't have been my old one.'

'You know what, I think you should ring the police. I'm sure they have IT people who deal with this stuff.'

'But they'll see the photo.'

'You can't just do nothing.'

'I know. But that doesn't alter the fact that more people will see it. If I just leave it, perhaps that'll be an end to it.'

'It won't if the person who sent it to you sends it to your friends or family or people you work with. If you do nothing, that could be a real possibility. Plus, you need to assume that if they found this one, maybe they found the others, too.'

'You don't think they have, do you? Sent them to other people? Oh my God. I'll never be able to leave this flat again.' Fresh tears tracked down her face.

My first thought was to ask Chris for help. That may not be the best move, though. Also, she'd never agree to him of all people seeing the picture when she wouldn't even show it to me.

'There's something else, Leanne. If someone has hacked your computer and got this off it, what about your bank details and stuff like that? You can't ignore this.'

She gasped. 'My money! Shit! What should I do?'

I was thinking fast now. 'Adam knew about this kind of thing, but he said he wasn't an expert. He spoke about online security sometimes, and I never really listened. Perhaps Nathan knows about it or may know someone who does. We should talk to him.'

'But he'll see it,' Lee said

She gnawed at her nails and fixed me with her tearful green eyes. Another tear brimmed over and spilled down her face. I took her hand and squeezed it.

'Not necessarily. He might be able to do it from just the email. I don't see what opening the picture will prove; he'll be more interested in where it's come from. Look, we'll sort this. But you can't just ignore it. You can't.'

'Erm, what about... could Chris help? He knows about computers, doesn't he?'

'Not him. Let's find someone else. In case they do have to open it. A professional, someone who does this exact thing for a living. I'll see if Nathan knows anyone.'

A niggling thought started up about my own laptop. Adam had asked me several times if my own computer was protected. I'd meant to let him take a look at it. I'd thought I had all the time in the world. All the emails I'd had in the past, when I'd clicked on links and nothing happened—were they more than they seemed?

I felt like something was crawling over my skin and I ran to my bedroom to do something I never normally did. I turned my computer off. Then unplugged it and closed the lid. Then I flipped it over, removed the battery and shoved it under the bed, with a pillow on it. It was going to stay like that until someone had looked at it. I'd talk to Nathan tomorrow. Already, even without knowing if anything had happened to it, I felt sick, violated. I returned to where Leanne was still sitting on her bed and did the same with hers.

'Right.' I felt slightly better now I'd done something positive. Perhaps it was just what we should have been doing all along and not been so blind or stupid. 'Do you have anti-virus on yours? Adam always said it was important.'

She shook her head. 'Not current, no. It ran out, and I never bothered to renew it. Someone told me you don't have to.'

'I don't either. I had a free trial thing ages ago and never did anything when it ran out. Lee, we've been really stupid. Our bank details, our shopping accounts and credit card stuff, our entire lives are on there. This is a wake-up call. I've seen things about it on TV and just assumed it wouldn't happen to me. I've even turned the channel over, thinking it was boring.'

'Me too. We need to change things, starting from now.'

'Let's try and get some sleep. The computers are off now, so nothing else can happen tonight. Tomorrow, we get help from wherever to sort it out.

Back in bed, I wondered whether to ring Chris and tell him what had happened but decided against it. It was late and he'd probably be asleep. If he wasn't, he'd only come charging over and want to see the email and take over. I'd tell him tomorrow. When the pain in my tummy subsided, I finally got some sleep.

52

I WAKE UP AFTER another boozy evening at Danny's feeling hungover but otherwise okay. Thank God I somehow managed to set the alarm properly, or I'd never have woken up on time. Just how much did I have to drink? I look down at myself; I'm fully dressed, on top of the duvet. Then I remember the email. The memory hits me like a slam in the chest. Fuck! When I got back here sometime after midnight, still drunk, I sent it. Then I collapsed onto the bed. It seemed like a laugh at the time. Now I'm regretting it. Way too impulsive. I wanted to be in control of when I sent it. She must have seen it by now.

I shower and make coffee. Can't face breakfast. There's just time to check the four-ways and assess the fall-out at Sarah's before I leave for my meeting. I look for my phone. It's not on the coffee table or in the bedroom anywhere. I check the pockets of the clothes I had on last night. It's not there. In fact, it's not anywhere.

Thirty minutes later and I've practically taken the flat apart. Shit! Where is it? It's a new iPhone, cost me a fortune. I've only had it a few months. It has to be here. I know it was in my pocket when I left the flat and when I got on the Tube.

So where is it? The last place I had it was... did I have it when I got to Danny's? I can't remember. But if I've lost it on the Tube, then it's gone for good. I could have lost it on the Tube on the way back.

Without it, I can't check what the four-ways have recorded. The numbers for the sims in the four-ways are stored on that phone. Without it, I know fuck all. Did I keep the boxes they came in? They had the numbers on the sides. In my panicked state, I can't remember. Why didn't I memorise them? My legs give way and I sink into the sofa, the leather giving its usual pfft noise as the air leaches out of it under my arse. I take deep, calming breaths. It's not the end of the world. I can get another phone, but it won't be today and then I'll have to get my old number changed over. The whole situation's just a bastard. I wish I could get my hands on whoever took my phone, the thieving little shitbag. Probably lifted it out of my pocket on the Underground and sold it for a vein full of crack. What's wrong with people these days? It's like no one's honest anymore.

By the time I leave the flat, encased in my armour of Hugo Boss, Armani and Calvin Klein, I feel better. Calmer. I'll have to not fixate on the email all day. There's nothing I can do about it now.

53

I RANG NATHAN BEFORE I left for work. The whole conversation was awkward, I mean, I'd only met the guy once, and that was at his best mate's funeral.

'Could you get here for two o'clock? There's a friend of mine, Gav, who'll look at them for you. This is his sort of thing. He's brilliant.'

'Thanks, Nathan.'

I rushed down the stairs from my flat, with two laptop bags weighing heavily on my shoulder. As I reached the main door, one of the downstairs flats opened and the Polish tenant I'd only met once before came out in a dressing gown with a fistful of mail. He held it out to me. I groaned inwardly as I recognised the gas bill with my name on.

'Sarah, yeah?' he said.

'Hi. Yes.' One of the laptop bags was slipping down my shoulder and I hitched it back up.

'Sorry. We have had these a few days.'

It happened several times a week here, that email ended up in the wrong flat.

'Shall I?' he asked, gesturing at my handbag.

'Yes. Thanks.' I turned my bag to face him and watched as he unzipped it, slipped the mail in and closed it back up again.

'No problem. Bye,' he said, returning to his flat and closing the door.

At work, I managed to sneak in while Jenny was outside on her phone and hide the laptops in a corner of the storeroom, under my coat.

'You're looking peaky, if you don't mind me saying,' she said when she came back in.

'Yes, um, is it alright if I go to the doctors this afternoon? I don't think it's anything serious, though. I can make up the time tomorrow.' I hated lying to her, but needs must and she'd just given me an out.

I worked until lunchtime, and when Jenny was out the back of the deli, emptying a bin, I picked up the laptops, called goodbye to her and left. I didn't want her asking questions, and it was bound to look fishy. It wasn't like I could hide them under my coat. By the time I got to Nathan's, out of breath and frantic with worry, I was half an hour late. I'd worked myself up into a frenzy on the way here, wondering what this Gav might discover.

'Hi Sarah, come through,' Nathan called when I opened the shop door. He was sitting in a room off to one side, looking incredibly small behind a huge desk littered with paper, wearing the same black polo shirt with the red A & N Security logo Adam used to wear.

'You okay?' He stood up, frowning. His eyes were hollow in his gaunt face.

'Yeah, sorry. It's just... nothing.' Bloody hell, tears were pricking my eyes. I slid the bags off my shoulder and rubbed where it hurt.

'Have a seat. Gav shouldn't be long.' He sat back down.

'Thanks, Nathan. I really appreciate this.' I hesitated. 'Um, how are you, anyway? You know, since everything...'

His eyes searched my face, then he looked down at his hands and was silent for a moment, gathering himself to speak. His shoulders slumped and his body seemed to shrink inwards.

'Not good. I'm really struggling, to tell you the truth. I don't know whether to keep the business going because it's what he would have wanted or sell it because I don't know if I can carry on. I don't know if I even want to. But I don't want to let him down, you know, throw away everything we worked for. We were a team. He was the nearest thing I had to a brother.'

I nodded. There was nothing for me to say.

'It's hard being here on my own, without him. That's actually the first time I've said that out loud and admitted it to myself.'

'It must be so hard for you.'

'He used to talk about you, you know, all the time. He really liked you.'

I closed my eyes briefly. *Please, Nathan, don't make me feel worse.*

Just then, a man burst through the door, making us both jump. At first glance, he looked like a tramp. He was small, with crooked teeth and straggly black hair that poked out from under a beanie. A little wisp of hair adorned the tip of his chin. His sweatshirt and black jeans had more slashes than fabric, and if I met him on the street, I'd be scared he might be about to mug me. But he had the most charming smile and I could see his crooked teeth were spotlessly clean. Not a bum, then. More like a skateboarder.

'Sarah, I presume. I'm Gav,' he said. He held out a hand with clean, neat fingernails and I shook it. His handshake was gentle, not like those people who crush your hand for no reason.

'Hello, Gav.'

He sat in the chair Nathan vacated for him. 'Right, Nath's filled me in. Let's take a look and see what's what.' He cleared a space, then took both laptops out and set them side by side on the desk.

'Er, first, Lee wanted me to ask if you need to see the picture. It's highly embarrassing for her and she's really worried about it.'

'No, I don't need to see it. I'm more bothered about how it got there. You can watch, make sure I don't open it, if you want. But she's absolutely sure it wasn't the bloke who took it who sent it to her?'

'No, it wasn't him. She sent him a message on Facebook this morning. They're still good friends. She believed him, said he was shocked when she told him what had happened.'

'Okay, fair enough.'

Nathan pulled up an empty chair and sat next to Gav, who was already busy with Leanne's laptop. On the screen was code and stuff I had no idea about. It seemed to take him ages and I grew more nervous by the minute.

'This'll take a while,' Nathan said. He must have sensed me getting jittery. 'Do you want some tea or something?'

'Coffee, one sugar for me,' said Gav, not taking his eyes off Leanne's computer. If he'd looked at the photo, I hadn't seen him. He certainly wasn't perving over it as Leanne had feared.

'I'll get them. It'll give me something to do. Nathan?'

'Tea, please. Two sugars. It's just through there.'

I went to the tiny area where the kitchen stuff was, boiled the kettle, and made their drinks. All the while, my mind was overloaded with thoughts of what they might find. Standing behind them, I chewed my lip and my fingernails in turn. What was taking so long? It must be bad news. I walked over to the window, watching the traffic on the busy street. Eventually, after what seemed like a thousand years, Gav turned to me, steepling his fingers. His face was grave.

'Well, we certainly have a problem. They've both got the same virus.'

I swallowed hard, feeling sick.

'But, basically, yours is worse. It's riddled with viruses and all sorts of spyware.' Gav's eyes locked onto mine.

'What sort of spyware? And viruses? Where've they come from?' My voice was shrill and rising.

'Let's go back to the beginning. Your computer has definitely been hacked. More than likely through an email you clicked on. It has a keylogger on it, probably installed through an email, so every key you press is recorded. The hacker can see what you're typing. Do you understand?' His eyes were serious.

I shook my head and wiped moist palms on my jeans. Was it hot in here? For the first time today, the pain in my abdomen started up, dull, griping, like wind. I rubbed where it hurt, low down on the left.

'It means that the hacker knows all your passwords. Your bank, where you shop, passwords for Facebook, emails, well—everything.'

He paused to let the implications of what he'd just said sink in. I opened my mouth to speak, but no words came. I tried again.

'Why would someone want to know where I shop and all the rest?'

'Hang on. There's more. Your webcam has been hacked as well.' He pointed to it. 'Someone can see you sitting at your laptop. Also, they can see everything behind you. Where do you normally keep your computer?'

The blood drained from my face, making me feel light-headed. 'In my bedroom, at the foot of my... my bed. Whoever it is can watch me in my bedroom as well?' My voice tailed off in a whisper.

'Yes. They take pictures of people and post them on websites. It's a thing. They're basically sick bastards who get a kick out of violating people.' Gav screwed up his face in disgust. 'It's a big problem and getting worse. Easy enough to sort by putting a piece of tape over the webcam.' He pointed to the tiny eye in the top of the screen then reached into his bag, pulled out a roll of black tape and ripped a small piece off, sticking it over the webcam. 'Still hacked, but at least they can't see you now.'

My mind was on overdrive, trying to process it all. I'd sit at my laptop for hours, and Gav was saying someone could have been watching me the whole time? Sometimes, I'd only been in my underwear. Sometimes I'd been naked when it was hot. Why wouldn't I, safe in my own bedroom? That meant I wasn't safe anywhere. They could see me in bed and... oh, dear God... it didn't bear thinking about. I felt like I might faint, and I clutched the edge of the table to steady myself.

'Are you alright?' asked Nathan, touching my shoulder from behind.

'Yes. I think. I mean, no, not really.'

Gav looked at me with concern. My stomach roiled wildly and blood pounded in my temples. His voice seemed faint and far-off. My fingers dug into my side, pressing, massaging the nagging pain.

'Can you think of anyone who would do this to you? Or it could be a total stranger, just chance. They do prey on the unaware, just for kicks.'

'No, I don't know anyone who would do this. Could it be someone who's followed my blog or Facebook or something like that? I had a troll on Twitter when I first started blogging. Could it be them?'

'It could be, yeah. But finding out who's responsible is hard if they're good enough. Now, don't freak out, but you need to see this.'

He tapped some keys on my laptop while I tried not to faint. Within a few seconds I was looking at dozens of images of people's faces, close up. They were sitting at their computers. Other images showed people doing all manner of things. One girl was asleep on her bed, with the covers kicked off. She was wearing little pyjama shorts and a vest. The whole thing—it was like looking through a window into hell. And, oh my God, there was one of me. I didn't know what I was looking at, but I was smiling. I was wearing my black G-Star T-shirt with the silver lettering spelling out RAW down the front, my hair was in a ponytail, and my bedroom was clearly visible in the background. My stomach dropped away at the thought and I sank onto a chair.

'All these people don't know?'

Gav shook his head. 'That's right. All with their privacy being violated, like yours has been. And if they put tape over their webcams when they're not using them...problem solved. Well, as far as the visual stuff is concerned, anyway. The audio's a different matter.'

I took some deep breaths, trying to put out of my mind the fact that I never turned off my laptop or put the lid down ever. I never moved it. Gav's next words were even more devastating.

'A hacked computer doesn't even have to be turned on at the time. These people are controlling and operating it, and do you know what? It's piss-easy to do.'

I nodded faintly. It was beginning to sink in. 'And they can hear things as well?'

'Yes, if they turn the microphone on.'

'And Lee's laptop? Who sent the email?'

'Hard to trace. Might not be able to. This person's good.'

'And all the stuff on mine?'

'I don't know. I only really scratched the surface. I need to keep it for a few days if I can and dig around more.'

'You can keep it for good. Put the damn thing on the fire for me. I'm never having a computer again.'

'That's a knee-jerk reaction, and it's not the answer. You need to be more aware of how to stay safe online, that's all. Find out the worst that can happen, then make sure it can't happen to you.'

I'd been so stupid. 'Can these pictures be removed?'

'Yes, but once they're out there, it's extremely difficult to find them all. We can remove them, but they have a habit of popping up on different websites that are hard to find. These twisted bastards know what they're doing. They're able to stay one step ahead all the time.'

'So there could be loads of me out there. When I've been in my bedroom and such like?'

I think of whatever pictures of Leanne are out there and make a decision: I'm not going to tell her. Whether it's a good or bad one, I don't know. I'll just say they've been removed and hope she never finds out. She'll spend the rest of her life worrying, otherwise.

He grimaced. 'It's more than likely. I can try and track down as many as I can. It's a weird world out there and the internet has made nasty things like this commonplace. Have you heard of the dark web?'

'Yeah. Vaguely. Child porn, snuff movies, that kind of thing, as far as I'm aware. I wouldn't even know how to get onto it.'

'No, but the sickos who use it do. There's a war going on out there and these,' he tapped my computer, 'Are weapons.'

I was beginning to see it now. 'Keep it as long as you like.'

'Okay. Give me a few more days and I'll ring you when I've looked into everything.'

When I got up to go, my legs were so shaky I could barely stand. Cold coffee slopped onto the desk when my knee knocked it.

'Sorry,' I said to Nathan.

'No worries.'

'I can't thank you enough for this. You too, Gav.'

'Will you be alright getting home?' asked Nathan, getting up. 'Is there anywhere I can drop you?'

'No, the bus stops at the end of the road. I'll get on it there. I'm going back to work. Thanks again.'

I could feel their eyes on me as I left, and I could just imagine what they were thinking. *Poor, ignorant idiot. How can people be so stupid? They always think it won't happen to them. They should learn about what computers are capable of if they're going to use one.* I wouldn't blame them, and I couldn't agree more. I was stupid and I had been ignorant.

It was raining hard outside and I waited at the bus stop, my mind in a complete fug. I could ring Chris and ask if he'd come and get me if he wasn't too busy. Pulling out my phone and bringing him up on speed dial, I paused with my thumb over it as a horrible thought entered my head and refused to go. The keylogger—some of the things Chris had said, the things he'd bought that were the exact ones I'd looked at online, like the dress from Next, the exact same one I had in my basket. The Jo Malone body cream, and the candle that he'd produced after I'd been looking at it online, saying I'd told him I liked it. I couldn't remember telling him that. Christ, the ASOS bag from ages ago. Lots of other little comments he'd made, telling me he knew me so well. And I'd believed him because I'd wanted to. But what if he'd been watching me the whole time and had access to my computer? It would explain it. He couldn't know me that well, as we hadn't been together that long. I'd been flattered, thinking we must be connected somehow, kindred spirits. But would he do something like this? He had the skills, no doubt about it; and all those computers in his flat. The more I thought about it, the more I felt sure it was him. There were just too many coincidences. He was very clever. And the bastard claimed to love me? What kind of love was that? A rage started deep inside me, and grew and grew until I was incandescent. Probably it was him who emailed the picture to Lee. If he could hack my computer, he could hack hers too. It was just the sort of thing he'd do for kicks and to get back at her. If he'd been listening through my laptop somehow when he'd been using the webcam, he would have heard her saying she didn't like him. That would explain a lot, too.

A taxi was coming up the road and I flagged it down, snapping Chris's address at the driver as I jumped in. He listened then nodded.

'Quick as you can, please.'

He drove off, muttering, *Where's the fire?*

He didn't hang about. I sat back with my eyes closed, trying to work out how I was going to play it at the other end. I didn't know if he'd be in or at work when I got there. Would he deny it? Course he would. But I was going to nail him. Then I was going to kill him.

I sat back and tried to relax. The mail from this morning that the Polish guy gave me was still in my bag. I took it out and shuffled through the letters. Nothing concerning, just the usual stuff. But one looked familiar; it was handwritten with my name on. It was a dirty brown envelope I was sure I'd seen before. The flap had been stuck down with Sellotape, as if it had been opened and resealed. I dropped the other letters back in my bag and opened it. Inside was a folded sheet of paper. It was a photocopy of a misspelt letter, a single sheet of paper, dated fifteen years ago. The letter was written in a shaky hand and was difficult to read in places.

On the night of 23rd Feb 2002, I wittnessed the accident on darley road that Joe Gillespie went to prison for, when that girl was killed. I was leeving the off-lisense at ten twenty when the car swurved out of control onto the path and hit the two children. I saw the drivers face it wasn't my ex-husband it was my son Colin. He had taken his dads car joyriding. Joe would have been passed out drunk as usuall and wouldn't have been able to remeber if he was gilty or not. He been dun for drink driving before. I dint go to the police at the time in order to protect my son and also I have no intrest in savin Joe Gillespie, who knokked me around all the time we were maried. If he gets sent down for something he dint do, I coudnt care les plus it keeps him out off our lifes. I have no prooff other than my own eyes but I have writ this down so there woud be a record of the truth on the ivent of my death.

Jane Gillespie 18th March 2002

I turned it over and scrawled on the back in a different but equally bad hand was a note from Shay.

I was guner give you this wen you came to leeds but you ran off. This is mainlie wot I wonted you to no. I have the mayne copie. Ring me. Shay.

If this was true, then it meant that Chris, not his father, killed that child. Oh. My. God.

54

AFTER MY MEETING, I *stay in the office to finish some stuff but clock off mid-afternoon when my headache returns and I can't concentrate. On the way home, I have to stop off and get a new iPhone. I pass my credit card over, pissed off at the amount of money it's about to cost me. Again, I wish I could wring the neck of the bastard who stole it. I've called my old one a few times from work, but it just goes straight to voicemail. I'll never get it back now.*

As I let myself in, Luisa is just leaving her flat. She's dressed smartly, in black trousers and jacket, and hasn't seen me yet. She's pulling the door shut behind her, looking at her phone, her scraggly blonde hair tied neatly back for once. When she sees me, she tries to scuttle back in, but I close the distance between us in a second.

'I want a word.' *I jam my boot in her door.*

She looks scared, blanching, bright red lipstick contrasting with her pale face. She puts her full weight against the door, a little gasp escaping her.

'Chris! Please! Move! What do you want? I'm going out.' *She's huffing with the effort of pushing the door against me. It has no effect.*

I put one hand on the door and push, easing my foot further inside. She stumbles back into the hallway.

'What do you think you're doing? You can't just force your way in here.' *Her eyes are wild and flitting about all over the place.*

'Jesus! Simmer down. What do you think I'm going to do? I just want to talk. I thought you liked talking to me, anyway. You were always fuckin' hanging around at one time. I couldn't get rid of you, remember?'

'What do you want to talk about?'

'You causing trouble all the time, sticking your oar in with my girlfriend, as if you don't know. Why did you ask her if I was burning clothes? You took some pictures, she said. And filmed me. What the fuck's it got to do with you?'

'I didn't mean anything by it. I swear.' Luisa swallows hard and backs up a step.

I take two slow steps inside and stop. She looks even more uneasy as the door shuts with a dull thud, propelled faster with the aid of my foot.

'So? Why do it then? It's none of your fuckin business, is it?'

She shakes her head, mute. Her usual flirtatiousness has deserted her. She looks like she's about to shit herself in fear. It would be funny if she wasn't causing me so much grief. When I move towards her, she takes a few steps back and pulls up short when the wall hits her back. Her shoes make a low thud when they meet the skirting board. She has nowhere left to go. I put the box containing the new phone on a small table in the hallway and advance until there's only a foot of space between us. She watches me as I look her up and down slowly, this woman who thinks she can manipulate people. Manipulate me. It would be easy to snap her neck with my bare hands. Maybe I will. Imagining how it would feel is making my fingers twitch.

'Where are the photos you took? And why did you take them in the first place?'

She puts her hands behind her back and splays them flat on the wall, shaking her head.

'I... I...'

'Where are the fuckin' photos?' I roar.

She points at a closed door to her right. 'In there.' Her voice is the squeak of a little mouse.

'Get them. Now.'

She nods and flees through the door into what looks like it should be a study but it's a shit tip, like her: untidy, shabby and lived-in. And no doubt well-used. A blind is pulled three-quarters of the way down, and the room is dark and dingy. There's a desk containing a laptop, printer, and loads of bits of paper. Her eyes shoot to the wall behind me and back to my face in a skittish way, almost as if imploring me not to look. I turn slowly to see dozens of pictures of me, pinned to a corkboard. It's like a slam in the guts. There must be over fifty of them. In some of them, I'm bare-chested in my flat, lifting weights. They've been taken through the front window. In others, I'm coming or going from the flat or in the street. In one, I'm getting into my car. All these and I never knew a damned thing.

I close my gaping mouth. 'What the fuck's this?' When I turn back to her, she's gazing at the floor, embarrassed.

'I'm sorry,' she says. 'I just liked looking at you. Yes, I fancied you. I'm not mental or anything...'

'You must be. I mean, who the fuck does this? Do you think this is normal?' I shake my head. What a violation! Just the thought of her creeping about watching me makes me want to throw up. I reach out and rip the corkboard off the wall in one tug, unable to look at the images for a second longer. The photos are only loosely attached and scatter all over the room. The corkboard clatters to the floor and is still.

'Pick them up,' I order her.

'I'm sorry. I'm sorry.' She's sobbing as she gets onto her knees and begins to scoop them frantically into a pile, aligning the edges and corners as quick as she can with trembling hands. From her position on the floor, she thrusts them at me, and I stuff them in my pockets. She squeals when I lunge and grab a handful of her hair, hauling her to her feet.

'No,' she gasps. Her hands fly up to her head, grabbing at where her hair is being pulled tight. It takes minimal effort to shake her about like a rag doll. She screams when I throw her into the desk. Her face hits it first and she careens off the edge, landing in a heap on the floor with a satisfying thump.

The photos I came for are on the desk, the ones she showed Sarah. They clearly show me burning stuff in the back garden. I can make out the jacket, the trousers and one trainer quite clearly, but there again, I know what I'm looking at. Maybe someone else wouldn't be able to tell. Still, these incriminate me more than anything else as regards Adam. You can see from the logo it's the jacket on the CCTV image, if you know what you're looking for. Now the jacket's gone, I need to get rid of these too. Just the sight of them is making my blood boil. Who does *this bitch think she is, trying to come between me and Sarah? She's pond life; scum. I shove them into my pocket with the rest.*

'Where's the digital file? What's it on? Computer? SD card?'

Luisa is groaning and pushing herself to her knees. She pauses, breathing heavily. 'SD card.'

There's a nasty swelling above her right eyebrow, where it hit the desk. Her hair is all over the place and her lipstick has smeared. She's looking at me with a clown face in absolute terror now, holding her hands up as if they'll form some sort of barrier. She yanks open a desk drawer too hard, and it falls to the floor, scattering its contents all over. She scrabbles frantically through the mess and takes out a small box of SD cards.

'I don't know which one. Take them all.'

I pocket the box and point to the computer. 'Any on here?'

She shakes her head. She could be lying, but I haven't got the time now to go looking through the thing. Maybe later.

'The video. Where's your phone?'

'In my bag.'

'Get it.'

I follow her to the front door where she dropped her bag on the floor, and then back to the study.

'Delete it,' I tell her.

I watch her delete it, satisfied.

'Why did you do it? Do you know what trouble you've caused me?' My voice is low, and she shrinks back as if I'm going to kill her or something. Fresh tears shine in her eyes.

'I don't know. Please don't hurt me anymore... I'm sorry... I never meant to…' she says. She's getting shrieky again. I can't risk anyone in the flat above hearing. She's already been screaming.

I pull her up by the arm this time and put my face close to hers. She sways on her feet, sobbing loudly now.

'Shut the fuck up, you stupid bitch. Or I'll shut you up. Okay?'

She nods quickly, her breath coming in great, ragged heaves, snot and tears mingling on her face. It's disgusting. Maybe she'll shut up if I frighten her enough, make her too scared to talk. I let go of her and she sags away, gasping and panting. Her hand goes to her head, and she gingerly touches the swelling above her eye, feeling all around it.

'I won't say anything. I promise. Please. Just take the pictures.'

She holds her hands out in a begging gesture. I've never really liked begging. It shows weakness. The pulse in her neck is throbbing under the white, smooth skin; it's mesmerising. The carotid artery; the most vulnerable part of a person. An easy target. Hers is like a butterfly trapped in a net, flitting about delicately but helpless all the same. Maybe just frightening her wouldn't be enough. How could I ever trust her to keep quiet? The butterfly jumps, enticing me to touch it, trap it. My hands slide around her neck and her eyes widen. Just one squeeze, one long, hard squeeze, and that could be it. She'd never be able to talk to anyone then or show them incriminating pictures of me. My thumbs rest lightly on the hollow of her throat and her pulse speeds up. I press ever so slightly, feeling her flesh give, and she goes rigid. She tries to shake her head but can't, in the tight grip I have on her. With a tiny squeeze, I exert more pressure. Her eyes are rolling wildly now, like a frightened horse. More, with both hands now. I can feel the cartilage and tissues in her throat yielding and a tiny, choking noise escapes her lips. A bubble of spittle appears at the corner of her mouth and I almost let go at the thought of it spilling onto my skin. It's revolting, the dribbling and gagging coming from her.

'Shut up,' I hiss in her face. 'Shut up, you vile bitch.'

I'm shaking her more now, pressing harder, and it feels good. This woman, who I've disliked for such a long time, has had this coming. I've told her to leave me alone so many times, but would she? No. She asked for this. It's her own fault. If only she'd listened, but no. I squeeze harder, harder. She deserves it. As her legs begin to give way, she slumps to the floor and I go with her, still clamping my hands around her throat. I crouch above her and press with all my strength. Her eyes close and tears slide from under the lids, tracking down her temples to the floor. Her hands open and close in fists, strong at first, then weaker, and her face is turning bright red. All I can focus on is squeezing, wringing the life out of her until she can't ever cause me trouble again. Her body is convulsing now and her heels drum frantically on the floor in a hypnotic dance. Then the drumming stops.

A loud bang brings me back, the front door slamming so loud it sounds like it's been ripped off its hinges. I sit back, shake my head to clear it, gulping in ragged breaths of air. My shirt is wet through.

There's a blurred shape beneath me and I have to blink several times to clear the red fog clouding my brain. Luisa doesn't move. Vivid red weals are clearly visible on her neck and her tongue is lolling out of her mouth, pink and thick. It's disgusting. She doesn't stir. I pull my hands away in shock, only vaguely recollecting what I've done. I stand up and stumble away from her while my mind screams at me to go. I can't be caught in here with her in this state. I check quickly around that I've got all the photos she's taken of me. Nauseous and dizzy now, I rush out of the room and down her hallway, stopping only to pick up the new phone. I wrench the door open. Two strides and I'll be at my own door. I pull up short. Sarah's unlocking my door. She turns sharply at the sound of me stumbling into the hallway. She looks as shocked to see me as I am to see her. Her eyes open wider as she looks me up and down and I check the front of my shirt surreptitiously for signs of blood even though I know there aren't any. She looks like shit, but I must look a thousand times worse. Her face is thunderous. I have no idea what I've done, but by the look of it, it must be bad.

55

WHAT WAS HE DOING leaving Luisa's flat? His hair was sticking up everywhere and his face was pale. He looked like he'd seen a ghost. Not like his usual overconfident self; he was nervous, jittery, his clothes creased and dishevelled. His shirt looked damp and stuck to him. For a moment, I was thrown off-balance and everything I'd been rehearsing in the taxi went out of my head. For a second, neither of us spoke. What was he doing in there? I peered around him but could see nothing in the gloom of her flat. He pulled the door closed behind him, his fingers clutching the door handle. The clunk it made echoed around the hallway.

'What are you doing here?' he asked in a strangled voice. He was obviously shocked to see me, and was breathing hard. A greasy sheen coated his forehead.

What *was* I doing here? The enormity of everything he'd done came flooding back. I swallowed hard. *Focus. Don't let him bullshit you.*

'You and I need to talk.'

'Sounds serious.' A nervous smile twitched his lips, and he let go of the door handle. In his other hand, he was clutching a box; a new iPhone. He saw me looking. 'Lost my phone,' he said, holding up the box. He walked past me and pushed open the door. 'Are you coming in?'

He held the door open and I stepped inside, closing it behind me. His bulk filled the space. The confidence I felt earlier was fading, but the feeling of being wronged and the hurt was even stronger. I'd have to draw on that to carry me through.

He put the phone down on the coffee table in the living room. I watched him all the way, still standing near the door. When he turned back, he was smiling, looking more like his normal self. Back in control. I took a few steps into the living room. Was he really capable of this? He reached for me, drew me to him and tried to kiss me.

His body didn't seem right. It smelled rank, sweaty, and not like him at all. And he was sort of clammy. Tiny tributaries of red veins formed a gossamer lacework on the whites of his eyeballs. I wriggled free, ducking out of his grasp.

'What's the matter?' he asked, his eyes following me as I went to stand at the window.

Outside, everything was normal. Three cars and a motorbike passed in quick succession but all I could hear was the blood pounding in my ears.

'You're acting all weird. What's up?' His voice was tight, strained. Like my nerves.

Just say it. I cleared my throat and faced him, flexing my fingers down by my sides. I wasn't wrong.

'Okay, the game's up, Chris. I know what you've been doing. I just need to know why.' I tossed my hair back in an attempt to look brave and confident, and stared at him defiantly. Seething white-hot anger flared deep inside me. The throbbing in my abdomen started up again. I ignored it, and searched his face for signs of his guilt; instead, there was a confused frown and a slight shake of his head.

He opened his mouth and closed it again. 'Eh? What you on about?'

I couldn't tell whether he was playing for time or genuinely baffled. *Come on, you know it's him.* I balled my fists and spoke through clenched teeth.

'Hazard a guess. What have you been doing that could make me feel this angry? And betrayed and let down. Think.'

'Sarah, can you stop talking in riddles? If I've done summat wrong, just say.' His Yorkshire accent got stronger and his eyes took on a guarded look.

'You total bastard! How long did you think you could get away with hacking my computer? It was you who sent Leanne that email, wasn't it? But you know the worst betrayal of all, Chris? Watching me through my webcam and taking pictures. That's unforgivable. In fact, it's downright pervy. So, come on—what have you got to say for yourself?'

I made myself pause and calm down. I didn't want to lose control. This man, this... creature... before me stood there totally frozen. Nothing on him moved for what seemed like forever. I could tell he was playing things through his mind, trying to come up with something that wouldn't make it seem so bad, a way to minimise it. Damage limitation. But there was nothing anyone could say to this. Nothing could ever make it acceptable.

Eventually he moved his head a fraction and his whole body seemed to thaw.

'Erm, what do you mean? I've done what?'

For a very brief, infinitesimal amount of time, I wondered if I'd made a mistake, but no. This was what he was good at, wasn't it, manipulating situations and people? Covering things up and lying about them?

'Don't lie to me anymore, Chris. I know everything. All of it.'

He sat down suddenly on the sofa, looking even paler than he did a moment ago.

'Did you think you could just carry on and I wouldn't find out? Just what do you take me for? Come on, man up and own up to it, at least.'

He stared at me for a long time, with a hurt look on his face. 'How could you suggest that I'd do that? Sarah, that's horrible.'

I bit my lip. He might be doing the wounded little boy thing, but it wasn't going to work. Not this time.

'My laptop's being looked at even as we speak. It's riddled with bugs and spyware that you put on it and it explains how you know everything I did and bought and stuff like that. Like that dress from Next, the Jo Malone stuff, the bag you sent me. You knew I was looking at it, all of it. You saw it in my basket. You could see all my Facebook messages because you logged in as me. My bank—you knew I was skint before you offered to help me. All my emails. All those little comments I've thought nothing of; until now. That's bad enough. But watching me and posting pictures of me on sick websites—seriously? You make my skin crawl.'

He said nothing. He didn't admit it, but he didn't deny it either. The betrayal was staggering; off the scale.

'Why would you do it? Was it just me or have you done it to other women? Was all this a game to you—us? And how you wouldn't speak to me after I came back from Leeds. You dared to talk to me about betrayal?' The pain in my abdomen gave a sudden stab, and I gasped, unable to breathe.

'Sarah... please. I love you. I haven't done anything...'

He was lying, panicking. I could see it in his eyes, his face, his whole body; the way the flush of colour crept up from the open neck of his shirt and into his cheeks, replacing the ashen skin with a scarlet stain. His Adam's apple bobbed up and down rapidly, and he pushed a hand through his hair, making it even wilder. Playing for time; it was obvious. I took a step away from the window. If all he was going to do was lie, I might as well go. To the police. Tell them about the hit and run as well.

'Okay, deny it. Whatever. I know it was you, Chris, and I'll prove it. It shouldn't be too hard. There are people out there who are cleverer than you, better than you, despite what you might think. They'll prove it for me.'

He didn't speak. I put my hand under my coat, under my jumper and pressed where it hurt. The pain was intense when I touched my side, but the words kept spilling from my mouth.

'It's a criminal offence, what you've done. Oh, but you know all about that, don't you? It's not your first, is it?' I threw the letter at him and he read it, turning white again.

'You killed that little girl all those years ago, didn't you? And let your dad go to prison. You actually *killed* someone.'

He still didn't speak. I could see the tremor that moved through his whole body. He wasn't denying it. Any of it. To think I'd slept with him, let him touch me, loved him. He was barely human.

'We're done here. I'll see myself out then, shall I? Oh, and what were you doing over there, at Luisa's? I thought you couldn't stand her. Coming out of there all mussed up...'

It was obvious. He must have been sleeping with her. God, the lowlife, after all the things he said. How could I have been so stupid? The thought of them together was making me sick; disgust, betrayal and hurt all vying for pole position. I couldn't wait to get out of there. He was bad, through and through. Lee was right not to trust him. I should've listened to her.

'Sarah, listen. Please...'

He advanced towards me, his massive shape bearing down on me, and suddenly I was scared. He was a killer and I was alone with him. I turned to go, hurrying back towards the door, and tripped on the doormat which had flipped over in one corner, possibly after I marched right over it in my haste to get in. Instinctively, I reached out to grab the jacket that always hung there, to break my fall before I hit the wall. My hand grabbed air and my nails scrabbled on the plaster: the jacket wasn't there. The coat hooks were empty. My head hit the wall and I went down, grazing my forehead and cheekbone hard. Through the pain that flared up in my face, something about the jacket, or its absence, rang a clanging bell in my brain. Then it came to me, falling into place like bars on a slot machine. The black jacket with the coloured logo that used to hang here was the one he was burning in the video and photos Luisa took. I knew where

I'd seen it before. The CCTV footage of Adam's attacker running away. The shape of the figure, the gait, everything about it—it was *him*. Chris attacked Adam. That was why he burned the clothes: to get rid of the evidence. He was angry with Luisa when I told him about the photos. Had he done something to her too, just now, when he was leaving her flat? He wouldn't sleep with her. He hated her.

My head was spinning but I had to get up. Now. Leave here. It wasn't safe. He was too dangerous. He reached for me, trying to help me stand.

'You're hurt. Let me help, for God's sake.'

I batted him away. He was blocking the door and I couldn't get out. I knew everything he'd done, and it was far worse than the hacking. This was murder. Or manslaughter or whatever. Chris's voice broke into my mind, imploring, hoarse.

'Sarah, please understand. I never meant to kill the girl. It was an accident. And your computer, I am guilty, and it did start out as a game but it's not like that now. I love you; you have to believe me. I've stopped it all, removed the pictures, it was stupid and...'

I struggled to my feet without his help. 'You didn't remove all the pictures. I've seen one. You must have missed it. And you killed Adam,' I whispered. The words were out before I realised I'd uttered them.

'What?' The hand he'd been reaching out withdrew sharply.

'It was you running away on that footage. The jacket that used to hang there. The one you got rid of. What have you done to Luisa?' My brain was screaming at me to stop talking. I was putting myself more at risk from him the more I said. I no longer knew what he'd do. I couldn't get past him and get out of there if he chose not to let me. And what could I do, anyway? He was a mountain compared to me. It was like David and Goliath but I had no stone with which to fell him. So, it didn't really matter what I did anymore. My legs trembled uncontrollably and I swayed, leaning against the wall. Despite the pain, I straightened up, sick with the realisation that Adam was dead because of him.

'What kind of an animal are you?' I whispered. I had to get away, but he was still blocking the door. I moved to push past him and his hand closed around my wrist, his grip tightening. It hurt.

'Listen. I can explain,' he said. I tried to yank my arm free and suddenly, it felt like something inside me burst open, low down in my pelvis and in my back. I was on fire, burning from within. I doubled up in the most excruciating agony I'd ever felt in my whole life. My knees buckled and I collapsed to the floor, the pain still tearing through me, getting worse and worse. When I looked down, my lower half was bathed in something dark red and glossy. There was a strong, metallic smell.

Chris was on his knees beside me, shouting, 'Oh my God, what is it? What's wrong? Please tell me, please... Oh God, oh God.'

I could just make him out through a red mist that was descending on me and I heard a cry like that of a wild animal, primal and guttural. As my senses dulled, I registered that it was coming from me. My abdomen felt like it was being torn to shreds by massive claws, burning and searing.

'Ambulance, please. Hurry. Yes. No. She's bleeding...' Chris's voice receded into the background as fresh pain ripped through me. Then, mercifully, everything went black.

56

A BANGING AND CLATTERING fought its way into my consciousness, and I stirred, but my body just wouldn't respond. My legs felt heavy, as if something was weighing them down. I slipped back to grey, then black, like floating underwater. Then I was kicking back up to the surface, trying to break through again.

Someone spoke. 'Don't try to move, darling. It's okay.'

Mum? I forced my eyes open to see her sitting beside me, looking terrified. She took my hand and squeezed it. 'Peter, she's awake. Get the doctor,' she hissed, and my dad rushed out of the room.

'What's happened? Where am I?' My hand hurt and I looked down to see a tube sticking out of the back of it. I was hooked up to something. Every time I moved, the needle dragged and I felt sick. I hated needles.

'You've had an operation, love. You're still groggy from the anaesthetic. Lie still.'

'What?'

I tried to sit up without moving my hand and gave it up as a bad job. There was a lump under the bedding on my stomach and I touched it gently with my other hand. Padding. A dressing? What happened? I hurt everywhere.

'Mum?' I glanced around the sparse room. The bedding was thin and scratchy, and there was a horrid boiled cabbage and sick smell. A nurse wheeled a metal trolley past, the squeaking and clattering hurting my head.

'Why am I in hospital?'

A man came in, with Dad following behind, and Mum got up from her chair.

'We'll leave you to talk to the doctor,' she said, leaning down and kissing my forehead.

'Hello Sarah. I'm Mr Evans. I did your operation. How much can you remember?'

He didn't look like a doctor. He wasn't wearing a white coat. Instead, he had on a mauve shirt and tie, and black trousers. He was thin, with a hooked nose and only a few sparse strands of hair. He looked at me over the top of his bi-focals, then down at the chart in his hand.

'Nothing. I don't know what I'm doing here. I'm sore.' A memory of me yelling at Chris popped into my head. What were we rowing about? I'd been hitting him, my arms flailing. Then, with horrible clarity, it all came rushing back. What he'd done. But why was I here? I could recall the harrowing pain in my abdomen and all that blood. Had Chris stabbed me?

'You've had to have a laparotomy, an incision into your abdomen; that's why you're sore. You were pregnant, but it was ectopic. Do you know what that means?'

Wasn't that where it grew in the tube, outside the uterus? I tried to process what he'd just said: I was having a baby?

He was speaking again. 'Did you know you were pregnant? Had you been having any pain before?'

'No, I didn't know. I've had some pain for the last week or so, though. I didn't know what it was.' I put my hand to my head, feeling dazed and weak. 'Ectopic is in the tube, isn't it?'

'Yes. Your tube ruptured and you were haemorrhaging. We had to remove it. You've had a blood transfusion.'

This was serious. This sort of thing could kill you. All that blood soaking my lower half, my legs sticky with it. How much did I lose? I could remember Chris calling an ambulance. Did he save my life? And where was he now? The doctor explained more about the condition, but I wasn't really taking in what he was saying. He questioned me about how I was feeling while a nurse took my temperature and blood pressure.

Twenty-four hours ago, my life was great. Now, everything I thought I knew was gone. My world had exploded and taken me with it.

After the nurse and doctor left, my parents came back in. Mum sat by my bed again with Dad at the other side. Tears glistened in her eyes and her poor, gnarled fingers trembled as they grasped mine.

'Darling, we were so worried. You could have died. Did you know you were pregnant?'

I shook my head. 'I had no idea.'

They'd never met Chris, and I hadn't told them much about him. I'd mentioned him once or twice, that's all. They looked stunned, to be honest. As must I. It didn't feel real. A baby? Mine? And now it was gone. Dad said nothing but watched me intently. His face was grey and drawn. I could tell he had questions, but he didn't ask them. Maybe Mum had ordered him not to. Because I couldn't relate to the thing with the baby yet, my mind spooled back to what I knew was real. Everything that happened with Chris. What I found out he did. My head snapped up. No one else knew yet.

'Mum, where's my phone? My bag?'

She blinked. 'I don't know.'

'Was I on my own when I came in? In the ambulance?'

'Yes. You were picked up from some flat in Fulham. Whose flat was it?'

'Chris's. I mentioned him, I think. The one who gave me a lift home from the wedding fair that day, so Dad didn't have to come back.'

She nodded, looking confused. 'Oh.'

'I need a phone or an iPad or something.'

'Well, I've got my mobile, but that's all. Are you allowed to turn it on in here?'

'I don't care. Let me have it.'

She retrieved it from her bag and handed it over, looking more bewildered than ever. I rang 999 and tried to explain everything to the woman on the other end.

'The man on the industrial estate who got mugged? I know who did it. I think he may have done something bad to two other people, as well. You need to send the police there or an ambulance.'

'Who did something bad? The man who was mugged?'

'No, the man who killed him.' *Was she stupid?*

'Okay, just slow down and take your time. What's the address for the ambulance?'

My mind was reeling frantically. I couldn't remember the name of the road. 'Erm, Flat 2, no, 1. It's in Fulham. Brookland Street... no, Brookland Road. No, Brookfield Road. 11 Brookfield Road, Flat 1. Please hurry. He's dangerous. And he ran over and killed a little girl fifteen years ago. In Leeds.'

Mum was looking at me with her eyes stretched wide. So was Dad. Mum mouthed 'she's delirious' to him.

'No Mum, I'm not. Just let me do this and I'll explain.'

'Sorry, what was that?' asked the voice over the phone.

'No, I was talking to someone else. Can you send some police to the hospital and I'll explain everything?'

'Which hospital?'

'Mum, where am I?'

'Chelsea and Westminster.'

'Okay, I got that.'

'Please hurry.'

I hung up, then immediately began to worry the woman might not have finished. But she could ring me back on Mum's phone. She must have got the number.

I looked across at the window and realised it was dark outside.

'What time is it?'

'One in the morning,' said Dad, checking his watch.

'Have you let Leanne know I'm here?'

'No. I never thought.'

I rang her and she answered immediately.

'Sarah, thank God. I've been worried sick. I was about to call the police. Jenny and Sandra say you didn't come back to work. Where are you? What happened after you dropped the computers off? Whose phone are you on?'

'Look, I'm okay. I'm in hospital but I'm fine. Mum and Dad are here. Can you let Jenny know? And can you visit in the morning? There's a lot to tell you. I'll text you which hospital and ward and visiting times later. There's no need to worry now. I've got to go.'

I handed the phone back to Mum, who was looking at me in alarm. 'Sarah, all that stuff you said to the police—what were you talking about?'

'Just a minute. Can I have your phone again?'

She passed it back with a look of disapproval. I knew Chris's number by heart, like I did Leanne's. I dialled it and got what I expected: nothing. Straight to voicemail. I didn't bother with a message. Then I remembered he had a new phone in his hand, said he'd lost his old one.

***

The next day, I pushed away the soup at lunchtime, too churned up to eat. I'd spent ages with the police last night, going over and over things, then again with my parents, then yet again with Lee and Nathan this morning until I was sick of thinking and talking about it. Mum and Dad had gone home to get something to eat, saying they'd be back for visiting later. I smoothed the bedcovers, thinking about the look on my dad's face as I relayed everything that had happened last night. Concern, worry, hurt and sorrow all melded together. He was hurting for me. And he looked like he wanted to hurt Chris badly. My dad had never been one for outward displays of emotion, but I had never ever doubted how much he loved me, his only child. And I'd seen how much what had happened to me had scared them. They were badly shaken up.

I'd waited all morning for the police to come back with an update. Finally, they returned, a man and a woman in uniform, carrying my phone and handbag. They sat on the plastic chairs newly vacated by my parents while I tried to pull myself up higher. I only managed a couple of inches.

The woman started to speak in sympathetic tones but the serious look on her face made my stomach twist. 'I hope you're feeling better, Sarah. We've been following up on your information from yesterday.'

I knew that. I wished she'd hurry up. 'Yes. And?'

'And after visiting Christopher Gillespie's flat, we can confirm there was no sign of him. Do you know if he had a passport? And if so, where would it be?'

'He has one in his bedside drawer. I saw it there once. Did you look there?'

I could tell by their faces that they had. So that was it then. He'd got away. He was probably out of the country by now. I might have guessed.

'And the neighbour? The woman?' I looked from one to the other. It wasn't going to be good news.

The woman nodded. 'I'm afraid we did find a body in her flat. She's been identified as Luisa Johnson.'

'Was she killed?'

'She was strangled, I'm afraid. That's all we can say at the moment.'

The rest of what they said went over my head. I didn't like Luisa, but she hadn't deserved that. What had she done that made him kill her? Then my heart gave an almighty lurch as I realised it must have been my fault. It happened after I told him what she'd said to me about him burning clothes. He'd seen her as a threat. I should have seen it coming, but I never thought him capable of such a thing. He probably attacked Adam because of me, too. I'd seen how jealous he was in the flat that day when Adam was doing the smoke alarm. He probably warned him off or wanted him out of the way, but to kill him? My God! It was unbelievable. Two people were dead because of me. I felt sick. The trembling that had been running in waves through my body now escalated into violent shaking.

The police were still speaking, asking if I knew where he might be. They took some convincing that I didn't have any idea as to where he could have gone.

'Seeing as you can't find his passport, I reckon he's gone abroad. Why else would he take it?' I said.

He wouldn't have gone back to Leeds, I was sure. If that was the last place on earth, he still wouldn't go there. I'd told the police last night about the car accident when Chris was a kid, and it was another line of enquiry they were following up. I told them his sister had the original his mum wrote as I didn't know what happened to my copy. How much was true, or how much evidence they had to suggest he committed any of the crimes, I didn't know, but I supposed it was their job to find out.

After the police had gone, I was left alone in my hospital bed, with nothing to do but brood. Pushing thoughts of Chris and the devastating fallout he'd left in his wake to one side, I tried to focus on what had happened to me. I had to deal with it sometime. I hadn't felt pregnant, so I still couldn't believe it. By my reckoning, I must have conceived the very first time we went to bed, after the wedding fair. We certainly did it enough times that weekend and didn't use condoms. I was sure it was the wrong time of the month for me to get pregnant. And we'd always been careful after that. *Stupid stupid stupid.*

A leaflet about ectopic pregnancy was by my bed, and I read it from cover to cover twice. As I read about what had happened to me, my emotions spilled over and I was in floods of tears. I'd been having a baby, an actual baby. I'd lost my fallopian tube, had life-saving surgery after extensive internal bleeding when the tube ruptured, and it would be six weeks before I could get back to normal. All this whilst also trying to come to terms with the fact that my boyfriend was a conniving, manipulative, spying bastard who'd used me for kicks. Did I believe he'd changed his mind and regretted it when he swore he loved me? I didn't know. Either way, it didn't change the fact that in his life he'd been responsible for the deaths of three people. And, in a roundabout way, I felt in some way responsible for two of them as well.

And he was still out there somewhere. Would he forget me? Somehow, I doubted it. He seemed so desperate when I found out what he'd done, trying to convince me he loved me. But, then, he would have, wouldn't he? My feelings for him were so mixed up. I hated him, but part of me still loved him. How did you make yourself fall out of love with someone?

But he was bad. He is bad. I shuddered as I looked out of the window, half expecting to see his face, despite being several floors up. If they didn't find him, would I spend the rest of my life looking over my shoulder? I tried to ignore the chill that crept up my spine. Maybe I'd never go on a computer again. It was that that had got me into this mess. But as I lay there, I recalled the conversation we'd had not long ago, about how much he wanted kids of his own. How badly he wanted two or three. And how he'd hinted that he wanted them with me. Maybe there was a way I could still hurt him. Maybe Facebook could still have its uses after all.

57

'*ANOTHER BEER, SIR?*'

At the sound of the soft Portuguese voice, I open my eyes.

'*Yeah.*'

She's lithe, curvy and young, and she wiggles for my benefit, knowing I'm watching her as she walks off to get my beer, some local Brazilian shit I can't pronounce. I pull my baseball cap down further over my eyes and lean back in my chair at one of the beachside tables, stretching my legs out and crossing them at the ankles. It's a comfortable twenty-six degrees, and the sea is crashing ferociously onto the beach. This place should be beautiful (golden-white sand, lush palm trees and rocks towering out of the ocean) but instead it's not. It's a dump. But it's still way better than Granford Towers in Leeds. Hell would be better than that. Even though the foam from the waves is swamped with bits of rubbish, skinny little tanned kids screech and jump with delight as the water swirls about their knees before receding, taking the scum with it. The beach is covered with litter, and sometimes the stench is overpowering. Mangy stray dogs, all skin and bone, run in packs, stealing what they can find to eat. The kids throw stones and sticks at them to keep them away.

I've been here two months now and the locals have got used to me being around, although I know some of them call me the 'Engleesh Peeg' behind my back. The people here have next to nothing. Poverty is king. Compared to them, I'm a millionaire. Correction, I was a millionaire. Now I'm the same as them. I have nothing left: no home, no job, no life and no Sarah. Course, no one here knows that. Round here, you don't ask questions, if you know what's good for you.

I turn my face to the sun. Every time I close my eyes, I relive that day. The day Sarah collapsed in my flat has to be the worst day of my life by a long way, and I've had some bad days in my time. I don't know how she found out, how she pieced it all together, nor could I stick around to find out. I was so stunned, my usual smart replies deserted me. When she went down, writhing in agony and screaming, I'd never been so scared. I actually thought she was dying. Apparently, she nearly did. With Luisa in the next flat (not knowing if she was dead or alive) I'd had to scarper straight after I called the ambulance. I grabbed my passports (I have three), the new phone and a few essentials, left everything else and got out of there. I didn't even have time to clean up my computers. The thought of someone else going through them was horrible.

I hated leaving her, but what else could I do? I can't go to prison—that would mean I'm no better than my old man.

So, I had to leave quickly. I had connections. You couldn't live my life and not learn a thing or two. Through Alex, at uni, I'd made and kept connections with some bad people, people who'll get you anything you want if you have the money. Such as fake documents. Within half an hour, my car was hidden in the back of a lorry, as payment for getting me out of the country as soon as possible. A few hours later it would have had a respray and new plates. Even I wouldn't have recognised it. Private planes and boats had me out of there in no time at all, no questions asked. Although, probably, if they'd known what I was really wanted for, it may have been different. Maybe they should have asked the right questions. I told them people were after me after I'd lost a lot of their money on a deal that had gone wrong. They fell for it and did the honours so here I am, in the arse-end of shitsville, in Brazil, putting my skills to the test in various scams and projects. I'm starting to make it pay, though. My new bank account under my new identity is beginning to rack up. My new passport and ID documents arrived two weeks after I got here. I am now Carl Frost.

But God, I miss Sarah. I can't, won't, forget her. I love her. She's The One. The Only Ten. Not long after I got here, I checked her Facebook page and found out she'd had an ectopic pregnancy and it had ruptured, causing her to haemorrhage in my flat, which accounted for all the blood. Ironically, I saved her life. And ended up in exile. I'm wanted back home for murder, both for Adam and Luisa, and she's also grassed me up for that kid fifteen years ago. I've seen it in the British papers online. So, three murders then. Murder, manslaughter, what's the difference? It all means prison. Probably, though, if Sarah hadn't talked, Shay would, so it would have made no difference either way, at least for the hit-and-run. If I go back, I'm fucked. But I don't want to stay here. There must be a way to go back to Britain someday, maybe under my new identity. I haven't worked it out yet, but one day I will.

The waitress, Angel, brings my beer and sets the bottle down on the table in front of me. She gives me the eye and I trail my hand up the inside of her firm, slender thigh, surreptitiously, so her father, the bar owner, won't see.

She stifles a smile and murmurs, 'You are very bad man.'

She moves away swiftly. I watch her arse in her tiny shorts as she goes back to the bar to resume her wiping and polishing. She has a fabulous body, a nine and a half, and she does anything I want in bed, she's so eager to please. She's not a ten. But she'll do for the meantime.

Angel's father's eyes slide to me, the sagging, red-rimmed lower lids mirroring the downward droop of his mouth. He frowns. He doesn't like the 'English bastard' as I've heard him refer to me. He doesn't want his nineteen-year-old daughter anywhere near me, but Angel has always been wilful and hard to control, so she says. If he forbids her to see me, he might as well push us together himself. I lift up my bottle in a silent greeting and nod. His lip curls and he turns away, barking something at Angel, who starts to clear the glasses at the other side of the bar.

I take a long slug of the cold beer and set it down. My shaved head itches like crazy. I pull the cap off and rake my nails across it. The stubble feels so different to the soft, bushy mop I used to have. It's not the only thing that's changed: I now have a beard, too. I've lost weight and muscle. Compared to before, I'm quite scrawny. My skin has now darkened; I could pass for one of the locals. At first glance, no one would recognise me from the old me, the one who left London in such a hurry. In the mirror, I barely recognise myself. The contact lenses I wear permanently took some getting used to, but now I have green eyes instead of brown.

I grab my tablet from off the table and turn it on. At least the Wi-Fi here works fine. I try to get onto Sarah's Facebook page again, but I'm blocked. It happened a few weeks ago, maybe after she realised I might still be reading it. But I don't think so. It's more likely that she put her pregnancy news on there, knowing I'd see it. She's gone into great detail about what had happened. She knew full well I wanted kids. So, as well as losing her, I've also lost the other thing I wanted most.

Angel wanders up to my table and places a small dish of nuts on it. She begins to speak, and I wave her away, my eyes fixed on the tablet, thinking. When I get back to Britain, the four-ways will still be there. I found the boxes with their numbers on before I went to my meeting that day. I wrote them down and put them in my wallet. They're now in my new phone and in my brain. Losing my iPhone turned out not to matter as I'd have had to get a new one, anyway. I wouldn't have been able to turn the old phone on. The police would have been alerted to it and triangulated the signal. Whoever nicked it would have had the police knocking on their door if they managed to use it. Poetic justice.

I've bugged her phone from my new one. It was still easy to get into. She obviously missed the fact it was hacked in the first place. Whoever she took the computers to didn't think of it either, and she'd said they were better than me. No. I would have thought about it. If she keeps the same phone and lives in the same flat, I can more or less pick up where I left off, minus the laptop. I could probably get back into that, too. There are always ways.

I pick up the bottle again and think about the baby. The dads always get neglected in these matters, and I've been devastated at what I've lost. It was my baby too. I can't stop looking at babies now, and there are certainly enough of them around here. The young girls seem to get knocked up while still at school.

I imagine what a newborn child would feel like snuggled up against my bare chest. The more I think about it, the more convinced I am that it will happen one day. Will it look like me or Sarah most? I picture a girl, a miniature version of Sarah and a boy, the image of me. Maybe a girl first, then a boy. According to Google, it's possible to get pregnant with only one fallopian tube.

I mess about with the tablet and Sarah's face looks out at me from her profile picture on Linked-In. It's a new one I've never seen. Her raven hair cascades over her shoulders and she's smiling, but she looks different, changed, somehow. I scrutinise every detail. Is that hurt I can see in her face after what's happened? I think it is. I can make it better.

And I can wait. I have time. All the time in the world. We'll be together one day. I'll be able to convince her I'm not the monster she thinks I am. Plus I know she still loves me. And I will always love her. She's my only ten. We belong together.

I drink some beer and toast myself—to going home. One day.

Read on for an excerpt from Look Again: The Webcam Watcher Book 2.

'Are you sure you want to do this?' Leanne asked. She folded her arms and leaned against the door frame to my bedroom. 'You don't seem too keen, if you don't mind me saying.'

I just shrugged. She'd hit the nail on the head but I wasn't about to admit it. I applied a second coat of mascara. In the mirror, the face looking back at me was more like Ann Boleyn might have looked as she walked to her execution rather than someone going on her first date in six months. I'd been cajoled into going and felt like a condemned woman.

'But he's such a nice, kind man.'

'He's mad keen on you, Sarah.'

'He's a good catch. He has a good job and a lovely house.'

These were all the things I'd been told by my bosses, Jenny and Sandra, as I worked, captive and unable to escape the barrage. Yet they meant well.

'Who is he again?' Leanne asked, scratching her nose.

'Sandra's friend's son. Apparently, he came into the deli one day, saw me, and has never stopped going on about me. Sandra says he's smitten.'

I don't like that word, smitten. It borders on obsession too much for my liking, and any crossover with obsession isn't good. I'd had enough obsession to last me a lifetime, thank you very much.

'Are you just going out with him to shut them up, then?' Lee asked.

I shrugged again. I couldn't really deny it.

'Well, you shouldn't be.'

I replaced the lid on the mascara and dropped it back into my make-up bag.

'I know. But I've been thinking, maybe they're right, and I have hidden away for too long.'

Lee didn't look convinced. 'Can't they see you're not keen?'

I turned to face her. 'It's not their fault, really. They don't know the full details of what happened, do they? They don't even know about the baby. I asked Mum to back me up when I told them it was just a stomach bug, and she did.'

At the mention of the baby, my throat tightened. I'd put it on Facebook, but only to get to *him*. And now I didn't even have a Facebook account. I'd closed it down ages ago.

Lee just shook her head. 'I think you're mad,' she said.

'Thanks.'

I was ready. She took in my ripped jeans and old sweater but didn't comment. It was clear I'd made no effort whatsoever. We both knew the old Sarah would have had every outfit out of the wardrobe and consulted with her on what to wear. She'd have sat on my bed with a glass of wine while we chatted. I would have had an expertly applied face full of make-up, crafted to make the most of my features whilst looking like there was barely any there, instead of the two coats of waterproof mascara I'd gone for tonight. My hair was unwashed and still in the low bun I'd pulled it back into for work this morning, and it wasn't what I'd call tidy.

'I won't be too long,' I told her, picking up my bag. 'Is Sam here?'

She nodded. 'He's staying over, if that's okay?'

'Yes, it's fine with me.'

'Well, dare I say, have fun.' She pulled a sarcastic face. 'What film are you seeing?'

I sighed. 'I let him pick, and he went for a rom-com with Cameron Diaz, so that's a black mark against him.'

She sniggered. 'Oh, dear.'

'Don't wait up,' I said, rolling my eyes.

'I thought you said you wouldn't be late.'

' Yeah, well. I won't be.' I pushed my feet into my battered old trainers. Lee said nothing.

'No funny business after the film, then?'

I stuck my fingers down my throat and mock-gagged. 'If he so much as touches my sleeve, he'll get a punch in the knackers.'

'Wow! I actually feel sorry for him now.'

She followed me to the door, and I waved to her as I left. It wasn't too late to text him and cancel. Except, of course, it was. I was going to be late (having taken so long deciding what to wear!) and he was probably going to be waiting outside for me any moment now. The cinema was a good ten- to fifteen-minute walk away.

It was dusk outside, and I zipped my jacket up, shivering at the thought that it would be dark when I got out. I couldn't see what the shadows may be hiding, but I felt there were eyes everywhere, watching, waiting. Sounded like paranoia, but once it had happened to you, the feeling never went away.

I'd arranged to meet David outside the cinema. I hated the cinema. All that popcorn-munching and bag-rustling and whispering. And that all-encompassing darkness so you couldn't tell who else might be in there, right behind you.

I tried to clear my mind. It was hardly a good state to turn up in, being on your guard and thinking about escaping or punching your date. I tried to relax and practised a smile. How hard could the next two hours be? And I was probably being too hard on him. He was a nice guy, by all accounts, and I needed to give him a chance. I'd met him twice in the deli and he seemed alright. He wasn't bad-looking.

FROM THE AUTHOR

I am a thriller writer living in Yorkshire in the UK. After years working as a dog groomer and musician (not usually at the same time), I discovered a love of writing that now won't go away. I recently decorated my office in a lovely shabby chic pink wallpaper, as I wanted to have a beautifully inspiring place in which to sit and plot how to inflict unspeakable suffering on my poor unsuspecting characters. Only they don't know that yet…

I love connecting with readers. As a writer, it's one of the best things about the job. It makes all the time spent thinking up stories to share worthwhile. I'd like to say a massive thank you for taking the time to read this lil' ol' book of mine. I hope you enjoyed reading it as much as I did writing it. If you feel moved to write a review, I would greatly appreciate. It really does make a difference to authors.

I strive for perfection. If you find a typo, I'd love you to tell me at info@stephanierogersauthor.com I hope you'll stay with me on this journey. We're gonna have a blast!

Printed in Great Britain
by Amazon